OUR MAGAZINE IS BORN!

The first number of *Our Magazine* was ready on New Year's Day. The Story Girl and I read it while others, except Felix, ate apples. It opened with a short "Editorial."

> With this number *Our Magazine* makes its first bow to the public. All the editors have done their best and the various departments are full of valuable information and amusement. The tasteful cover is by a famous artist, Mr. Blair Stanley, who sent it to us all the way from Europe at the request of his daughter. Mr. Peter Craig, our enterprising literary editor, contributes a touching love story. Miss Felicity King's essay on Shakespeare is none the worse for being an old school composition, as it is new to most of our readers. Miss Cecily King contributes a thrilling article of adventure.
>
> The various departments are ably edited, and we feel that we have reason to be proud of *Our Magazine*. But we shall not rest on our oars. "Excelsior" shall ever be our motto . . .

Don't miss any of the titles in the ROAD TO AVONLEA
series, published by Bantam Books:

THE STORY GIRL
THE GOLDEN ROAD
CHRONICLES OF AVONLEA
FURTHER CHRONICLES OF AVONLEA

The
Golden
Road

L. M. MONTGOMERY

BANTAM BOOKS
TORONTO · NEW YORK · LONDON · SYDNEY · AUCKLAND

ROAD TO AVONLEA: THE GOLDEN ROAD
A BANTAM BOOK 0 553 40387 7

First published 1910 by L.C. Page & Company (Incorporated)

First publication in Great Britain

PRINTING HISTORY
Bantam edition published 1990

Bantam Books are published by Transworld Publishers
Ltd., 61–63 Uxbridge Road, Ealing, London W5 5SA, in
Australia by Transworld Publishers (Australia) Pty. Ltd.,
15–23 Helles Avenue, Moorebank, NSW 2170, and in New
Zealand by Transworld Publishers (N.Z.) Ltd., Cnr. Moselle
and Waipareira Avenues, Henderson, Auckland.

Printed and bound in Great Britain by
Cox & Wyman Ltd., Reading, Berks.

Foreword

ONCE upon a time we all walked on the golden road. It was a fair highway, through the Land of Lost Delight; shadow and sunshine were blessedly mingled, and every turn and dip revealed a fresh charm and a new loveliness to eager hearts and unspoiled eyes.

On that road we heard the song of morning stars; we drank in fragrances aerial and sweet as a May mist; we were rich in gossamer fancies and iris hopes; our hearts sought and found the boon of dreams; the years waited beyond and they were very fair; life was a rose-lipped comrade with purple flowers dripping from her fingers.

We may long have left the golden road behind, but its memories are the dearest of our eternal possessions; and those who cherish them as such may haply find a pleasure in the pages of this book, whose people are pilgrims on the golden road of youth.

Contents

CHAPTER I

A New Departure

"I'VE thought of something amusing for the winter," I said as we drew into a half-circle around the glorious wood-fire in Uncle Alec's kitchen.

It had been a day of wild November wind, closing down into a wet, eerie twilight. Outside, the wind was shrilling at the windows and around the eaves, and the rain was playing on the roof. The old willow at the gate was writhing in the storm and the orchard was a place of weird music, born of all the tears and fears that haunt the halls of night. But little we cared for the gloom and the loneliness of the outside world; we kept them at bay with the light of the fire and the laughter on our young lips.

We had been having a splendid game of Blind-Man's Buff. That is, it had been splendid at first; but later the fun went out of it because we found that Peter was, of malice prepense, allowing himself to be caught too easily, in order that he might have the pleasure of catching Felicity—which he never failed to do, no matter how tightly his eyes were bound. What remarkable goose said that love is blind? Love can see through five folds of closely-woven muffler with ease!

"I'm getting tired," said Cecily, whose breath was coming rather quickly and whose pale cheeks had bloomed into scarlet. "Let's sit down and get the Story Girl to tell us a story."

But as we dropped into our places the Story Girl shot a significant glance at me which intimated that this was the psychological moment for introducing the scheme she and I had been secretly developing for some days. It was really the Story Girl's idea and none of mine. But she had insisted that I should make the suggestion as coming wholly from myself.

"If you don't, Felicity won't agree to it. You know yourself, Bev, how contrary she's been lately over anything I mention.

And if she goes against it Peter will too—the ninny!—and it wouldn't be any fun if we weren't all in it."

"What is it?" asked Felicity, drawing her chair slightly away from Peter's.

"It is this. Let us get up a newspaper of our own—write it all ourselves, and have all we do in it. Don't you think we can get a lot of fun out of it?"

Everyone looked rather blank and amazed, except the Story Girl. She knew what she had to do, and she did it.

"What a silly idea!" she exclaimed, with a contemptuous toss of her long brown curls. "Just as if *we* could get up a newspaper!"

Felicity fired up, exactly as we had hoped.

"*I* think it's a splendid idea," she said enthusiastically. "I'd like to know why we couldn't get up as good a newspaper as they have in town! Uncle Roger says the *Daily Enterprise* has gone to the dogs—all the news it prints is that some old woman has put a shawl on her head and gone across the road to have tea with another old woman. I guess we could do better than that. You needn't think, Sara Stanley, that nobody but you can do anything."

"I think it would be great fun," said Peter decidedly. "My Aunt Jane helped edit a paper when she was at Queen's Academy, and she said it was very amusing and helped her a great deal."

The Story Girl could hide her delight only by dropping her eyes and frowning.

"Bev wants to be editor," she said, "and I don't see how he can, with no experience. Anyhow, it would be a lot of trouble."

"Some people are so afraid of a little bother," retorted Felicity.

"I think it would be nice," said Cecily timidly, "and none of us have any experience of being editors, any more than Bev, so that wouldn't matter."

"Will it be printed?" asked Dan.

"Oh, no," I said. "We can't have it printed. We'll just have to write it out—we can buy foolscap from the teacher."

"I don't think it will be much of a newspaper if it isn't printed," said Dan scornfully.

"It doesn't matter very much what *you* think," said Felicity.

"Thank you," retorted Dan.

"Of course," said the Story Girl hastily, not wishing to have Dan turned against our project, "if all the rest of you want it I'll go in for it too. I daresay it would be real good fun, now that I come to think of it. And we'll keep the copies, and when we become famous they'll be quite valuable."

"I wonder if any of us ever will be famous," said Felix.

"The Story Girl will be," I said.

"I don't see how she can be," said Felicity skeptically. "Why, she's just one of us."

"Well, it's decided, then, that we're to have a newspaper," I resumed briskly. "The next thing is to choose a name for it. That's a very important thing."

"How often are you going to publish it?" asked Felix.

"Once a month."

"I thought newspapers came out every day, or every week at least," said Dan.

"We couldn't have one every week," I explained. "It would be too much work."

"Well, that's an argument," admitted Dan. "The less work you can get along with the better, in my opinion. No, Felicity, you needn't say it. I know exactly what you want to say, so save your breath to cool your porridge. I agree with you that I never work if I can find anything else to do."

> " 'Remember it is harder still
> To have no work to do,' "

quoted Cecily reprovingly.

"I don't believe *that*," rejoined Dan. "I'm like the Irishman who said he wished the man who begun work had stayed and finished it."

"Well, is it decided that Bev is to be editor?" asked Felix.

"Of course it is," Felicity answered for everybody.

"Then," said Felix, "I move that the name be *The King Monthly Magazine*."

"That sounds fine," said Peter, hitching his chair a little nearer Felicity's.

"But," said Cecily timidly, "that will leave out Peter and the Story Girl and Sara Ray, just as if they didn't have a share in it. I don't think that would be fair."

"You name it then, Cecily," I suggested.

"Oh!" Cecily threw a deprecating glance at the Story Girl and Felicity. Then, meeting the contempt in the latter's gaze, she raised her head with unusual spirit.

"I think it would be nice just to call it *Our Magazine*," she said. "Then we'd all feel as if we had a share in it."

"*Our Magazine* it will be, then," I said. "And as for having a share in it, you bet we'll all have a share in it. If I'm to be editor you'll all have to be sub-editors, and have charge of a department."

"Oh, I couldn't," protested Cecily.

"You must," I said inexorably. " 'England expects everyone to do his duty.' That's our motto—only we'll put Prince Edward Island in place of England. There must be no shirking. Now, what departments will we have? We must make it as much like a real newspaper as we can."

"Well, we ought to have an etiquette department, then," said Felicity. "The *Family Guide* has one."

"Of course we'll have one," I said, "and Dan will edit it."

"Dan!" exclaimed Felicity, who had fondly expected to be asked to edit it herself.

"I can run an etiquette column as well as that idiot in the *Family Guide*, anyhow," said Dan defiantly. "But you can't have an etiquette department unless questions are asked. What am I to do if nobody asks any?"

"You must make some up," said the Story Girl. "Uncle Roger says that is what the *Family Guide* man does. He says it is impossible that there can be as many hopeless fools in the world as that column would stand for otherwise."

"We want you to edit the household department, Felicity," I said, seeing a cloud lowering on that fair lady's brow. "Nobody can do that as well as you. Felix will edit the jokes and the Information Bureau, and Cecily must be fashion editor. Yes, you must, Sis. It's easy as wink. And the Story Girl will attend to the personals. They're very important. Anyone can contribute a personal, but the Story Girl is to see there are some in every issue, even if she has to make them up, like Dan with the etiquette."

"Bev will run the scrap book department, besides the editorials," said the Story Girl, seeing that I was too modest to say it myself.

"Aren't you going to have a story page?" asked Peter.

"We will, if you'll be fiction and poetry editor," I said.

Peter, in his secret soul, was dismayed, but he would not blanch before Felicity.

"All right," he said, recklessly.

"We can put anything we like in the scrap book department," I explained, "but all the other contributions must be original, and all must have the name of the writer signed to them, except the personals. We must all do our best. *Our Magazine* is to be 'a feast of reason and flow of soul.'"

I felt that I had worked in two quotations with striking effect. The others, with the exception of the Story Girl, looked suitably impressed.

"But," said Cecily, reproachfully, "haven't you anything for Sara Ray to do? She'll feel awful bad if she is left out."

I had forgotten Sara Ray. Nobody, except Cecily, ever did remember Sara Ray unless she was on the spot. But we decided to put her in as advertising manager. That sounded well and really meant very little.

"Well, we'll go ahead then," I said, with a sigh of relief that the project had been so easily launched. "We'll get the first issue out about the first of January. And whatever else we do we mustn't let Uncle Roger get hold of it. He'd make such fearful fun of it."

"I hope we can make a success of it," said Peter moodily. He had been moody ever since he was entrapped into being fiction editor.

"It will be a success if we are determined to succeed," I said. "'Where there is a will there is always a way.'"

"That's just what Ursula Townley said when her father locked her in her room the night she was going to run away with Kenneth MacNair," said the Story Girl.

We pricked up our ears, scenting a story.

"Who were Ursula Townley and Kenneth MacNair?" I asked.

"Kenneth MacNair was a first cousin of the Awkward Man's grandfather, and Ursula Townley was the belle of the Island in her day. Who do you suppose told me the story—no, read it to me, out of his brown book?"

"Never the Awkward Man himself!" I exclaimed incredulously.

"Yes, he did," said the Story Girl triumphantly. "I met him one day last week back in the maple woods when I was looking for ferns. He was sitting by the spring, writing in his brown book. He hid it when he saw me and looked real silly; but after I had talked to him awhile I just asked him about it, and told him that the gossips said he wrote poetry in it, and if he did would he tell me, because I was dying to know. He said he wrote a little of everything in it; and then I begged him to read me something out of it, and he read me the story of Ursula and Kenneth."

"I don't see how you ever had the face," said Felicity; and even Cecily looked as if she thought the Story Girl had gone rather far.

"Never mind that," cried Felix, "but tell us the story. That's the main thing."

"I'll tell it just as the Awkward Man read it, as far as I can," said the Story Girl, "but I can't put all his nice poetical touches in, because I can't remember them all, though he read it over twice for me."

CHAPTER II

A Will,
A Way
and
A Woman

"ONE day, over a hundred years ago, Ursula Townley was waiting for Kenneth MacNair in a great beechwood, where brown nuts were falling and an October wind was making the leaves dance on the ground like pixy-people."

"What are pixy-people?" demanded Peter, forgetting the Story Girl's dislike of interruptions.

"Hush," whispered Cecily. "That is only one of the Awkward Man's poetical touches, I guess."

"There were cultivated fields between the grove and the dark blue gulf; but far behind and on each side were woods, for Prince Edward Island a hundred years ago was not what it is today. The settlements were few and scattered, and the population so scanty that old Hugh Townley boasted that he knew every man, woman and child in it.

"Old Hugh was quite a noted man in his day. He was noted for several things—he was rich, he was hospitable, he was proud, he was masterful—and he had for daughter the handsomest young woman in Prince Edward Island.

"Of course, the young men were not blind to her good looks, and she had so many lovers that all the other girls hated her—"

"You bet!" said Dan, aside—

"But the only one who found favour in her eyes was the very last man she should have pitched her fancy on, at least if old Hugh were the judge. Kenneth MacNair was a dark-eyed young sea-captain of the next settlement, and it was to meet him that Ursula stole to the beechwood on that autumn day of crisp wind and ripe sunshine. Old Hugh had forbidden his house to the young man, making such a scene of fury about it that even

Ursula's high spirit quailed. Old Hugh had really nothing against Kenneth himself; but years before either Kenneth or Ursula was born, Kenneth's father had beaten Hugh Townley in a hotly contested election. Political feeling ran high in those days, and old Hugh had never forgiven the MacNair his victory. The feud between the families dated from that tempest in the provincial teapot, and the surplus of votes on the wrong side was the reason why, thirty years later, Ursula had to meet her lover by stealth if she met him at all."

"Was the MacNair a Conservative or a Grit?" asked Felicity.

"It doesn't make any difference what he was," said the Story Girl impatiently. "Even a Tory would be romantic a hundred years ago. Well, Ursula couldn't see Kenneth very often, for Kenneth lived fifteen miles away and was often absent from home in his vessel. On this particular day it was nearly three months since they had met.

"The Sunday before, young Sandy MacNair had been in Carlyle church. He had risen at dawn that morning, walked bare-footed for eight miles along the shore, carrying his shoes, hired a harbour fisherman to row him over the channel, and then walked eight miles more to the church at Carlyle, less, it is to be feared, from a zeal for holy things than that he might do an errand for his adored brother, Kenneth. He carried a letter which he contrived to pass into Ursula's hand in the crowd as the people came out. This letter asked Ursula to meet Kenneth in the beechwood the next afternoon, and so she stole away there when suspicious father and watchful stepmother thought she was spinning in the granary loft."

"It was very wrong of her to deceive her parents," said Felicity primly.

The Story Girl couldn't deny this, so she evaded the ethical side of the question skilfully.

"I am not telling you what Ursula Townley *ought* to have done," she said loftily. "I am only telling you what she *did* do. If you don't want to hear it you needn't listen, of course. There wouldn't be many stories to tell if nobody ever did anything she shouldn't do.

"Well, when Kenneth came, the meeting was just what might have been expected between two lovers who had taken their last kiss three months before. So it was a good half-hour before Ursula said,

" 'Oh, Kenneth, I cannot stay long—I shall be missed. You said in your letter that you had something important to talk of. What is it?'

" 'My news is this, Ursula. Next Saturday morning my vessel, *The Fair Lady*, with her captain on board, sails at dawn from Charlottetown harbour, bound for Buenos Ayres. At this season this means a safe and sure return—next May.'

" 'Kenneth!' cried Ursula. She turned pale and burst into tears. 'How can you think of leaving me? Oh, you are cruel!'

" 'Why, no, sweetheart,' laughed Kenneth. 'The captain of *The Fair Lady* will take his bride with him. We'll spend our honeymoon on the high seas, Ursula, and the cold Canadian winter under southern palms.'

" 'You want me to run away with you, Kenneth?' exclaimed Ursula.

" 'Indeed, dear girl, there's nothing else to do!'

" 'Oh, I cannot!' she protested. 'My father would—'

" 'We'll not consult him—until afterward. Come, Ursula, you know there's no other way. We've always known it must come to this. *Your* father will never forgive me for *my* father. You won't fail me now. Think of the long parting if you send me away alone on such a voyage. Pluck up your courage, and we'll let Townleys and MacNairs whistle their mouldy feuds down the wind while we sail southward in *The Fair Lady*. I have a plan.'

" 'Let me hear it,' said Ursula, beginning to get back her breath.

" 'There is to be a dance at The Springs Friday night. Are you invited, Ursula?"

" 'Yes.'

" 'Good. I am not—but I shall be there—in the fir grove behind the house, with two horses. When the dancing is at its height you'll steal out to meet me. Then 'tis but a fifteen mile ride to Charlottetown, where a good minister, who is a friend of mine, will be ready to marry us. By the time the dancers have tired their heels you and I will be on our vessel, able to snap our fingers at fate.'

" 'And what if I do not meet you in the fir grove?' said Ursula, a little impertinently.

" 'If you do not, I'll sail for South America the next morning, and many a long year will pass ere Kenneth MacNair comes home again.'

"Perhaps Kenneth didn't mean that, but Ursula thought he did, and it decided her. She agreed to run away with him. Yes, of course that was wrong, too, Felicity. She ought to have said, 'No, I shall be married respectably from home, and have a wedding and a silk dress and bridesmaids and lots of presents.' But she didn't. She wasn't as prudent as Felicity King would have been."

"She was a shameless hussy," said Felicity, venting on the long-dead Ursula that anger she dare not visit on the Story Girl.

"Oh, no, Felicity dear, she was just a lass of spirit. I'd have done the same. And when Friday night came she began to dress for the dance with a brave heart. She was to go to The Springs with her uncle and aunt, who were coming on horseback that afternoon, and would then go on to The Springs in old Hugh's carriage, which was the only one in Carlyle then. They were to leave in time to reach The Springs before nightfall, for the October nights were dark and the wooded roads rough for travelling.

"When Ursula was ready she looked at herself in the glass with a good deal of satisfaction. Yes, Felicity, she was a vain baggage, that same Ursula, but that kind didn't all die out a hundred years ago. And she had good reason for being vain. She wore the sea-green silk which had been brought out from England a year before and worn but once—at the Christmas ball at Government House. A fine, stiff, rustling silk it was, and over it shone Ursula's crimson cheeks and gleaming eyes, and masses of nut brown hair.

"As she turned from the glass she heard her father's voice below, loud and angry. Growing very pale, she ran out into the hall. Her father was already half way upstairs, his face red with fury. In the hall below Ursula saw her stepmother, looking troubled and vexed. At the door stood Malcolm Ramsay, a homely neighbour youth who had been courting Ursula in his clumsy way ever since she grew up. Ursula had always hated him.

"'Ursula!' shouted old Hugh, 'come here and tell this scoundrel he lies. He says that you met Kenneth MacNair in the beechgrove last Tuesday. Tell him he lies! Tell him he lies!'

"Ursula was no coward. She looked scornfully at poor Ramsay.

" 'The creature is a spy and a tale-bearer,' she said, 'but in this he does not lie. I *did* meet Kenneth MacNair last Tuesday.'

" 'And you dare to tell me this to my face!' roared old Hugh. 'Back to your room, girl! Back to your room and stay there! Take off that finery. You go to no more dances. You shall stay in that room until I choose to let you out. No, not a word! I'll put you there if you don't go. In with you—aye, and take your knitting with you. Occupy yourself with that this evening instead of kicking your heels at The Springs!'

"He snatched a roll of gray stocking from the hall table and flung it into Ursula's room. Ursula knew she would have to follow it, or be picked up and carried in like a naughty child. So she gave the miserable Ramsay a look that made him cringe, and swept into her room with her head in the air. The next moment she heard the door locked behind her. Her first proceeding was to have a cry of anger and shame and disappointment. That did no good, and then she took to marching up and down her room. It did not calm her to hear the rumble of the carriage out of the gate as her uncle and aunt departed.

" 'Oh, what's to be done?' she sobbed. 'Kenneth will be furious. He will think I have failed him and he will go away hot with anger against me. If I could only send a word of explanation I know he would not leave me. But there seems to be no way at all—though I have heard that there's always a way when there's a will. Oh, I shall go mad! If the window were not so high I would jump out of it. But to break my legs or my neck would not mend the matter.'

"The afternoon passed on. At sunset Ursula heard hoof-beats and ran to the window. Andrew Kinnear of The Springs was tying his horse at the door. He was a dashing young fellow, and a political crony of old Hugh. No doubt he would be at the dance that night. Oh, if she could get speech for but a moment with him!

"When he had gone into the house, Ursula, turning impatiently from the window, tripped and almost fell over the big ball of homespun yarn her father had flung on the floor. For a moment she gazed at it resentfully—then, with a gay little laugh, she pounced on it. The next moment she was at her table, writing a brief note to Kenneth MacNair. When it was written, Ursula unwound the gray ball to a considerable depth, pinned the note on it, and rewound the yarn over it. A gray ball, the color of the twilight, might escape observation, where a white missive fluttering down from an upper window would surely be seen by someone. Then she softly opened her window and waited.

"It was dusk when Andrew went away. Fortunately old Hugh did not come to the door with him. As Andrew untied his horse Ursula threw the ball with such good aim that it struck him, as she had meant it to do, squarely on the head. Andrew looked up at her window. She leaned out, put her finger warningly on her lips, pointed to the ball, and nodded. Andrew, looking somewhat puzzled, picked up the ball, sprang to his saddle, and galloped off.

"So far, well, thought Ursula. But would Andrew understand? Would he have wit enough to think of exploring the big, knobby ball for its delicate secret? And would he be at the dance after all?

"The evening dragged by. Time had never seemed so long to Ursula. She could not rest or sleep. It was midnight before she heard the patter of a handful of gravel on her window-panes. In a trice she was leaning out. Below in the darkness stood Kenneth MacNair.

"'Oh, Kenneth, did you get my letter? And is it safe for you to be here?'

"'Safe enough. Your father is in bed. I've waited two hours down the road for his light to go out, and an extra half-hour to put him to sleep. The horses are there. Slip down and out, Ursula. We'll make Charlottetown by dawn yet.'

"'That's easier said than done, lad. I'm locked in. But do you go out behind the new barn and bring the ladder you will find there.'

"Five minutes later, Miss Ursula, hooded and cloaked, scrambled soundlessly down the ladder, and in five more minutes she and Kenneth were riding along the road.

"'There's a stiff gallop before us, Ursula,' said Kenneth.

"'I would ride to the world's end with you, Kenneth MacNair,' said Ursula. Oh, of course she shouldn't have said anything of the sort, Felicity. But you see people had no etiquette departments in those days. And when the red sunlight of a fair October dawn was shining over the gray sea *The Fair Lady* sailed out of Charlottetown harbour. On her deck stood Kenneth and Ursula MacNair, and in her hand, as a most precious treasure, the bride carried a ball of gray homespun yarn."

"Well," said Dan, yawning, "I like that kind of a story. Nobody goes and dies in it, that's one good thing."

"Did old Hugh forgive Ursula?" I asked.

"The story stopped there in the brown book," said the Story Girl, "but the Awkward Man says he did, after awhile."

"It must be rather romantic to be run away with," remarked Cecily, wistfully.

"Don't you get such silly notions in your head, Cecily King," said Felicity, severely.

CHAPTER III

The Christmas Harp

GREAT was the excitement in the houses of King as Christmas drew nigh. The air was simply charged with secrets. Everybody was very penurious for weeks beforehand and hoards were counted scrutinizingly every day. Mysterious pieces of handiwork were smuggled in and out of sight, and whispered consultations were held, about which nobody thought of being jealous, as might have happened at any other time. Felicity was in her element, for she and her mother were deep in preparations for the day. Cecily and the Story Girl were excluded from these doings with indifference on Aunt Janet's part and what seemed ostentatious complacency on Felicity's. Cecily took this to heart and complained to me about it.

"I'm one of this family as much as Felicity is," she said, with as much indignation as Cecily could feel, "and I don't think she need shut me out of everything. When I wanted to stone the raisins for the mince-meat she said, no, she would do it herself, because Christmas mince-meat was *very* particular—as if I couldn't stone raisins right! The airs Felicity puts on about her cooking just make me sick," concluded Cecily wrathfully

"It's a pity she doesn't make a mistake in cooking once in a while herself," I said. "Then maybe she wouldn't think she knew so much more than other people."

All parcels that came in the mail from distant friends were taken charge of by Aunts Janet and Olivia, not to be opened until the great day of the feast itself. How slowly the last week passed! But even watched pots will boil in the fullness of time, and finally Christmas day came, gray and dour and frost-bitten without, but full of revelry and rose red mirth within. Uncle Roger and Aunt Olivia and the Story Girl came over early for the day; and Peter came too, with his shining, morning face, to be hailed with joy, for we had been afraid that Peter would not be able to spend Christmas with us. His mother had wanted him home with her.

"Of course I ought to go," Peter had told me mournfully, "but we won't have turkey for dinner, because ma can't afford it. And ma always cries on holidays because she says they make her think of father. Of course she can't help it, but it ain't cheerful. Aunt Jane wouldn't have cried. Aunt Jane used to say she never saw the man who was worth spoiling her eyes for. But I guess I'll have to spend Christmas at home."

At the last moment, however, a cousin of Mrs. Craig's in Charlottetown invited her for Christmas, and Peter, being given his choice of going or staying, joyfully elected to stay. So we were all together, except Sara Ray, who had been invited but whose mother wouldn't let her come.

"Sara Ray's mother is a nuisance," snapped the Story Girl. "She just lives to make that poor child miserable, and she won't let her go to the party tonight, either."

"It is just breaking Sara's heart that she can't," said Cecily compassionately. "I'm almost afraid I won't enjoy myself for thinking of her, home there alone, most likely reading the Bible, while we're at the party."

"She might be worse occupied than reading the Bible," said Felicity rebukingly.

"But Mrs. Ray makes her read it as a punishment," protested Cecily. "Whenever Sara cries to go anywhere—and of course she'll cry tonight—Mrs. Ray makes her read seven chapters in the Bible. I wouldn't think that would make her very fond of it. And I'll not be able to talk the party over with Sara afterwards— and that's half the fun gone."

"You can tell her all about it," comforted Felix.

"Telling isn't a bit like talking it over," retorted Cecily. "It's too one-sided."

We had an exciting time opening our presents. Some of us had more than others, but we all received enough to make us feel comfortably that we were not unduly neglected in the matter. The contents of the box which the Story Girl's father had sent her from Paris made our eyes stick out. It was full of beautiful things, among them another red silk dress—not the bright, flame-hued tint of her old one, but a rich, dark crimson, with the most distracting flounces and bows and ruffles; and with it were little red satin slippers with gold buckles, and heels that made Aunt Janet hold up her hands in horror. Felicity remarked scornfully that she would have thought the Story Girl would get tired wearing red so much, and even Cecily commented apart to me that she thought when you got so many things all at once you didn't appreciate them as much'as when you only got a few.

"I'd never get tired of red," said the Story Girl. "I just love it—it's so rich and glowing. When I'm dressed in red I always feel ever so much cleverer than in any other colour. Thoughts just crowd into my brain one after the other. Oh, you darling dress—you dear, sheeny, red-rosy, glistening, silky thing!"

She flung it over her shoulder and danced around the kitchen.

"Don't be silly, Sara," said Aunt Janet, a little stiffly. She was a good soul, that Aunt Janet, and had a kind, loving heart in her ample bosom. But I fancy ther were times when she thought it rather hard that the daughter of a roving adventurer—as she considered him—like Blair Stanley should disport herself in silk dresses, while her own daughters must go clad in gingham and muslin—for those were the days when a feminine creature got one silk dress in her lifetime, and seldom more than one.

The Story Girl also got a present from the Awkward Man—a little, shabby, worn volume with a great many marks on the leaves.

"Why, it isn't new—it's an old book!" exclaimed Felicity. "I didn't think the Awkward Man was mean, whatever else he was."

"Oh, you don't understand, Felicity," said the Story Girl patiently. "And I don't suppose I can make you understand. But I'll try. I'd ten times rather have this than a new book. It's one of his own, don't you see—one that he has read a hundred times and loved and made a friend of. A new book, just out of a shop, wouldn't be the same thing at all. It wouldn't *mean* anything. I consider it a great compliment that he has given me this book. I'm prouder of it than of anything else I've got."

"Well, you're welcome to it," said Felicity. "I don't understand and I don't want to. *I* wouldn't give anybody a Christmas present that wasn't new, and I wouldn't thank anybody who gave me one."

Peter was in the seventh heaven because Felicity had given him a present—and, moreover, one that she had made herself. It was a bookmark of perforated cardboard, with a gorgeous red and yellow worsted goblet worked on it, and below, in green letters, the solemn warning, "Touch Not The Cup." As Peter was not addicted to habits of intemperance, not even to looking on dandelion wine when it was pale yellow, we did not exactly see why Felicity should have selected such a device. But Peter was perfectly satisfied, so nobody cast any blight on his happiness by carping criticism. Later on Felicity told me she had worked the bookmark for him because his father used to drink before he ran away.

"I thought Peter ought to be warned in time," she said.

Even Pat had a ribbon of blue, which he clawed off and lost half an hour after it was tied on him. Pat did not care for vain adornments of the body.

We had a glorious Christmas dinner, fit for the halls of Lucullus, and ate far more than was good for us, none daring to make us afraid on that one day of the year. And in the evening—oh, rapture and delight!—we went to Kitty Marr's party.

It was a fine December evening; the sharp air of morning had mellowed until it was as mild as autumn. There had been no snow, and the long fields, sloping down from the homestead, were brown and mellow. A weird, dreamy stillness had fallen on the purple earth, the dark fir woods, the valley rims, the sere meadows. Nature seemed to have folded satisfied hands to rest, knowing that her long wintry slumber was coming upon her.

At first, when the invitations to the party had come, Aunt Janet had said we could not go; but Uncle Alec interceded in our favour, perhaps influenced thereto by Cecily's wistful eyes. If Uncle Alec had a favourite among his children it was Cecily, and he had grown even more indulgent toward her of late. Now and then I saw him looking at her intently, and, following his eyes and thought, I had, somehow, seen that Cecily was paler and thinner than she had been in the summer, and that her soft eyes seemed larger, and that over her little face in moments of repose there was a certain languor and weariness that made it very sweet and pathetic. And I heard him tell Aunt Janet that he did not like to see the child getting so much the look of her Aunt Felicity.

"Cecily is perfectly well," said Aunt Janet sharply. "She's only growing very fast. Don't be foolish, Alec."

But after that Cecily had cups of cream where the rest of us got only milk; and Aunt Janet was very particular to see that she had her rubbers on whenever she went out.

On this merry Christmas evening, however, no fears or dim foreshadowings of any coming event clouded our hearts or faces. Cecily looked brighter and prettier than I had ever seen her, with her softly shining eyes and the nut brown gloss of her hair. Felicity was too beautiful for words; and even the Story Girl, between excitement and the crimson silk array, blossomed out with a charm and allurement more potent than any regular loveliness—and this in spite of the fact that Aunt Olivia had tabooed the red satin slippers and mercilessly decreed that stout shoes should be worn.

"I know just how you feel about it, you daughter of Eve," she said, with gay sympathy, "but December roads are damp, and if you are going to walk to Marrs' you are not going to do it in those frivolous Parisian concoctions, even with overboots on; so be brave, dear heart, and show that you have a soul above little red satin shoes."

"Anyhow," said Uncle Roger, "that red silk dress will break the hearts of all the feminine small fry at the party. You'd break their spirits, too if you wore the slippers. Don't do it, Sara. Leave them one wee loophole of enjoyment."

"What does Uncle Roger mean?" whispered Felicity.

"He means you girls are all dying of jealousy because of the Story Girl's dress," said Dan.

"I am not of a jealous disposition," said Felicity loftily, "and she's entirely welcome to the dress—with a complexion like that."

But we enjoyed that party hugely, every one of us. And we enjoyed the walk home afterwards, through dim, enshadowed fields where silvery star-beams lay, while Orion trod his stately march above us, and a red moon climbed up the black horizon's rim. A brook went with us part of the way, singing to us through the dark—a gay, irresponsible vagabond of valley and wilderness.

Felicity and Peter walked not with us. Peter's cup must surely have brimmed over that Christmas night. When we left the Marr house, he had boldly said to Felicity, "May I see you home?" And Felicity, much to our amazement, had taken his arm and marched off with him. The primness of her was indescribable, and was not at all ruffled by Dan's hoot of derision. As for me, I was consumed by a secret and burning desire to ask the Story Girl if I might see *her* home; but I could not screw my courage to the sticking point. How I envied Peter his easy, insouciant manner! I could not emulate him, so Dan and Felix and Cecily and the Story Girl and I all walked hand in hand, huddling a little closer together as we went through James Frewen's woods—for there are strange harps in a fir grove, and who shall say what fingers sweep them? Mighty and sonorous was the music above our heads as the winds of the night stirred the great boughs tossing athwart the starlit sky. Perhaps it was that æolian harmony which recalled to the Story Girl a legend of elder days.

"I read such a pretty story in one of Aunt Olivia's books last night," she said. "It was called 'The Christmas Harp.' Would you like to hear it? It seems to me it would just suit this part of the road."

"There isn't anything about—about ghosts in it, is there?" said Cecily timidly.

"Oh, no, I wouldn't tell a ghost story here for anything. I'd frighten myself too much. This story is about one of the shepherds who saw the angels on the first Christmas night. He was just a youth, and he loved music with all his heart, and he longed to be able to express the melody that was in his soul. But he could not; he had a harp and he often tried to play on it; but his clumsy fingers only made such discord that his companions laughed at him and mocked him, and called him a madman because he would not give it up, but would rather sit apart by himself, with his arms about his harp, looking up into the sky, while they gathered around their fire and told tales to wile away their long night vigils as they watched their sheep on the hills. But to him the thoughts that came out of the great silence were far sweeter than their mirth; and he never gave up the hope, which sometimes left his lips as a prayer, that some day he might be able to express those thoughts in music to the tired, weary, forgetful world. On the first Christmas night he was out with his fellow shepherds on the hills. It was chill and dark, and all, except him, were glad to gather around the fire. He sat, as usual, by himself, with his harp on his knee and a great longing in his heart. And there came a marvellous light in the sky and over the hills, as if the darkness of the night had suddenly blossomed into a wonderful meadow of flowery flame; and all the shepherds saw the angels and heard them sing. And as they sang, the harp that the young shepherd held began to play softly by itself, and as he listened to it he realized that it was playing the same music that the angels sang and that all his secret longings and aspirations and strivings were expressed in it. From that night, whenever he took the harp in his hands, it played the same music; and he wandered all over the world carrying it; wherever the sound of its music was heard hate and discord fled away and peace and good-will reigned. No one who heard it could think an evil thought; no one could feel hopeless or despairing or bitter or angry. When a man had once heard that music it entered into his soul and heart and life and became a part of him for ever. Years went by; the shepherd grew old and bent and feeble; but still he roamed over land and sea, that his harp might carry the message of the Christmas night and the angel song to all mankind. At last his strength failed him and he fell by the wayside in the darkness; but his harp played as his spirit passed; and it seemed to him that a Shining One stood by him, with wonderful starry eyes, and said to him, 'Lo, the music thy harp has played for so many years has been but the echo of the love and sympathy and purity and beauty in thine own soul; and if at any time in the wanderings thou hadst opened the door of that soul to evil or envy or selfishness thy harp would have ceased to play. Now thy life is ended; but what thou hast given to mankind has no end; and as long as the world lasts, so long will the heavenly music of the Christmas harp ring in the ears of men.' When the sun rose the old shepherd lay dead by the roadside, with a smile on his face; and in his hands was a harp with all its strings broken."

We left the fir woods as the tale was ended, and on the opposite hill was home. A dim light in the kitchen window betokened that Aunt Janet had no idea of going to bed until all her young fry were safely housed for the night.

"Ma's waiting up for us," said Dan. "I'd laugh if she happened to go to the door just as Felicity and Peter were strutting up. I guess she'll be cross. It's nearly twelve."

"Christmas will soon be over," said Cecily, with a sigh. "Hasn't it been a nice one? It's the first we've all spent together. Do you suppose we'll ever spend another together?"

"Lots of 'em," said Dan cheerily. "Why not?"

"Oh, I don't know," answered Cecily, her footsteps lagging somewhat. "Only things seem just a little too pleasant to last."

"If Willy Fraser had had as much spunk as Peter, Miss Cecily King mightn't be so low spirited," quoth Dan, significantly.

Cecily tossed her head and disdained reply. There are really some remarks a self-respecting young lady must ignore.

CHAPTER IV

New Year Resolutions

IF we did not have a white Christmas we had a white New Year. Midway between the two came a heavy snowfall. It was winter in our orchard of old delights then,—so truly winter that it was hard to believe summer had ever dwelt in it, or that spring would ever return to it. There were no birds to sing the music of the moon; and the path where the apple blossoms had fallen were heaped with less fragrant drifts. But it was a place of wonder on a moonlight night, when the snowy arcades shone like avenues of ivory and crystal, and the bare trees cast fairy-like traceries upon them. Over Uncle Stephen's Walk, where the snow had fallen smoothly, a spell of white magic had been woven. Taintless and wonderful it seemed, like a street of pearl in the new Jerusalem.

On New Year's Eve we were all together in Uncle Alec's kitchen, which was tacitly given over to our revels during the winter evenings. The Story Girl and Peter were there, of course, and Sara Ray's mother had allowed her to come up on condition that she should be home by eight sharp. Cecily was glad to see her, but the boys never hailed her arrival with over-much delight, because, since the dark began to come down early, Aunt Janet always made one of us walk down home with her. We hated this, because Sara Ray was always so maddeningly self-conscious of having an escort. We knew perfectly well that next day in school she would tell her chums as a "dead" secret that "So-and-So King saw her home" from the hill farm the night before. Now, seeing a young lady home from choice, and being sent home with her by your aunt or mother are two entirely different things, and we thought Sara Ray ought to have sense enough to know it.

Outside there was a vivid rose of sunset behind the cold hills of fir, and the long reaches of snowy fields glowed fairily pink in the western light. The drifts along the edges of the meadows and down the lane looked as if a series of breaking waves had, by the lifting of a magician's wand, been suddenly transformed into marble, even to their toppling curls of foam.

Slowly the splendour died, giving place to the mystic beauty of a winter twilight when the moon is rising. The hollow sky was a cup of blue. The stars came out over the white glens and the earth was covered with a kingly carpet for the feet of the young year to press.

"I'm so glad the snow came," said the Story Girl. "If it hadn't the New Year would have seemed just as dingy and worn out as the old. There's something very solemn about the idea of a New Year, isn't there? Just think of three hundred and sixty-five whole days, with not a thing happened in them yet."

"I don't suppose anything very wonderful will happen in them," said Felix pessimistically. To Felix, just then, life was flat, stale and unprofitable because it was his turn to go home with Sara Ray.

"It makes me a little frightened to think of all that may happen in them," said Cecily. "Miss Marwood says it is what we put into a year, not what we get out of it, that counts."

"I'm always glad to see a New Year," said the Story Girl. "I wish we could do as they do in Norway. The whole family sits up until midnight, and then, just as the clock is striking twelve, the father opens the door and welcomes the New Year in. Isn't it a pretty custom?"

"If ma would let us stay up till twelve we might do that too," said Dan, "but she never will. I call it mean."

"If I ever have children I'll let them stay up to watch the New Year in," said the Story Girl decidedly.

"So will I," said Peter, "but other nights they'll have to go to bed at seven."

"You ought to be ashamed, speaking of such things," said Felicity, with a scandalized face.

Peter shrank into the background abashed, no doubt believing that he had broken some *Family Guide* precept all to pieces.

"I didn't know it wasn't proper to mention children," he muttered apologetically.

"We ought to make some New Year resolutions," suggested the Story Girl. "New Year's Eve is the time to make them."

"I can't think of any resolutions I want to make," said Felicity, who was perfectly satisfied with herself.

"I could suggest a few to you," said Dan sarcastically.

"There are so many I would like to make," said Cecily, "that I'm afraid it wouldn't be any use trying to keep them all."

"Well, let's all make a few, just for the fun of it, and see if we can keep them," I said. "And let's get paper and ink and write them out. That will make them seem more solemn and binding."

"And then pin them up on our bedroom walls, where we'll see them every day," suggested the Story Girl, "and every time we break a resolution we must put a cross opposite it. That will show us what progress we are making, as well as make us ashamed if we have too many crosses."

"And let's have a Roll of Honour in *Our Magazine*," suggested Felix, "and every month we'll publish the names of those who keep their resolutions perfect."

"I think it's all nonsense," said Felicity. But she joined our circle around the table, though she sat for a long time with a blank sheet before her.

"Let's each make a resolution in turn," I said. "I'll lead off."

And, recalling with shame certain unpleasant differences of opinion I had lately had with Felicity, I wrote down in my best hand,

"I shall try to keep my temper always."

"You'd better," said Felicity tactfully.

It was Dan's turn next.

"I can't think of anything to start with," he said, gnawing his penholder fiercely.

"You might make a resolution not to eat poison berries," suggested Felicity.

"You'd better make one not to nag people everlastingly," retorted Dan.

"Oh, don't quarrel the last night of the old year," implored Cecily.

"You might resolve not to quarrel any time," suggested Sara Ray.

"No, sir," said Dan emphatically. "There's no use making a resolution you *can't* keep. There are people in this family you've just *got* to quarrel with if you want to live. But I've thought of one—I won't do things to spite people."

Felicity—who really was in an unbearable mood that night—laughed disagreeably; but Cecily gave her a fierce nudge, which probably restrained her from speaking.

"I will not eat any apples," wrote Felix.

"What on earth do you want to give up eating apples for?" asked Peter in astonishment.

"Never mind," returned Felix.

"Apples make people fat, you know," said Felicity sweetly.

"It seems a funny kind of resolution," I said doubtfully. "I think our resolutions ought to be giving up wrong things or doing right ones."

"You make your resolutions to suit yourself and I'll make mine to suit myself," said Felix defiantly.

"I shall never get drunk," wrote Peter painstakingly.

"But you never do," said the Story Girl in astonishment.

"Well, it will be all the easier to keep the resolution," argued Peter.

"That isn't fair," complained Dan. "If we all resolved not to do the things we never do we'd all be on the Roll of Honour."

"You let Peter alone," said Felicity severely. "It's a very good resolution and one everybody ought to make."

"I shall not be jealous," wrote the Story Girl.

"But are you?" I asked, surprised.

The Story Girl coloured and nodded. "Of one thing," she confessed, "but I'm not going to tell what it is."

"I'm jealous sometimes, too," confessed Sara Ray, "and so my first resolution will be 'I shall try not to feel jealous when I hear the other girls in school describing all the sick spells they've had.'"

"Goodness, do you want to be sick?" demanded Felix in astonishment.

"It makes a person important," explained Sara Ray.

"I am going to try to improve my mind by reading good books and listening to older people," wrote Cecily.

"You got that out of the Sunday School paper," cried Felicity.

"It doesn't matter where I got it," said Cecily with dignity. "The main thing is to keep it."

"It's your turn, Felicity," I said.

Felicity tossed her beautiful golden head.

"I told you I wasn't going to make any resolutions. Go on yourself."

"I shall always study my grammar lesson," I wrote—I, who loathed grammar with a deadly loathing.

"I hate grammar too," sighed Sara Ray. "It seems so unimportant."

Sara was rather fond of a big word, but did not always get hold of the right one. I rather suspected that in the above instance she really meant uninteresting.

"I won't get mad at Felicity, if I can help it," wrote Dan.

"I'm sure I never do anything to make you mad," exclaimed Felicity.

"I don't think it's polite to make resolutions about your sisters," said Peter.

"He can't keep it anyway," scoffed Felicity. "He's got such an awful temper."

"It's a family failing," flashed Dan, breaking his resolution ere the ink on it was dry.

"There you go," taunted Felicity.

"I'll work all my arithmetic problems without any help," scribbled Felix.

"I wish I could resolve that, too," sighed Sara Ray, "but it wouldn't be any use. I'd never be able to do those compound multiplication sums the teacher gives us to do at home every night if I didn't get Judy Pineau to help me. Judy isn't a good reader and she can't spell *at all,* but you can't stick her in arithmetic as far as she went herself. I feel sure," concluded poor Sara, in a hopeless tone, "that I'll *never* be able to understand compound multiplication."

> "'Multiplication is vexation,
>   Division is as bad,
> The rule of three perplexes me,
>   And fractions drive me mad,'"

quoted Dan.

"I haven't got as far as fractions yet," sighed Sara, "and I hope I'll be too big to go to school before I do. I hate arithmetic, but I am *passionately* fond of geography."

"I will not play tit-tat-x on the fly leaves of my hymn book in church," wrote Peter.

"Mercy, did you ever do such a thing?" exclaimed Felicity in horror.

Peter nodded shamefacedly.

"Yes—that Sunday Mr. Bailey preached. He was so long-winded, I got awful tired, and, anyway, he was talking about things I couldn't understand, so I played tit-tat-x with one of the Markdale boys. It was the day I was sitting up in the gallery."

"Well, I hope if you ever do the like again you won't do it in *our* pew," said Felicity severely.

"I ain't going to do it at all," said Peter. "I felt sort of mean all the rest of the day."

"I shall try not to be vexed when people interrupt me when I'm telling stories," wrote the Story Girl. "But it will be hard," she added with a sigh.

"*I* never mind being interrupted," said Felicity.

"I shall try to be cheerful and smiling all the time," wrote Cecily.

"You are, anyway," said Sara Ray loyally.

"I don't believe we ought to be cheerful *all* the time," said the Story Girl. "The Bible says we ought to weep with those who weep."

"But maybe it means that we're to weep cheerfully," suggested Cecily.

"Sorter as if you were thinking, 'I'm very sorry for you but I'm mighty glad I'm not in the scrape too,'" said Dan.

"Dan, don't be irreverent," rebuked Felicity.

"I know a story about old Mr. and Mrs. Davidson of Markdale," said the Story Girl. "She was always smiling and it used to aggravate her husband, so one day he said very crossly, 'Old lady, what *are* you grinning at?' 'Oh, well, Abiram, everything's so bright and pleasant, I've just got to smile.'

"Not long after there came a time when everything went wrong—the crop failed and their best cow died, and Mrs. Davidson had rheumatism; and finally Mr. Davidson fell and broke his leg. But still Mrs. Davidson smiled. 'What in the dickens are you grinning about now, old lady?' he demanded. 'Oh, well, Abiram,' she said, 'everything is so dark and unpleasant I've just got to smile.' 'Well,' said the old man crossly, 'I think you might give your face a rest sometimes.'"

"I shall not talk gossip," wrote Sara Ray with a satisfied air.

"Oh, don't you think that's a little *too* strict?" asked Cecily anxiously. "Of course, it's not right to talk *mean* gossip, but the harmless kind doesn't hurt. If I say to you that Emmy MacPhail is going to get a new fur collar this winter, *that* is harmless gossip, but if I say I don't see how Emmy MacPhail can afford a new fur collar when her father can't pay my father for the oats he got from him, that would be *mean* gossip. If I were you, Sara, I'd put *mean* gossip."

Sara consented to this amendment.

"I will be polite to everybody," was my third resolution, which passed without comment.

"I'll try not to use slang since Cecily doesn't like it," wrote Dan.

"*I* think some slang is real cute," said Felicity.

"The *Family Guide* says it's very vulgar," grinned Dan. "Doesn't it, Sara Stanley?"

"Don't disturb me," said the Story Girl dreamily. "I'm just thinking a beautiful thought."

"I've thought of a resolution to make," cried Felicity. "Mr. Marwood said last Sunday we should always try to think beautiful thoughts and then our lives would be very beautiful. So I shall resolve to think a beautiful thought every morning before breakfast."

"Can you only manage one a day?" queried Dan.

"And why before breakfast?" I asked.

"Because it's easier to think on an empty stomach," said Peter, in all good faith. But Felicity shot a furious glance at him.

"I selected that time," she explained with dignity, "because when I'm brushing my hair before my glass in the morning I'll see my resolution and remember it."

"Mr. Marwood meant that *all* our thoughts ought to be beautiful," said the Story Girl. "If they were, people wouldn't be afraid to say what they think."

"They oughtn't to be afraid to, anyhow," said Felix stoutly. "I'm going to make a resolution to say just what I think always."

"And do you expect to get through the year alive if you do?" asked Dan.

"It might be easy enough to say what you think if you could always be sure just what you *do* think," said the Story Girl. "So often I can't be sure."

"How would you like it if people always said just what they think to you?" asked Felicity.

"I'm not very particular what *some* people think of me," rejoined Felix.

"I notice you don't like to be told by anybody that you're fat," retorted Felicity.

"Oh, dear me, I do wish you wouldn't all say such sarcastic things to each other," said poor Cecily plaintively. "It sounds so horrid the last night of the old year. Dear knows where we'll all be this night next year. Peter, it's your turn."

"I will try," wrote Peter, "to say my prayers every night regular, and not twice one night because I don't expect to have time the next,—like I did the night before the party," he added.

"I s'pose you never said your prayers until we got you to go to church," said Felicity—who had had no hand in inducing Peter to go to church, but had stoutly opposed it, as recorded in the first volume of our family history.

"I did, too," said Peter. "Aunt Jane taught me to say my prayers. Ma hadn't time, being as father had run away; ma had to wash at night same as in day-time."

"I shall learn to cook," wrote the Story Girl, frowning.

"You'd better resolve not to make puddings of—" began Felicity, then stopped as suddenly as if she had bitten off the rest of her sentence and swallowed it. Cecily had nudged her, so she had probably remembered the Story Girl's threat that she would never tell another story if she was ever twitted with the pudding she had made from sawdust. But we all knew what Felicity had started to say and the Story Girl dealt her a most uncousinly glance.

"I will not cry because mother won't starch my aprons," wrote Sara Ray.

"Better resolve not to cry about anything," said Dan kindly.

Sara Ray shook her head forlornly.

"That would be too hard to keep. There are times when I *have* to cry. It's a relief."

"Not to the folks who have to hear you," muttered Dan aside to Cecily.

"Oh, hush," whispered Cecily back. "Don't go and hurt her feelings the last night of the old year. Is it my turn again? Well, I'll resolve not to worry because my hair is not curly. But, oh, I'll never be able to help wishing it was."

"Why don't you curl it as you used to do, then?" asked Dan.

"You know very well that I've never put my hair up in curl papers since the time Peter was dying of the measles," said Cecily reproachfully. "I resolved then I wouldn't because I wasn't sure it was quite right."

"I will keep my finger-nails neat and clean," I wrote. "There, that's four resolutions. I'm not going to make any more. Four's enough."

"I shall always think twice before I speak," wrote Felix.

"That's an awful waste of time," commented Dan, "but I guess you'll need to if you're always going to say what you think."

"I'm going to stop with three," said Peter.

"I will have all the good times I can," wrote the Story Girl.

"*That's* what *I* call sensible," said Dan.

"It's a very easy resolution to keep, anyhow," commented Felix.

"I shall try to like reading the Bible," wrote Sara Ray.

"You ought to like reading the Bible without trying to," exclaimed Felicity.

"If you had to read seven chapters of it every time you were naughty I don't believe you would like it either," retorted Sara Ray with a flash of spirit.

"I shall try to believe only half of what I hear," was Cecily's concluding resolution.

"But which half?" scoffed Dan.

"The best half," said sweet Cecily simply.

"I'll try to obey mother *always,*" wrote Sara Ray, with a tremendous sigh, as if she fully realized the difficulty of keeping such a resolution. "And that's all I'm going to make."

"Felicity has made only one," said the Story Girl.

"I think it better to make just one and keep it than make a lot and break them," said Felicity loftily

She had the last word on the subject, for it was time for Sara Ray to go, and our circle broke up. Sara and Felix departed and we watched them down the lane in the moonlight—Sara walking demurely in one runner track, and Felix stalking grimly along in the other. I fear the romantic beauty of that silver shining night was entirely thrown away on my misanthropic brother.

And it was, as I remember it, a most exquisite night—a white poem, a frosty, starry lyric of light. It was one of those nights on which one might fall asleep and dream happy dreams of gardens of mirth and song, feeling all the while through one's sleep the soft splendour and radiance of the white moon-world outside, as one hears soft, far-away music sounding through the thoughts and words that are born of it.

As a matter of fact, however, Cecily dreamed that night that she saw three full moons in the sky, and wakened up crying with the horror of it.

CHAPTER V

The First Number of Our Magazine

THE first number of *Our Magazine* was ready on New Year's Day, and we read it that evening in the kitchen. All our staff had worked nobly and we were enormously proud of the result, although Dan still continued to scoff at a paper that wasn't printed. The Story Girl and I read it turnabout while the others, except Felix, ate apples. It opened with a short

EDITORIAL

With this number *Our Magazine* makes its first bow to the public. All the editors have done their best and the various departments are full of valuable information and amusement. The tastefully designed cover is by a famous artist, Mr. Blair Stanley, who sent it to us all the way from Europe at the request of his daughter. Mr. Peter Craig, our enterprising literary editor, contributes a touching love story. (*Peter, aside, in a gratified pig's whisper:* "I never was called 'Mr.' before.") Miss Felicity King's essay on Shakespeare is none the worse for being an old school composition, as it is new to most of our readers. Miss Cecily King contributes a thrilling article of adventure. The various departments are ably edited, and we feel that we have reason to be proud of *Our Magazine*. But we shall not rest on our oars. "Excelsior'" shall ever be our motto. We trust that each succeeding issue will be better than the one that went before. We are well aware of many defects, but it is easier to see them than to remedy them. Any suggestion that would tend to the improvement of *Our Magazine* will be thankfully received, but we trust that no criticism will be made that will hurt anyone's feelings. Let us all work together in harmony, and strive to make *Our*

Magazine an influence for good and a source of innocent pleasure, and let us always remember the words of the poet.

> "The heights by great men reached and kept
>   Were not attained by sudden flight,
> But they, while their companions slept,
>   Were toiling upwards in the night."

(*Peter, impressively:*—"I've read many a worse editorial in the *Enterprise*.")

ESSAY ON SHAKESPEARE

Shakespeare's full name was William Shakespeare. He did not always spell it the same way. He lived in the reign of Queen Elizabeth and wrote a great many plays. His plays are written in dialogue form. Some people think they were not written by Shakespeare but by another man of the same name. I have read some of them because our school teacher says everybody ought to read them, but I did not care much for them. There are some things in them I cannot understand. I like the stories of Valeria H. Montague in the *Family Guide* ever so much better. They are more exciting and truer to life. *Romeo and Juliet* was one of the plays I read. It was very sad. Juliet dies and I don't like stories where people die. I like it better when they all get married especially to dukes and earls. Shakespeare himself was married to Anne Hatheway. They are both dead now. They have been dead a good while. He was a very famous man.

F<small>ELICITY</small> K<small>ING</small>

(*Peter, modestly:* "I don't know much about Shakespeare myself but I've got a book of his plays that belonged to my Aunt Jane, and I guess I'll have to tackle him as soon as I finish with the Bible.")

THE STORY OF AN ELOPEMENT FROM CHURCH

This is a true story. It happened in Markdale to an uncle of my mothers. He wanted to marry Miss Jemima Parr. Felicity says Jemima is not a romantic name for a heroin of a story but I cant help it in this case because it is a true story and her name realy was Jemima. My mothers uncle was named Thomas Taylor. He was poor at that time and so the father of Miss Jemima Parr did not want him for a soninlaw and told him he was not to come near the house or he would set the dog on him. Miss Jemima Parr was very pretty and my mothers uncle Thomas was just crazy about her and she wanted him too. She cried almost every night after her father forbid him to come to the house except the nights she had to sleep or she would have died. And she was so frightened he might try to come for all and get tore up by the dog and it was a bull-dog too that would never let go. But mothers uncle Thomas was too cute for that. He waited till one day there was preaching in the Markdale church in the middle of the week because it was sacrament time and Miss Jemima Parr and her family all went because her father was an elder. My mothers uncle Thomas went too and set in the pew just behind Miss Jemima Parrs family. When they all bowed their heads at prayer time Miss Jemima Parr didnt but set bolt uprite and my mothers uncle Thomas bent over and wispered in her ear. I dont know what he said so I cant right it but Miss Jemima Parr blushed that is turned red and nodded her head. Perhaps some people may think that my mothers uncle Thomas shouldnt of wispered at prayer time in church but you must remember that Miss Jemima Parrs father had thretened to set the dog on him and that was hard lines when he was a respektable young man though not rich. Well when they were singing the last sam my mothers uncle Thomas got up and went out very quietly and as soon as church was out Miss Jemima Parr walked out too real quick. Her family never suspekted anything and they hung round talking to folks and shaking hands while Miss Jemima Parr and my mothers uncle Thomas were eloping outside. And what do you suppose they eloped in. Why in Miss Jemima Parrs fathers slay. And when he went out they were gone and his slay was gone also his horse. Of course my mothers uncle Thomas didnt steal the horse. He just borroed it and sent it home the next day. But before Miss Jemima Parrs father could get another rig to follow them they were so far away he couldent catch them before they got married. And they lived happy together forever afterwards. Mothers uncle Thomas lived to be a very old man. He died very suddent. He felt quite well when he went to sleep and when he woke up he was dead.

PETER CRAIG.

MY MOST EXCITING ADVENTURE

The editor says we must all write up our most exciting adventure for *Our Magazine*. My most exciting adventure happened a year ago last November. I was nearly frightened to death. Dan says he wouldn't of been scared and Felicity says she would of known what it was but it's easy to talk.

It happened the night I went down to see Kitty Marr. I thought when I went that Aunt Olivia was visiting there and I could come home with her. But she wasn't there and I had to come home alone. Kitty came a piece of the way but she wouldn't come any further than Uncle James Frewen's gate. She said it was because it was so windy she was afraid she would get the tooth-ache and not because she was frightened of the ghost of the dog that haunted the bridge in Uncle James' hollow. I did wish she hadn't said anything about the dog because I mightn't of thought about it if she hadn't. I had to go on alone thinking of it. I'd heard the story often but I'd never believed in it. They said the dog used to appear at one end of the bridge and walk across it with people and vanish when he got to the other end. He never tried to bite anyone but one wouldn't want to meet the ghost of a dog even if one didn't believe in him. I knew there was no such thing as ghosts and I kept saying a paraphrase over to myself and the Golden Text of the next Sunday School lesson but oh, how my heart beat when I got near the hollow! It was so dark. You could just see things dim-like but you couldn't see what they were. When I got to the bridge I walked along sideways with my back to the railing so I couldn't think the dog was behind me. And then just in the middle of the bridge I met something. It was right before me and it was big and black, just about the size of a Newfoundland dog, and I thought I could see a white nose. And it kept jumping about from one side of the bridge to the other. Oh, I hope none of my readers will ever be so frightened as I was then. I was too frightened to run back because I was afraid it would chase me and I couldn't get past it, it moved so quick, and then it just made one spring right on me and I felt its claws and I screamed and fell down. It rolled off to one side and laid there quite quiet but I didn't dare move and I don't know what would have become of me if Amos Cowan hadn't come along that very minute with a lantern. And there was me sitting in the middle of the bridge and that awful thing beside me. And what do you think it was but a big umbrella with a white handle? Amos said it was his umbrella and it had blown away from him and he had to go back and get the lantern to look for it. I felt like asking him what on earth he was going about with an umbrella open when it wasent raining. But the Cowans do such queer things. You remember the time Jerry Cowan sold us God's picture. Amos took me right home and I was thankful for I don't know what would have become of me if he hadn't come along. I couldn't sleep all night and I never want to have any more adventures like that one.

CECILY KING.

PERSONALS

Mr. Dan King felt somewhat indisposed the day after Christmas—probably as the result of too much mince pie. (*Dan, indignantly:*—"I wasn't. I only et one piece!")

Mr. Peter Craig thinks he saw the Family Ghost on Christmas Eve. But the rest of us think all he saw was the white calf with the red tail. (*Peter, muttering sulkily:*—"It's a queer calf that would walk up on end and wring its hands.")

Miss Cecily King spent the night of Dec. 20th with Miss Kitty Marr. They talked most of the night about new knitted lace patterns and their beaus and were very sleepy in school next day. (*Cecily, sharply:*—"We never mentioned such things!")

Patrick Grayfur, Esq., was indisposed yesterday, but seems to be enjoying his usual health to-day.

The King family expect their Aunt Eliza to visit them in January. She is really our great-aunt. We have never seen her but we are told she is very deaf and does not like children. So Aunt Janet says we must make ourselves scarce when she comes.

Miss Cecily King has undertaken to fill with names a square of the missionary quilt which the Mission Band is making. You pay five cents to have your name embroidered in a corner, ten cents to have it in the centre, and a quarter if you want it left off altogether. (*Cecily, indignantly:*—"That isn't the way at all.")

WANTED—A remedy to make a fat boy thin. Address, "Patient Sufferer, care of *Our Magazine.*"

(*Felix, sourly:*—"Sara Ray never got that up. I'll bet it was Dan. He'd better stick to his own department.")

HOUSEHOLD DEPARTMENT

Mrs. Alexander King killed all her geese the twentieth of December. We all helped pick them. We had one Christmas Day and will have one every fortnight the rest of the winter.

The bread was sour last week because mother wouldn't take my advice. I told her it was too warm for it in the corner behind the stove

Miss Felicity King invented a new recete for date cookies recently, which everybody said were excelent. I am not going to publish it though, because I don't want other people to find it out.

ANXIOUS INQUIRER:—If you want to remove inkstains place the stain over steam and apply salt and lemon juice. If it was Dan who sent this question in I'd advise him to stop wiping his pen on his shirt sleeves and then he wouldn't have so many stains.

FELICITY KING.

ETIQUETTE DEPARTMENT

F-l-x:—Yes, you should offer your arm to a lady when seeing her home. but don't keep her standing too long at the gate while you say good night.

(*Felix, enraged:*—"I never asked such a question.")

C-c-l-y:—No, it is not polite to use "Holy Moses" or "dodgasted" in ordinary conversation.

(Cecily had gone down cellar to replenish the apple plate, so this passed without protest.)

S-r-a:—No, it isn't polite to cry all the time. As to whether you should ask a young man in, it all depends on whether he went home with you of his own accord or was sent by some elderly relative.

F-l-t-y:—It does not break any rule of etiquette if you keep a button off your best young man's coat for a keepsake. But don't take more than one or his mother might miss them.

DAN KING.

FASHION NOTES

Knitted mufflers are much more stylish than crocheted ones this winter. It is nice to have one the same colour as your cap.

Red mittens with a black diamond pattern on the back are much run after. Em Frewen's grandma knits hers for her. She can knit the double diamond pattern and Em puts on such airs about it, but I think the single diamond is in better taste.

The new winter hats at Markdale are very pretty. It is so exciting to pick a hat. Boys can't have that fun. Their hats are so much alike.

CECILY KING.

FUNNY PARAGRAPHS

This is a true joke and really happened.

There was an old local preacher in New Brunswick one time whose name was Samuel Clask. He used to preach and pray and visit the sick just like a regular minister. One day he was visiting a neighbour who was dying and he prayed the Lord to have mercy on him because he was very poor and had worked so hard all his life that he hadn't much time to attend to religion.

"And if you don't believe me, O Lord," Mr. Clask finished up with, "just take a look at his hands."

FELIX KING.

GENERAL INFORMATION BUREAU

DAN:—Do porpoises grow on trees or vines?
Ans. Neither. They inhabit the deep sea.

FELIX KING.

(*Dan, aggrieved:*—"Well, I'd never heard of porpoises and it sounded like something that grew. But you needn't have gone and put it in the paper."

Felix:—"It isn't any worse than the things you put in about me that I never asked at all."

Cecily, soothingly:—"Oh, well, boys, it's all in fun, and I think *Our Magazine* is perfectly elegant."

Felicity, failing to see the Story Girl and Beverley exchanging winks behind her back:—"It certainly is, though *some people* were so opposed to starting it.")

What harmless, happy fooling it all was! How we laughed as we read and listened and devoured apples! Blow high, blow low, no wind can ever quench the ruddy glow of that faraway winter night in our memories. And though *Our Magazine* never made much of a stir in the world, or was the means of hatching any genius, it continued to be capital fun for us throughout the year.

CHAPTER VI

Great-Aunt Eliza's Visit

IT was a diamond winter day in February—clear, cold, hard, brilliant. The sharp blue sky shone, the white fields and hills glittered, the fringe of icicles around the eaves of Uncle Alec's house sparkled. Keen was the frost and crisp the snow over our world; and we young fry of the King households were all agog to enjoy life—for was it not Saturday, and were we not left all alone to keep house?

Aunt Janet and Aunt Olivia had had their last big "kill" of market poultry the day before; and early in the morning all our grown-ups set forth to Charlottetown, to be gone the whole day. They left us many charges as usual, some of which we remembered and some of which we forgot; but with Felicity in command none of us dared stray far out of line. The Story Girl and Peter came over, of course, and we all agreed that we would haste and get the work done in the forenoon, that we might have an afternoon of uninterrupted enjoyment. A taffy-pull after dinner and then a jolly hour of coasting on the hill field before supper were on our programme. But disappointment was our portion. We did manage to get the taffy made but before we could sample the result satisfactorily, and just as the girls were finishing with the washing of the dishes, Felicity glanced out of the window and exclaimed in tones of dismay,

"Oh, dear me, here's Great-aunt Eliza coming up the lane! Now, isn't that too mean?"

We all looked out to see a tall, gray-haired lady approaching the house, looking about her with the slightly puzzled air of a stranger. We had been expecting Great-aunt Eliza's advent for some weeks, for she was visiting relatives in Markdale. We knew she was liable to pounce down on us any time, being one of those delightful folk who like to "surprise" people, but we had never thought of her coming that particular day. It must be confessed that we did not look forward to her visit with any pleasure. None of us had ever seen her, but we knew she was very deaf, and had very decided opinions as to the way in which children should behave.

"Whew!" whistled Dan. "We're in for a jolly afternoon. She's deaf as a post and we'll have to split our throats to make her hear at all. I've a notion to skin out."

"Oh, don't talk like that, Dan," said Cecily reproachfully. "She's old and lonely and has had a great deal of trouble. She has buried three husbands. We must be kind to her and do the best we can to make her visit pleasant."

"She's coming to the back door," said Felicity, with an agitated glance around the kitchen. "I told you, Dan, that you should have shovelled the snow away from the front door this morning. Cecily, set those pots in the pantry quick—hide those boots, Felix—shut the cupboard door, Peter—Sara, straighten up the lounge. She's awfully particular and ma says her house is always as neat as wax."

To do Felicity justice, while she issued orders to the rest of us, she was flying busily about herself, and it was amazing how much was accomplished in the way of putting the kitchen in perfect order during the two minutes in which Great-aunt Eliza was crossing the yard.

"Fortunately the sitting-room is tidy and there's plenty in the pantry," said Felicity, who could face anything undauntedly with a well-stocked larder behind her.

Further conversation was cut short by a decided rap at the door. Felicity opened it.

"Why, how do you do, Aunt Eliza?" she said loudly.

A slightly bewildered look appeared on Aunt Eliza's face. Felicity perceived she had not spoken loudly enough.

"How do you do, Aunt Eliza," she repeated at the top of her voice. "Come in—we are glad to see you. We've been looking for you for ever so long."

"Are your father and mother at home?" asked Aunt Eliza, slowly.

"No, they went to town today. But they'll be home this evening."

"I'm sorry they're away," said Aunt Eliza, coming in, "because I can stay only a few hours."

"Oh, that's too bad," shouted poor Felicity, darting an angry glance at the rest of us, as if to demand why we didn't help her out. "Why, we've been thinking you'd stay a week with us anyway. You *must* stay over Sunday."

"I really can't. I have to go to Charlottetown tonight," returned Aunt Eliza.

"Well, you'll take off your things and stay to tea, at least," urged Felicity, as hospitably as her strained vocal chords would admit.

"Yes, I think I'll do that. I want to get acquainted with my—my nephews and nieces," said Aunt Eliza, with a rather pleasant glance around our group. If I could have associated thought of such a thing with my preconception of Great-aunt Eliza I could have sworn there was a twinkle in her eye. But of course it was impossible. "Won't you introduce yourselves, please?"

Felicity shouted our names and Great-aunt Eliza shook hands all round. She performed the duty grimly and I concluded I must have been mistaken about the twinkle. She was certainly very tall and dignified and imposing—altogether a great-aunt to be respected.

Felicity and Cecily took her to the spare room and then left her in the sitting-room while they returned to the kitchen, to discuss the matter in family conclave.

"Well, and what do you think of dear Aunt Eliza?" asked Dan.

"S-s-s-sh," warned Cecily, with a glance at the half-open hall door.

"Pshaw," scoffed Dan, "She can't hear us. There ought to be a law against anyone being as deaf as that."

"She's not so old-looking as I expected," said Felix. "If her hair wasn't so white she wouldn't look much older than your mother."

"You don't have to be very old to be a great-aunt," said Cecily. "Kitty Marr has a great-aunt who is just the same age as her mother. I expect it was burying so many husbands turned her hair white. But Aunt Eliza doesn't look just as I expected she would either."

"She's dressed more stylishly than I expected," said Felicity. "I thought she'd be real old-fashioned, but her clothes aren't too bad at all."

"She wouldn't be bad-looking if 'tweren't for her nose," said Peter. "It's too long, and crooked besides."

"You needn't criticize our relations like that," said Felicity tartly.

"Well, aren't you doing it yourselves?" expostulated Peter.

"That's different," retorted Felicity. "Never you mind Great-aunt Eliza's nose."

"Well, don't expect me to talk to her," said Dan, " 'cause I won't."

"I'm going to be very polite to her," said Felicity. "She's rich. But how are we to entertain her, that's the question."

"What does the *Family Guide* say about entertaining your rich, deaf old aunt?" queried Dan ironically.

"The *Family Guide* says we should be polite to *everybody*," said Cecily, with a reproachful look at Dan.

"The worst of it is," said Felicity, looking worried, "that there isn't a bit of old bread in the house and she can't eat new, I've heard father say it gives her indigestion. What will we do?"

"Make a pan of rusks and apologize for having no old bread," suggested the Story Girl, probably by way of teasing Felicity. The latter, however, took it in all good faith.

"The *Family Guide* says we should never apologize for things we can't help. It says it's adding insult to injury to do it. But you run over home for a loaf of stale bread, Sara, and it's a good idea about the rusks. I'll make a panful."

"Let me make them," said the Story Girl, eagerly. "I can make real good rusks now."

"No, it wouldn't do to trust you," said Felicity mercilessly. "You might make some queer mistake and Aunt Eliza would tell it all over the country. She's a fearful old gossip. I'll make the rusks myself. She hates cats, so we mustn't let Paddy be seen. And she's a Methodist, so mind nobody says anything against Methodists to her."

"Who's going to say anything, anyhow?" asked Peter belligerently.

"I wonder if I might ask her for her name for my quilt square?" speculated Cecily. "I believe I will. She looks so much friendlier than I expected. Of course she'll choose the five-cent section. She's an estimable old lady, but very economical."

"Why don't you say she's so mean she'd skin a flea for its hide and tallow?" said Dan. "That's the plain truth."

"Well, I'm going to see about getting tea," said Felicity, "so the rest of you will have to entertain her. You better go in and show her the photographs in the album. Dan, you do it."

"Thank you, that's a girl's job," said Dan. "I'd look nice sitting up to Aunt Eliza and yelling out that this was Uncle Jim and 'tother Cousin Sarah's twins, wouldn't I? Cecily or the Story Girl can do it."

"I don't know all the pictures in your album," said the Story Girl hastily.

"I s'pose I'll have to do it, though I don't like to," sighed Cecily. "But we ought to go in. We've left her alone too long now. She'll think we have no manners."

Accordingly we all filed in rather reluctantly. Great-aunt Eliza was toasting her toes—clad, as we noted, in very smart and shapely shoes—at the stove and looking quite at her ease. Cecily, determined to do her duty even in the face of such fearful odds as Great-aunt Eliza's deafness, dragged a ponderous, plush-covered album from its corner and proceeded to display and explain the family photographs. She did her brave best but she could not shout like Felicity, and half the time, as she confided to me later on, she felt that Great-aunt Eliza did not hear one word she said, because she didn't seem to take in who the people were, though, just like all deaf folks, she wouldn't let on. Great-aunt Eliza certainly didn't talk much; she looked at the photographs in silence, but she smiled now and then. That smile bothered me. It was so twinkly and so very un-great-aunt-Elizaish. But I felt indignant with her. I thought she might have shown a little more appreciation of Cecily's gallant efforts to entertain.

It was very dull for the rest of us. The Story Girl sat rather sulkily in her corner; she was angry because Felicity would not let her make the rusks, and also, perhaps, a little vexed because she could not charm Great-aunt Eliza with her golden voice and story-telling gift. Felix and I looked at each other and wished ourselves out in the hill field, careering gloriously adown its gleaming crust.

But presently a little amusement came our way. Dan, who was sitting behind Great-aunt Eliza, and consequently out of her view, began making comments on Cecily's explanation of this one and that one among the photographs. In vain Cecily implored him to stop. It was too good fun to give up. For the next half-hour the dialogue ran after this fashion, while Peter and Felix and I, and even the Story Girl, suffered agonies trying to smother our bursts of laughter—for Great-aunt Eliza could see if she couldn't hear:

Cecily, shouting:—"That is Mr. Joseph Elliott of Markdale, a second cousin of mother's."

Dan:—"Don't brag of it, Sis. He's the man who was asked if somebody else said something in sincerity and old Joe said, 'No, he said it in my cellar.'"

Cecily:—"This isn't anybody in *our* family. It's little Xavy Gautier who used to be hired with Uncle Roger."

Dan:—"Uncle Roger sent him to fix a gate one day and scolded him because he didn't do it right, and Xavy was mad as hops and said 'How you 'spect me to fix dat gate? I never learned jogerfy.'"

Cecily, with an anguished glance at Dan:—"This is Great-uncle Robert King."

Dan:—"He's been married four times. Don't you think that's often enough, dear great-aunty?"

Cecily:—"(Dan!!) This is a nephew of Mr. Ambrose Marr's. He lives out west and teaches school."

Dan:—"Yes, and Uncle Roger says he doesn't know enough not to sleep in a field with the gate open."

Cecily:—"This is Miss Julia Stanley, who used to teach in Carlisle a few years ago."

Dan:—"When she resigned the trustees had a meeting to see if they'd ask her to stay and raise her supplement. Old Highland Sandy was alive then and he got up and said, 'If she for go let her for went. Perhaps she for marry.'"

Cecily, with the air of a martyr:—"This is Mr. Layton, who used to travel around selling Bibles and hymn books and Talmage's sermons."

Dan:—"He was so thin Uncle Roger used to say he always mistook him for a crack in the atmosphere. One time he stayed here all night and went to prayer meeting and Mr. Marwood asked him to lead in prayer. It had been raining 'most every day for three weeks, and it was just in haymaking time, and everybody thought the hay was going to be ruined, and old Layton got up and prayed that God would send gentle showers on the growing crops, and I heard Uncle Roger whisper to a fellow behind me, 'If somebody don't choke him off we won't get the hay made this summer.' "

Cecily, in exasperation:—"(Dan, shame on you for telling such irreverent stories.) This is Mrs. Alexander Scott of Markdale. She has been very sick for a long time."

Dan:—"Uncle Roger says all that keeps her alive is that she's scared her husband will marry again."

Cecily:—"This is old Mr. James MacPherson who used to live behind the graveyard."

Dan:—"He's the man who told mother once that he always made his own iodine out of strong tea and baking soda."

Cecily:—"This is Cousin Ebenezer MacPherson on the Markdale road."

Dan:—"Great temperance man! He never tasted rum in his life. He took the measles when he was forty-five and was crazy as a loon with them, and the doctor ordered them to give him a dose of brandy. When he swallowed it he looked up and says, solemn as an owl, 'Give it to me oftener and more at a time.' "

Cecily, imploringly:—"(Dan, do stop. You make me so nervous I don't know what I'm doing.) This is Mr. Lemuel Goodridge. He is a minister."

Dan:—"You ought to see his mouth. Uncle Roger says the drawing string has fell out of it. It just hangs loose—so fashion."

Dan, whose own mouth was far from being beautiful, here gave an imitation of the Rev. Lemuel's, to the utter undoing of Peter, Felix, and myself. Our wild guffaws of laughter penetrated even Great-aunt Eliza's deafness, and she glanced up with a startled face. What we would have done I do not know had not Felicity at that moment appeared in the doorway with panic-stricken eyes and exclaimed,

"Cecily, come here for a moment."

Cecily, glad of even a temporary respite, fled to the kitchen and we heard her demanding what was the matter.

"Matter!" exclaimed Felicity, tragically. "Matter enough! Some of you left a soup plate with molasses in it on the pantry table and Pat got into it and what do you think? He went into the spare room and walked all over Aunt Eliza's things on the bed. You can see his tracks plain as plain. What in the world can we do? She'll be simply furious."

I looked apprehensively at Great-aunt Eliza; but she was

gazing intently at a picture of Aunt Janet's sister's twins, a most stolid, uninteresting pair; but evidently Great-aunt Eliza found them amusing for she was smiling widely over them.

"Let us take a little clean water and a soft bit of cotton," came Cecily's clear voice from the kitchen, "and see if we can't clean the molasses off. The coat and hat are both cloth, and molasses isn't like grease."

"Well, we can try, but I wish the Story Girl would keep her cat home," grumbled Felicity.

The Story Girl here flew out to defend her pet, and we four boys stayed on, miserably conscious of Great-aunt Eliza, who never said a word to us, despite her previously expressed desire to become acquainted with us. She kept on looking at the photographs and seemed quite oblivious of our presence.

Presently the girls returned, having, as transpired later, been so successful in removing the traces of Paddy's mischief that it was not deemed necessary to worry Great-aunt Eliza with any account of it. Felicity announced tea and, while Cecily conveyed Great-aunt Eliza out to the dining-room, lingered behind to consult with us for a moment.

"Ought we to ask her to say grace?" she wanted to know.

"I know a story," said the Story Girl, "about Uncle Roger when he was just a young man. He went to the house of a very deaf old lady and when they sat down to the table she asked him to say grace. Uncle Roger had never done such a thing in his life and he turned as red as a beet and looked down and muttered, 'E-r-r, please excuse me—I—I'm not accustomed to doing that.' Then he looked up and the old lady said 'Amen,' loudly and cheerfully. She thought Uncle Roger was saying grace all the time."

"I don't think it's right to tell funny stories about such things," said Felicity coldly. "And I asked for your opinion, not for a story."

"If we don't ask her, Felix must say it, for he's the only one who can, and we must have it, or she'd be shocked."

"Oh, ask her—ask her," advised Felix hastily.

She was asked accordingly and said grace without any hesitation, after which she proceeded to eat heartily of the excellent supper Felicity had provided. The rusks were especially good and Great-aunt Eliza ate three of them and praised them. Apart from that she said little and during the first part of the meal we sat in embarrassed silence. Toward the last, however, our tongues were loosened, and the Story Girl told us a tragic tale of old Charlottetown and a governor's wife who had died of a broken heart in the early days of the colony.

"They say that story isn't true," said Felicity. "They say what she really died of was indigestion. The Governor's wife who lives there now is a relation of our own. She is a second cousin of father's but we've never seen her. Her name was Agnes Clark. And mind you, when father was a young man he was dead in love with her and so was she with him."

"Who ever told you that?" exclaimed Dan.

"Aunt Olivia. And I've heard ma teasing father about it, too. Of course, it was before father got acquainted with mother."

"Why didn't your father marry her?" I asked.

"Well, she just simply wouldn't marry him in the end. She got over being in love with him. I guess she was pretty fickle. Aunt Olivia said father felt awful about it for awhile, but he got over it when he met ma. Ma was twice as good-looking as Agnes Clark. Agnes was a sight for freckles, so Aunt Olivia says. But she and father remained real good friends. Just think, if she had married him we would have been the children of the Governor's wife."

"But she wouldn't have been the Governor's wife then," said Dan.

"I guess it's just as good being father's wife," declared Cecily loyally.

"You might think so if you saw the Governor," chuckled Dan. "Uncle Roger says it would be no harm to worship him because he doesn't look like anything in the heavens above or on the earth beneath or the waters under the earth."

"Oh, Uncle Roger just says that because he's on the opposite side of politics," said Cecily. "The Governor isn't really so very ugly. I saw him at the Markdale picnic two years ago. He's very fat and bald and red-faced, but I've seen far worse looking men."

"I'm afraid your seat is too near the stove, Aunt Eliza," shouted Felicity.

Our guest, whose face was certainly very much flushed, shook her head.

"Oh, no, I'm very comfortable," she said. But her voice had the effect of making us uncomfortable. There was a queer, uncertain little sound in it. Was Great-aunt Eliza laughing at us? We looked at her sharply but her face was very solemn. Only her eyes had a suspicious appearance. Somehow, we did not talk much more the rest of the meal.

When it was over Great-aunt Eliza said she was very sorry but she must really go. Felicity politely urged her to stay, but was much relieved when Great-aunt Eliza adhered to her intention of going. When Felicity took her to the spare room Cecily slipped upstairs and presently came back with a little parcel in her hand.

"What have you got there?" demanded Felicity suspiciously.

"A—a little bag of rose-leaves," faltered Cecily. "I thought I'd give them to Aunt Eliza."

"The idea! Don't you do such a thing," said Felicity contemptuously. "She'd think you were crazy."

"She was awfully nice when I asked her for her name for the quilt," protested Cecily, "and she took a ten-cent section after all. So I'd like to give her the rose-leaves—and I'm going to, too, Miss Felicity."

Great-aunt Eliza accepted the little gift quite graciously, bade us all good-bye, said she had enjoyed herself very much, left messages for father and mother, and finally betook herself away. We watched her cross the yard, tall, stately, erect, and disappear down the lane. Then, as often aforetime, we gathered together in the cheer of the red hearth-flame, while outside the wind of a winter twilight sang through fair white valleys brimmed with a reddening sunset, and a faint, serene, silver-cold star glimmered over the willow at the gate.

"Well," said Felicity, drawing a relieved breath, "I'm glad she's gone. She certainly is queer, just as mother said."

"It's a different kind of queerness from what I expected, though," said the Story Girl meditatively. "There's something I can't quite make out about Aunt Eliza. I don't think I altogether like her."

"I'm precious sure I don't," said Dan.

"Oh, well, never mind. She's gone now and that's the last of it," said Cecily comfortingly.

But it wasn't the last of it—not by any manner of means was it! When our grown-ups returned almost the first words Aunt Janet said were,

"And so you had the Governor's wife to tea?"

We all stared at her.

"I don't know what you mean," said Felicity. "We had nobody to tea except Great-aunt Eliza. She came this afternoon and—"

"Great-aunt Eliza? Nonsense," said Aunt Janet. "Aunt Eliza was in town today. She had tea with us at Aunt Louisa's. But wasn't Mrs. Governor Lesley here? We met her on her way back to Charlottetown and she told us she was. She said she was visiting a friend in Carlisle and thought she would call to see father for old acquaintance sake. What in the world are all you children staring like that for? Your eyes are like saucers."

"There was a lady here to tea," said Felicity miserably, "but we thought it was Great-aunt Eliza—she never *said* she wasn't—I thought she acted queer—and we all yelled at her as if she was deaf—and said things to each other about her nose—and Pat running over her clothes—"

"She must have heard all you said while I was showing her the photographs, Dan," cried Cecily.

"And about the Governor at tea time," chuckled unrepentant Dan.

"I want to know what all this means," said Aunt Janet sternly.

She knew in due time, after she had pieced the story together from our disjointed accounts. She was horrified, and Uncle Alec was mildly disturbed, but Uncle Roger roared with laughter and Aunt Olivia echoed it.

"To think you should have so little sense!" said Aunt Janet in a disgusted tone.

"I think it was real mean of her to pretend she was deaf," said Felicity, almost on the verge of tears.

"That was Agnes Clark all over," chuckled Uncle Roger. "How she must have enjoyed this afternoon!"

She had enjoyed it, as we learned the next day, when a letter came from her.

"Dear Cecily and all the rest of you," wrote the Governor's wife, "I want to ask you to forgive me for pretending to be Aunt Eliza. I suspect it was a little horrid of me, but really I couldn't resist the temptation, and if you will forgive me for it I will forgive you for the things you said about the Governor, and we will all be good friends You know the Governor is a very nice man, though he has the misfortune not to be handsome.

"I had just a splendid time at your place, and I envy your

Aunt Eliza her nephews and nieces. You were all so nice to me, and I didn't dare to be a bit nice to you lest I should give myself away. But I'll make up for that when you come to see me at Government House, as you all must the very next time you come to town. I'm so sorry I didn't see Paddy, for I love pussy cats, even if they do track molasses over my clothes. And, Cecily, thank you ever so much for that little bag of pot-pourri. It smells like a hundred rose gardens, and I have put it between the sheets for my very sparest room bed, where you shall sleep when you come to see me, you dear thing. And the Governor wants you to put his name on the quilt square, too, in the ten-cent section.

"Tell Dan I enjoyed his comments on the photographs very much. They were quite a refreshing contrast to the usual explanations of 'who's who.' And Felicity, your rusks were perfection. Do send me your recipe for them, there's a darling.

"Yours most cordially,

"AGNES CLARK LESLEY."

"Well, it was decent of her to apologize, anyhow," commented Dan.

"If we only hadn't said that about the Governor," moaned Felicity.

"How did you make your rusks?" asked Aunt Janet. "There was no baking-powder in the house, and I never could get them right with soda and cream of tartar."

"There was plenty of baking-powder in the pantry," said Felicity.

"No, there wasn't a particle. I used the last making those cookies Thursday morning."

"But I found another can nearly full, away back on the top shelf, ma,—the one with the yellow label. I guess you forgot it was there."

Aunt Janet stared at her pretty daughter blankly. Then amazement gave place to horror.

"Felicity King!" she exclaimed. "You don't mean to tell me that you raised those rusks with the stuff that was in that old yellow can?"

"Yes, I did," faltered Felicity, beginning to look scared. "Why, ma, what was the matter with it?"

"Matter! That stuff was *tooth-powder*, that's what it was. Your

Cousin Myra broke the bottle her tooth-powder was in when she was here last winter and I gave her that old can to keep it in. She forgot to take it when she went away and I put it on that top shelf. I declare you must all have been bewitched yesterday."

Poor, poor Felicity! If she had not always been so horribly vain over her cooking and so scornfully contemptuous of other people's aspirations and mistakes along that line, I could have found it in my heart to pity her.

The Story Girl would have been more than human if she had not betrayed a little triumphant amusement, but Peter stood up for his lady manfully.

"The rusks were splendid, anyhow, so what difference does it make what they were raised with?"

Dan, however, began to taunt Felicity with her tooth-powder rusks, and kept it up for the rest of his natural life.

"Don't forget to send the Governor's wife the recipe for them," he said.

Felicity, with eyes tearful and cheeks crimson from mortification, rushed from the room, but never, never did the Governor's wife get the recipe for those rusks.

CHAPTER VII

We
Visit
Cousin
Mattie's

ONE Saturday in March we walked over to Baywater, for a long-talked-of visit to Cousin Mattie Dilke. By the road, Baywater was six miles away, but there was a short cut across hills and fields and woods which was scantly three. We did not look forward to our visit with any particular delight, for there was nobody at Cousin Mattie's except grown-ups who had been grown up so long that it was rather hard for them to remember they had ever been children. But, as Felicity told us, it was necessary to visit Cousin Mattie at least once a year, or else she would be "huffed," so we concluded we might as well go and have it over.

"Anyhow, we'll get a splendiferous dinner," said Dan. "Cousin Mattie's a great cook and there's nothing stingy about her."

"You are always thinking of your stomach," said Felicity pleasantly.

"Well, you know I couldn't get along very well without it, darling," responded Dan who, since New Year's, had adopted a new method of dealing with Felicity—whether by way of keeping his resolution or because he had discovered that it annoyed Felicity far more than angry retorts, deponent sayeth not. He invariably met her criticisms with a good-natured grin and a flippant remark with some tender epithet tagged on to it. Poor Felicity used to get hopelessly furious over it.

Uncle Alec was dubious about our going that day. He looked abroad on the general dourness of gray earth and gray air and gray sky, and said a storm was brewing. But Cousin Mattie had been sent word that we were coming, and she did not like to be disappointed, so he let us go, warning us to stay with Cousin Mattie all night if the storm came on while we were there.

We enjoyed our walk—even Felix enjoyed it, although he

had been appointed to write up the visit for *Our Magazine* and was rather weighed down by the responsibility of it. What mattered it though the world were gray and wintry? We walked the golden road and carried spring time in our hearts, and we beguiled our way with laughter and jest, and the tales the Story Girl told us—myths and legends of elder time.

The walking was good, for there had lately been a thaw and everything was frozen. We went over fields, crossed by spidery trails of gray fences, where the withered grasses stuck forlornly up through the snow; we lingered for a time in a group of hill pines, great, majestic tree-creatures, friends of evening stars; and finally struck into the belt of fir and maple which intervened between Carlisle and Baywater. It was in this locality that Peg Bowen lived, and our way lay near her house though not directly in sight of it. We hoped we would not meet her, for since the affair of the bewitchment of Paddy we did not know quite what to think of Peg; the boldest of us held his breath as we passed her haunts, and drew it again with a sigh of relief when they were safely left behind.

The woods were full of the brooding stillness that often precedes a storm, and the wind crept along their white, cone-sprinkled floors with a low, wailing cry. Around us were solitudes of snow, arcades picked out in pearl and silver, long avenues of untrodden marble whence sprang the cathedral columns of the firs. We were all sorry when we were through the woods and found ourselves looking down into the snug, commonplace, farmstead-dotted settlement of Baywater.

"There's Cousin Mattie's house—that big white one at the turn of the road," said the Story Girl. "I hope she has that dinner ready, Dan. I'm hungry as a wolf after our walk."

"I wish Cousin Mattie's husband was still alive," said Dan. "He was an awful nice old man. He always had his pockets full of nuts and apples. I used to like going there better when he was alive. Too many old women don't suit me."

"Oh, Dan, Cousin Mattie and her sisters-in-law are just as nice and kind as they can be," reproached Cecily.

"Oh, they're kind enough, but they never seem to see that a fellow gets over being five years old if he only lives long enough," retorted Dan.

"I know a story about Cousin Mattie's husband," said the Story Girl. "His name was Ebenezer, you know—"

"Is it any wonder he was thin and stunted looking?" said Dan.

"Ebenezer is just as nice a name as Daniel," said Felicity.

"Do you *really* think so, my angel?" inquired Dan, in honey-sweet tones.

"Go on. Remember your second resolution," I whispered to the Story Girl, who was stalking along with an outraged expression.

The Story Girl swallowed something and went on.

"Cousin Ebenezer had a horror of borrowing. He thought it was simply a dreadful disgrace to borrow *anything*. Well, you know he and Cousin Mattie used to live in Carlisle, where the Rays now live. This was when Grandfather King was alive. One day Cousin Ebenezer came up the hill and into the kitchen where all the family were. Uncle Roger said he looked as if he had been stealing sheep. He sat for a whole hour in the kitchen and hardly spoke a word, but just looked miserable. At last he got up and said in a desperate sort of way, 'Uncle Abraham, can I speak with you in private for a minute?' 'Oh, certainly,' said grandfather, and took him into the parlour. Cousin Ebenezer shut the door, looked all around him and then said imploringly, '*More private still.*' So grandfather took him into the spare room and shut that door. He was getting frightened. He thought something terrible must have happened to Cousin Ebenezer. Cousin Ebenezer came right up to grandfather, took hold of the lapel of his coat, and said in a whisper, 'Uncle Abraham, can—you—lend—me—an—axe?'"

"He needn't have made such a mystery about it," said Cecily, who had missed the point entirely, and couldn't see why the rest of us were laughing. But Cecily was such a darling that we did not mind her lack of a sense of humour.

"It's kind of mean to tell stories like that about people who are dead," said Felicity.

"Sometimes it's safer than when they're alive though, sweetheart," commented Dan.

We had expected good dinner at Cousin Mattie's—may it be counted unto her for righteousness. She and her sister-in-law, Miss Louisa Jane and Miss Caroline, were very kind to us. We had quite a nice time, although I understood why Dan objected to them when they patted us all on the head and told us whom we resembled and gave us peppermint lozenges.

CHAPTER VIII

We
Visit
Peg Bowen

WE left Cousin Mattie's early, for it still looked like a storm, though no more so than it had in the morning. We intended to go home by a different path—one leading through cleared land overgrown with scrub maple, which had the advantage of being farther away from Peg Bowen's house. We hoped to be home before it began to storm, but we had hardly reached the hill above the village when a fine, driving snow began to fall. It would have been wiser to have turned back even then; but we had already come a mile and we thought we would have ample time to reach home before it became really bad. We were sadly mistaken; by the time we had gone another half-mile we were in the thick of a bewildering, blinding snowstorm. But it was by now just as far back to Cousin Mattie's as it was to Uncle Alec's, so we struggled on, growing more frightened at every step. We could hardly face the stinging snow, and we could not see ten feet ahead of us. It had turned bitterly cold and the tempest howled all around us in white desolation under the fast-darkening night. The narrow path we were trying to follow soon became entirely obliterated and we stumbled blindly on, holding to each other, and trying to peer through the furious whirl that filled the air. Our plight had come upon us so suddenly that we could not realize it. Presently Peter, who was leading the van because he was supposed to know the path best, stopped.

"I can't see the road any longer," he shouted. "I don't know where we are."

We all stopped and huddled together in a miserable group. Fear filled our hearts. It seemed ages ago that we had been snug and safe and warm at Cousin Mattie's. Cecily began to cry with cold. Dan, in spite of her protests, dragged off his overcoat and made her put it on.

"We can't stay here," he said. "We'll all freeze to death if we do. Come on—we've got to keep moving. The snow ain't so deep yet. Take hold of my hand, Cecily. We must all hold together. Come, now."

"It won't be nice to be frozen to death, but if we get through alive think what a story we'll have to tell," said the Story Girl between her chattering teeth.

In my heart I did not believe we would ever get through alive. It was almost pitch dark now, and the snow grew deeper every moment. We were chilled to the heart. I thought how nice it would be to lie down and rest; but I remembered hearing that that was fatal, and I endeavoured to stumble on with the others. It was wonderful how the girls kept up, even Cecily. It occurred to me to be thankful that Sara Ray was not with us.

But we were wholly lost now. All around us was a horror of great darkness. Suddenly Felicity fell. We dragged her up, but she declared she could not go on—she was done out.

"Have you any idea where we are?" shouted Dan to Peter.

"No," Peter shouted back, "the wind is blowing every which way. I haven't any idea where home is."

Home! Would we ever see it again? We tried to urge Felicity on, but she only repeated drowsily that she must lie down and rest. Cecily, too, was reeling against me. The Story Girl still stood up staunchly and counselled struggling on, but she was numb with cold and her words were hardly distinguishable. Some wild idea was in my mind that we must dig a hole in the snow and all creep into it. I had read somewhere that people had thus saved their lives in snowstorms. Suddenly Felix gave a shout.

"I see a light," he cried.

"Where? Where?" We all looked but could see nothing.

"I don't see it now but I saw it a moment ago," shouted Felix. "I'm sure I did. Come on—over in this direction."

Inspired with fresh hope we hurried after him. Soon we all saw the light—and never shone a fairer beacon. A few more steps and, coming into the shelter of the woodland on the further side, we realized where we were.

"That's Peg Bowen's house," exclaimed Peter, stopping short in dismay.

"I don't care whose house it is," declared Dan. "We've got to go to it."

"I s'pose so," acquiesced Peter ruefully. "We can't freeze to death even if she is a witch."

"For goodness' sake don't say anything about witches so close to her house," gasped Felicity. "I'll be thankful to get in anywhere."

We reached the house, climbed the flight of steps that led to that mysterious second story door, and Dan rapped. The door opened promptly and Peg Bowen stood before us, in what seemed exactly the same costume she had worn on the memorable day when we had come, bearing gifts, to propitiate her in the matter of Paddy.

Behind her was a dim room scantly illumined by the one small candle that had guided us through the storm; but the old Waterloo stove was colouring the gloom with tremulous, rose-red whorls of light, and warm and cosy indeed seemed Peg's retreat to us snow-covered, frost-chilled, benighted wanderers.

"Gracious goodness, where did yez all come from?" exclaimed Peg. "Did they turn yez out?"

"We've been over to Baywater, and we got lost in the storm coming back," explained Dan. "We didn't know where we were till we saw your light. I guess we'll have to stay here till the storm is over—if you don't mind."

"And it won't inconvenience you," said Cecily timidly.

"Oh, it's no inconvenience to speak of. Come in. Well, yez *have* got some snow on yez. Let me get a broom. You boys stomp your feet well and shake your coats. You girls give me your things and I'll hang them up. Guess yez are most froze. Well, sit up to the stove and git het up."

Peg bustled away to gather up a dubious assortment of chairs, with backs and rungs missing, and in a few minutes we were in a circle around her roaring stove, getting dried and thawed out. In our wildest flights of fancy we had never pictured ourselves as guests at the witch's hearthstone. Yet here we were; and the witch herself was actually brewing a jorum of ginger tea for Cecily, who continued to shiver long after the rest of us were roasted to the marrow. Poor Sis drank that scalding draught, being in too great awe of Peg to do aught else.

"That'll soon fix your shivers," said our hostess kindly. "And now I'll get yez all some tea."

"Oh, please don't trouble," said the Story Girl hastily.

"'Taint any trouble," said Peg briskly; then, with one of the sudden changes to fierceness which made her such a terrifying personage, "Do yez think my vittels ain't clean?"

"Oh, no, no," cried Felicity quickly, before the Story Girl could speak, "none of us would ever think *that*. Sara only meant she didn't want you to go to any bother on our account."

"It ain't any bother," said Peg, mollified. "I'm spry as a cricket this winter, though I have the realagy sometimes. Many a good bite I've had in your ma's kitchen. I owe yez a meal."

No more protests were made. We sat in awed silence, gazing with timid curiosity about the room, the stained, plastered walls of which were well-nigh covered with a motley assortment of pictures, chromos, and advertisements, pasted on without much regard for order or character. We had heard much of Peg's pets and now we saw them. Six cats occupied various cosy corners; one of them, the black goblin which had so terrified us in the summer, blinked satirically at us from the centre of Peg's bed. Another, a dilapidated, striped beastie, with both ears and one eye gone, glared at us from the sofa in the corner. A dog, with only three legs, lay behind the stove; a crow sat on a roost above our heads, in company with a matronly old hen; and on the clock shelf were a stuffed monkey and a grinning skull. We had heard that a sailor had given Peg the monkey. But where had she got the skull? And whose was it? I could not help puzzling over these gruesome questions.

Presently tea was ready and we gathered around the festal board—a board literally as well as figuratively, for Peg's table was the work of her own unskilled hands. The less said about the viands of that meal, and the dishes they were served in, the better. But we ate them—bless you, yes!—as we would have eaten any witch's banquet set before us. Peg might or might not be a witch—common sense said not; but we knew she was quite capable of turning every one of us out of doors in one of her sudden fierce fits if we offended her; and we had no mind to trust ourselves again to that wild forest where we had fought a losing fight with the demon forces of night and storm.

But it was not an agreeable meal in more ways than one. Peg was not at all careful of anybody's feelings. She hurt Felix's cruelly as she passed him his cup of tea.

"You've gone too much to flesh, boy. So the magic seed didn't work hey?"

How in the world had Peg found out about that magic seed? Felix looked uncommonly foolish.

"If you'd come to me in the first place I'd soon have told you how to get thin," said Peg, nodding wisely.

"Won't you tell me now?" asked Felix eagerly, his desire to melt his too solid flesh overcoming his dread and shame.

"No, I don't like being second fiddle," answered Peg with a crafty smile. "Sara, you're too scrawny and pale—not much like your ma. I knew her well. She was counted a beauty, but she made no great things of a match. Your father had some money but he was a tramp like meself. Where is he now?"

"In Rome," said the Story Girl rather shortly.

"People thought your ma was crazy when she took him. But she'd a right to please herself. Folks is too ready to call other folks crazy. There's people who say *I'm* not in my right mind. Did yez ever"—Peg fixed Felicity with a piercing glance—"hear anything so ridiculous?"

"Never," said Felicity, white to the lips.

"I wish everybody was as sane as I am," said Peg scornfully. Then she looked poor Felicity over critically. "You're good-looking but proud. And your complexion won't wear. It'll be like your ma's yet—too much red in it."

"Well, that's better than being the colour of mud," muttered Peter, who wasn't going to hear his lady traduced, even by a witch. All the thanks he got was a furious look from Felicity, but Peg had not heard him and now she turned her attention to Cecily.

"You look delicate. I daresay you'll never live to grow up."

Cecily's lip trembled and Dan's face turned crimson.

"Shut up," he said to Peg. "You've no business to say such things to people."

I think my jaw dropped. I know Peter's and Felix's did. Felicity broke in wildly.

"Oh, don't mind him, Miss Bowen. He's got *such* a temper—that's just the way he talks to us all at home. *Please* excuse him."

"Bless you, I don't mind him," said Peg, from whom the unexpected seemed to be the thing to expect. "I like a lad of spurrit. And so your father run away, did he, Peter? He used to be a beau of mine—he seen me home three times from singing school when we was young. Some folks said he did it for a dare.

There's such a lot of jealousy in the world, ain't there? Do you know where he is now?"

"No," said Peter.

"Well, he's coming home before long," said Peg mysteriously.

"Who told you that?" cried Peter in amazement.

"Better not ask," responded Peg, looking up at the skull.

If she meant to make the flesh creep on our bones she succeeded. But now, much to our relief, the meal was over and Peg invited us to draw our chairs up to the stove again.

"Make yourselves at home," she said, producing her pipe from her pocket. "I ain't one of the kind who thinks their houses too good to live in. Guess I won't bother washing the dishes. They'll do yez for breakfast if yez don't forget your places. I s'pose none of yez smokes."

"No," said Felicity, rather primly.

"Then yez don't know what's good for yez," retorted Peg, rather grumpily. But a few whiffs of her pipe placated her and, observing Cecily sigh, she asked her kindly what was the matter.

"I'm thinking how worried they'll be at home about us," explained Cecily.

"Bless you, dearie, don't be worrying over that. I'll send them word that yez are all snug and safe here."

"But how can you?" cried amazed Cecily.

"Better not ask," said Peg again, with another glance at the skull.

An uncomfortable silence followed, finally broken by Peg, who introduced her pets to us and told how she had come by them. The black cat was her favourite.

"That cat knows more than I do, if yez'll believe it," she said proudly. "I've got a rat too, but he's a bit shy when strangers is round. Your cat got all right again that time, didn't he?"

"Yes," said the Story Girl.

"Thought he would," said Peg, nodding sagely. "I seen to that. Now, don't yez all be staring at the hole in my dress."

"We weren't," was our chorus of protest.

"Looked as if yez were. I tore that yesterday but I didn't mend it. I was brought up to believe that a hole was an accident but a patch was a disgrace. And so your Aunt Olivia is going to be married after all?"

This was news to us. We felt and looked dazed.

"I never heard anything of it," said the Story Girl.

"Oh, it's true enough. She's a great fool. I've no faith in husbands. But one good thing is she ain't going to marry that Henry Jacobs of Markdale. He wants her bad enough. Just like his presumption,—thinking himself good enough for a King. His father is the worst man alive. He chased me off his place with his dog once. But I'll get even with him yet."

Peg looked very savage, and visions of burned barns floated through our minds.

"He'll be punished in hell, you know," said Peter timidly.

"But I won't be there to see that," rejoined Peg. "Some folks say I'll go there because I don't go to church oftener. But *I* don't believe it."

"Why don't you go?" asked Peter, with a temerity that bordered on rashness.

"Well, I've got so sunburned I'm afraid folks might take me for an Injun," explained Peg, quite seriously. "Besides, your minister makes such awful long prayers. Why does he do it?"

"I suppose he finds it easier to talk to God than to people," suggested Peter reflectively.

"Well, anyway, I belong to the round church," said Peg comfortably, "and so the devil can't catch *me* at the corners. I haven't been to Carlisle church for over three years. I thought I'd a-died laughing the last time I was there. Old Elder Marr took up the collection that day. He'd on a pair of new boots and they squeaked all the way up and down the aisles. And every time the boots squeaked the elder made a face, like he had toothache. It was awful funny. How's your missionary quilt coming on, Cecily?"

Was there anything Peg didn't know?

"Very well," said Cecily.

"You can put my name on it, if you want to."

"Oh, thank you. Which section—the five-cent one or the ten-cent one?" asked Cecily timidly.

"The ten-cent one, of course. The best is none too good for me. I'll give you the ten cents another time. I'm short of change just now—not being as rich as Queen Victory. There's her picture up there—the one with the blue sash and diamint crown and the lace curting on her head. Can any of yez tell me this—is Queen Victory a married woman?"

"Oh, yes, but her husband is dead," answered the Story Girl.

"Well, I s'pose they couldn't have called her an old maid, seeing she was a queen, even if she'd never got married. Sometimes I sez to myself, 'Peg, would you like to be Queen Victory?' But I never know what to answer. In summer, when I can roam anywhere in the woods and the sunshine—I wouldn't be Queen Victory for anything. But when it's winter and cold and I can't git nowheres—I feel as if I wouldn't mind changing places with her."

Peg put her pipe back in her mouth and began to smoke fiercely. The candle wick burned long, and was topped by a little cap of fiery red that seemed to wink at us like an impish gnome. The most grotesque shadow of Peg flickered over the wall behind her. The one-eyed cat remitted his grim watch and went to sleep. Outside the wind screamed like a ravening beast at the window. Suddenly Peg removed her pipe from her mouth, bent forward, gripped my wrist with her sinewy fingers until I almost cried out with pain, and gazed straight into my face. I felt horribly frightened of her. She seemed an entirely different creature. A wild light was in her eyes, a furtive, animal-like expression was on her face. When she spoke it was in a different voice and in different language.

"Do you hear the wind?" she asked in a thrilling whisper. "What *is* the wind? What *is* the wind?"

"I—I—don't know," I stammered.

"No more do I," said Peg, "and nobody knows. Nobody knows what the wind is. I wish I could find out. I mightn't be so afraid of the wind if I knew what it was. I *am* afraid of it. When the blasts come like that I want to crouch down and hide me. But I can tell you one thing about the wind—it's the only free thing in the world—*the—only—free—thing*. Everything else is subject to some law, but the wind is *free*. It bloweth where it listeth and no man can tame it. It's free—that's why I love it, though I'm afraid of it. It's a grand thing to be free—free—free—free!"

Peg's voice rose almost to a shriek. We were dreadfully frightened, for we knew there were times when she was quite crazy and we feared one of her "spells" was coming on her. But with a swift movement she turned the man's coat she wore up over her shoulders and head like a hood, completely hiding her face. Then she crouched forward, elbows on knees, and relapsed into silence. None of us dared speak or move. We sat thus for half an hour. Then Peg jumped up and said briskly in her usual tone,

"Well, I guess yez are all sleepy and ready for bed. You girls can sleep in my bed over there, and I'll take the sofy. Yez can put the cat off if yez like, though he won't hurt yez. You boys can go downstairs. There's a big pile of straw there that'll do yez for a bed, if yez put your coats on. I'll light yez down, but I ain't going to leave yez a light for fear yez'd set fire to the place."

Saying good-night to the girls, who looked as if they thought their last hour was come, we went to the lower room. It was quite empty, save for a pile of fire wood and another of clean straw. Casting a stealthy glance around, ere Peg withdrew the light, I was relieved to see that there were no skulls in sight. We four boys snuggled down in the straw. We did not expect to sleep, but we were very tired and before we knew it our eyes were shut, to open no more till morning. The poor girls were not so fortunate. They always averred they never closed an eye. Four things prevented them from sleeping. In the first place Peg snored loudly; in the second place the fitful gleams of firelight kept flickering over the skull for half the night and making gruesome effects on it; in the third place Peg's pillows and bedclothes smelled rankly of tobacco smoke; and in the fourth place they were afraid the rat Peg had spoken of might come out to make their acquaintance. Indeed, they were sure they heard him skirmishing about several times.

When we wakened in the morning the storm was over and a young morning was looking through rosy eyelids across a white world. The little clearing around Peg's cabin was heaped with dazzling drifts, and we boys fell to and shovelled out a road to her well. She gave us breakfast—stiff oatmeal porridge without milk, and a boiled egg apiece. Cecily could *not* eat her porridge; she declared she had such a bad cold that she had no appetite; a cold she certainly had; the rest of us choked our messes down and after we had done so Peg asked us if we had noticed a soapy taste.

"The soap fell into the porridge while I was making it," she said. "But,"—smacking her lips,—"I'm going to make yez an Irish stew for dinner. It'll be fine."

An Irish stew concocted by Peg! No wonder Dan said hastily,

"You are very kind but we'll have to go right home."

"Yez can't walk," said Peg.

"Oh, yes, we can. The drifts are so hard they'll carry, and the snow will be pretty well blown off the middle of the fields. It's only three-quarters of a mile. We boys will go home and get a pung and come back for you girls."

But the girls wouldn't listen to this. They must go with us, even Cecily.

"Seems to me yez weren't in such a hurry to leave last night," observed Peg sarcastically.

"Oh, it's only because they'll be so anxious about us at home, and it's Sunday and we don't want to miss Sunday School," explained Felicity.

"Well, I hope your Sunday School will do yez good," said Peg, rather grumpily. But she relented again at the last and gave Cecily a wishbone.

"Whatever you wish on that will come true," she said. "But you only have the one wish, so don't waste it."

"We're so much obliged to you for all your trouble," said the Story Girl politely.

"Never mind the trouble. The expense is the thing," retorted Peg grimly.

"Oh!" Felicity hesitated. "If you would let us pay you—give you something—"

"No, thank yez," responded Peg loftily. "There is people who take money for their hospitality, I've heerd, but I'm thankful to say I don't associate with that class. Yez are welcome to all yez have had here, if yez *are* in a big hurry to get away."

She shut the door behind us with something of a slam, and her black cat followed us so far, with stealthy, furtive footsteps, that we were frightened of it. Eventually it turned back; then, and not till then, did we feel free to discuss our adventure.

"Well, I'm thankful we're out of *that*," said Felicity, drawing a long breath. "Hasn't it just been an awful experience?"

"We might all have been found frozen stark and stiff this morning," remarked the Story Girl with apparent relish.

"I tell you, it was a lucky thing we got to Peg Bowen's," said Dan.

"Miss Marwood says there is no such thing as luck," protested Cecily. "We ought to say it was Providence instead."

"Well, Peg and Providence don't seem to go together very well, somehow," retorted Dan. "If Peg is a witch it must be the Other One she's in co. with."

"Dan, it's getting to be simply scandalous the way you talk," said Felicity. "I just wish ma could hear you."

"Is soap in porridge any worse than tooth-powder in rusks, lovely creature?" asked Dan.

"Dan, Dan," admonished Cecily, between her coughs, "remember it's Sunday."

"It seems hard to remember that," said Peter. "It doesn't seem a mite like Sunday and it seems awful long since yesterday."

"Cecily, you've got a dreadful cold," said the Story Girl anxiously.

"In spite of Peg's ginger tea," added Felix.

"Oh, that ginger tea was *awful*," exclaimed poor Cecily. "I thought I'd never get it down—it was so hot with ginger—and there was so much of it! But I was so frightened of offending Peg I'd have tried to drink it all if there had been a bucketful. Oh, yes, it's very easy for you all to laugh! *You* didn't have to drink it."

"We had to eat two meals, though," said Felicity with a shiver. "And I don't know when those dishes of hers were washed. I just shut my eyes and took gulps."

"Did you notice the soapy taste in the porridge?" asked the Story Girl.

"Oh, there were so many queer tastes about it I didn't notice one more than another," answered Felicity wearily.

"What bothers me," remarked Peter absently, "is that skull. Do you suppose Peg really finds things out by it?"

"Nonsense! How could she?" scoffed Felix, bold as a lion in daylight.

"She didn't *say* she did, you know," I said cautiously.

"Well, we'll know in time if the things she said were going to happen do," mused Peter.

"Do you suppose your father is really coming home?" queried Felicity.

"I hope not," answered Peter decidedly.

"You ought to be ashamed of yourself," said Felicity severely.

"No, I oughtn't. Father got drunk all the time he was

home, and wouldn't work and was bad to mother," said Peter defiantly. "She had to support him as well as herself and me. I don't want to see any father coming home, and you'd better believe it. Of course, if he was the right sort of a father it'd be different."

"What *I* would like to know is if Aunt Olivia is going to be married," said the Story Girl absently. "I can hardly believe it. But now that I think of it—Uncle Roger has been teasing her ever since she was in Halifax last summer."

"If she does get married you'll have to come and live with us," said Cecily delightedly.

Felicity did not betray so much delight and the Story Girl remarked with a weary little sigh that she hoped Aunt Olivia wouldn't. We all felt rather weary, somehow. Peg's predictions had been unsettling, and our nerves had all been more or less strained during our sojourn under her roof. We were glad when we found ourselves at home.

The folks had not been at all troubled about us, but it was because they were sure the storm had come up before we would think of leaving Cousin Mattie's and not because they had received any mysterious message from Peg's skull. We were relieved at this, but on the whole, our adventure had not done much towards clearing up the vexed question of Peg's witchcraft.

CHAPTER IX

Extracts from the February and March Numbers of Our Magazine

Miss Felicity King.

HONOURABLE MENTION

Mr. Felix King.
Mr. Peter Craig.
Miss Sara Ray.

EDITORIAL

THE editor wishes to make a few remarks about the Resolution Honour Roll. As will be seen, only one name figures on it. Felicity says she has thought a beautiful thought every morning before breakfast without missing one morning, not even the one we were at Peg Bowen's. Some of our number think it not fair that Felicity should be on the honour roll (*Felicity, aside:* "That's Dan, of course.") when she only made one resolution and won't tell us what any of the thoughts were. So we have decided to give honourable mention to everybody who has kept one resolution perfect. Felix has worked all his arithmetic problems by himself. He complains that he never got more than a third of them right and the teacher has marked him away down; but one cannot keep resolutions without some inconvenience. Peter has never played tit-tat-x in church or got drunk and says it wasn't as bad as he expected. (*Peter, indignantly:* "I never said it." *Cecily, soothingly:* "Now, Peter, Bev only meant that as a joke.") Sara Ray has never talked any mean gossip, but does not find conversation as interesting as it used to be. (*Sara Ray, wonderingly:* "I don't remember of saying that.")

Felix did not eat any apples until March, but forgot and ate seven the day we were at Cousin Mattie's. (*Felix:* "I only ate five!") He soon gave up trying to say what he thought always. He got into too much trouble. We think Felix ought to change to old Grandfather King's rule. It was, "Hold your tongue when you can, and when you can't tell the truth." Cecily feels she has not read all the good books she might, because some she tried to read were very dull and the *Pansy* books were so much more interesting. And it is no use trying not to feel bad because her hair isn't curly and she has marked that resolution out. The Story Girl came very near to keeping her resolution to have all the good times possible, but she says she missed two, if not three, she might have had. Dan refuses to say anything about his resolutions and so does the editor.

PERSONALS

We regret that Miss Cecily King is suffering from a severe cold.

Mr. Alexander Marr of Markdale died very suddenly last week. We never heard of his death till he was dead.

Miss Cecily King wishes to state that she did not ask the question about "Holy Moses" and the other word in the January number. Dan put it in for a mean joke.

The weather has been cold and fine. We have only had one bad storm. The coasting on Uncle Roger's hill continues good.

Aunt Eliza did not favour us with a visit after all. She took cold and had to go home. We were sorry that she had a cold but glad that she had to go home. Cecily said she thought it wicked of us to be glad. But when we asked her "cross her heart" if she wasn't glad herself she had to say she was.

Miss Cecily King has got three very distinguished names on her quilt square. They are the Governor and his wife and a witch's.

The King family had the honour of entertaining the Governor's wife to tea on February the seventeenth. We are all invited to visit Government House but some of us think we won't go.

A tragic event occurred last Tuesday. Mrs. James Frewen came to tea and there was no pie in the house. Felicity has not yet fully recovered.

A new boy is coming to school. His name is Cyrus Brisk and his folks moved up from Markdale. He says he is going to punch Willy Fraser's head if Willy keeps on thinking he is Miss Cecily King's beau.

(*Cecily:* "I haven't *any* beau! I don't mean to think of such a thing for at least eight years yet!")

Miss Alice Reade of Charlottetown Royalty has come to Carlisle to teach music. She boards at Mr. Peter Armstrong's. The girls are all going to take music lessons from her. Two descriptions of her will be found in another column. Felix wrote one, but the girls thought he did not do her justice, so Cecily wrote another one. She admits she copied most of the description out of Valeria H. Montague's story *Lord Marmaduke's First, Last, and Only Love; or the Bride of the Castle by the Sea,* but says they fit Miss Reade better than anything she could make up.

HOUSEHOLD DEPARTMENT

Always keep the kitchen tidy and then you needn't mind if company comes unexpectedly.

ANXIOUS INQUIRER: We don't know anything that will take the stain out of a silk dress when a soft-boiled egg is dropped on it. Better not wear your silk dress so often, especially when boiling eggs.

Ginger tea is good for colds.

OLD HOUSEKEEPER: Yes, when the baking-powder gives out you can use tooth-powder instead.

(*Felicity:* "I never wrote that! I don't care, I don't think it's fair for other people to be putting things in my department!")

Our apples are not keeping well this year. They are rotting; and besides father says we eat an awful lot of them.

PERSERVERANCE: I will give you the recipe for dumplings you ask for. But remember it is not everyone who can make dumplings, even from the recipe. There's a knack in ..

If the soap falls into the porridge do not tell your guests

about it until they have finished eating it because it might take away their appetite.

FELICITY KING.

ETIQUETTE DEPARTMENT

P-r C-g:—Do not criticize people's noses unless you are sure they can't hear you, and don't criticize your best girl's great-aunt's nose in any case.

(*Felicity, tossing her head:* "Oh, my! I s'pose Dan thought that was extra smart.")

C-y K-g:—When my most intimate friend walks with another girl and exchanges lace patterns with her, what ought I to do? Ans. Adopt a dignified attitude.

F-y K-g:—It is better not to wear your second best hat to church, but if your mother says you must it is not for me to question her decision.

(*Felicity:* "Dan just copied that word for word out of the *Family Guide,* except about the hat part.")

P-r C-g:—Yes, it would be quite proper to say good evening to the family ghost if you met it.

F-x K-g:—No, it is not polite to sleep with your mouth open. What's more, it isn't safe. Something might fall into it.

DAN KING.

FASHION NOTES

Crocheted watch pockets are all the rage now. If you haven't a watch they do to carry your pencil in or a piece of gum.

It is stylish to have hair ribbons to match your dress. But it is hard to match gray drugget. I like scarlet for that.

It is stylish to pin a piece of ribbon on your coat the same colour as your chum wears in her hair. Mary Martha Cowan saw them doing it in town and started us doing it here. I always wear Kitty's ribbon and Kitty wears mine, but the Story Girl thinks it is silly.

CECILY KING.

AN ACCOUNT OF OUR VISIT TO COUSIN MATTIE'S

We all walked over to Cousin Mattie's last week. They were all well there and we had a fine dinner. On our way back a snow-storm came up and we got lost in the woods. We didn't know where we were or nothing. If we hadn't seen a light I guess we'd all have been frozen and snowed over, and they would never have found us till spring and that would be very sad. But we saw a light and made for it and it was Peg Bowen's. Some people think she is a witch and it's hard to tell, but she was real hospitable and took us all in. Her house was very untidy but it was warm. She has a skull. I mean a loose skull, not her own. She lets on it tells her things, but Uncle Alec says it couldn't because it was only an Indian skull that old Dr. Beecham had and Peg stole it when he died, but Uncle Roger says he wouldn't trust himself with Peg's skull for anything. She gave us supper. It was a horrid meal. The Story Girl says I must not tell what I found in the bread and butter because it would be too disgusting to read in *Our Magazine* but it don't matter because we were all there, except Sara Ray, and know what it was. We stayed all night and us boys slept in straw. None of us had ever slept on straw before. We got home in the morning. That is all I can write about our visit to Cousin Mattie's.

Felix King.

MY WORST ADVENTURE

It's my turn to write it so I suppose I must. I guess my worst adventure was two years ago when a whole lot of us were coasting on Uncle Rogers hill. Charlie Cowan and Fred Marr had started, but half-way down their sled got stuck and I run down to shove them off again. Then I stood there just a moment to watch them with my back to the top of the hill. While I was standing there Rob Marr started Kitty and Em Frewen off on his sled. His sled had a wooden tongue in it and it slanted back over the girls' heads. I was right in the way and they yelled to me to get out, but just as I heard them it struck me. The sled took me between the legs and I was histed back over the tongue and dropped in a heap behind before I knew what had happened to me. I thought a tornado had struck me. The girls couldn't stop though they thought I was killed, but Rob came tearing down and helped me up. He was awful scared but I wasn't killed nor my back wasn't broken but my nose bled something awful and kept on bleeding for three days. Not all the time but by spells.

Dan King.

THE STORY OF HOW CARLISLE GOT ITS NAME

This is a true story to. Long ago there was a girl lived in charlotte town. I dont know her name so I cant right it and maybe it is just as well for Felicity might think it wasnt romantik like Miss Jemima Parrs. She was awful pretty and a young englishman who had come out to make his fortune fell in love with her and they were engaged to be married the next spring. His name was Mr. Carlisle. In the winter he started off to hunt cariboo for a spell. Cariboos lived on the island then. There aint any here now. He got to where it is Carlisle now. It wasn't anything then only woods and a few indians. He got awful sick and was sick for ever so long in a indian camp and only an old micmac squaw to wait on him. Back in town they all thought he was dead and his girl felt bad for a little while and then got over it and took up with another beau. The girls say that wasnt romantik but I think it was sensible but if it had been me that died I'd have felt bad if she forgot me so soon. But he hadnt died and when he got back to town he went right to her house and walked in and there she was standing up to be married to the other fellow. Poor Mr. Carlisle felt awful. He was sick and week and it went to his head. He just turned and run and run till he got back to the old micmac's camp and fell in front of it. But the indians had gone because it was spring and it didnt matter because he really was dead this time and people come looking for him from town and found him and buryed him there and called the place after him. They say the girl was never happy again and that was hard lines on her but maybe she deserved it.

PETER CRAIG.

MISS ALICE READE

Miss Alice Reade is a very pretty girl. She has kind of curly blackish hair and big gray eyes and a pale face. She is tall and thin but her figure is pretty fair and she has a nice mouth and a sweet way of speaking. The girls are crazy about her and talk about her all the time.

FELIX KING.

BEAUTIFUL ALICE

That is what we girls call Miss Reade among ourselves. She is divinely beautiful. Her magnificent wealth of raven hair flows back in glistening waves from her sun-kissed brow. (*Dan:* "If Felix had said she was sunburned you'd have all jumped on him." (*Cecily, coldly:* "Sun-kissed doesn't mean sunburned." *Dan:* "What does it mean then?" *Cecily, embarrassed:* "I—I don't know. But Miss Montague says the Lady Geraldine's brow was sun-kissed and of course an earl's daughter wouldn't be sunburned." *The Story Girl:* "Oh, don't interrupt the reading like this. It spoils it.") Her eyes are gloriously dark and deep, like midnight lakes mirroring the stars of heaven. Her features are like sculptured marble and her mouth is a trembling, curving Cupid's bow. (*Peter, aside:* "What kind of a thing is that?") Her creamy skin is as fair and flawless as the petals of a white lily. Her voice is like the ripple of a woodland brook and her slender form is matchless in its symmetry. (*Dan:* "That's Valeria's way of putting it, but Uncle Roger says she don't show her feed much." *Felicity:* "Dan! if Uncle Roger is vulgar you needn't be!") Her hands are like a poet's dreams. She dresses so nicely and looks so stylish in her clothes. Her favourite colour is blue. Some people think she is stiff and some say she is stuck-up, but she isn't a bit. It's just that she is different from them and they don't like it. She is just lovely and we adore her.

CECILY KING.

CHAPTER X

Disappearance of Paddy

As I remember, the spring came late that year in Carlisle. It was May before the weather began to satisfy the grown-ups. But we children were more easily pleased, and we thought April a splendid month because the snow all went early and left gray, firm, frozen ground for our rambles and games. As the days slipped by they grew more gracious; the hillsides began to look as if they were thinking of mayflowers; the old orchard was washed in a bath of tingling sunshine and the sap stirred in the big trees; by day the sky was veiled with delicate cloud drift, fine and filmy as woven mist; in the evenings a full, low moon looked over the valleys, as pallid and holy as some aureoled saint; a sound of laughter and dream was on the wind and the world grew young with the mirth of April breezes.

"It's so nice to be alive in the spring," said the Story Girl one twilight as we swung on the boughs of Uncle Stephen's walk.

"It's nice to be alive any time," said Felicity, complacently.

"But it's nicer in the spring," insisted the Story Girl. "When I'm dead I think I'll *feel* dead all the rest of the year, but when spring comes I'm sure I'll feel like getting up and being alive again."

"You do say such queer things," complained Felicity. "You won't be really dead any time. You'll be in the next world. And I think it's horrid to talk about people being dead anyhow."

"We've all got to die," said Sara Ray solemnly, but with a certain relish. It was as if she enjoyed looking forward to something in which nothing, neither an unsympathetic mother, nor the cruel fate which had made her a colourless little nonentity, could prevent her from being the chief performer.

"I sometimes think," said Cecily, rather wearily, "that it isn't so dreadful to die young as I used to suppose."

She prefaced her remark with a slight cough, as she had been all too apt to do of late, for the remnants of the cold she had caught the night we were lost in the storm still clung to her.

"Don't talk such nonsense, Cecily," cried the Story Girl with unwonted sharpness, a sharpness we all understood. All of us, in our hearts, though we never spoke of it to each other, thought Cecily was not as well as she ought to be that spring, and we hated to hear anything said which seemed in any way to touch or acknowledge the tiny, faint shadow which now and again showed itself dimly athwart our sunshine.

"Well, it was you began talking of being dead," said Felicity angrily. "*I* don't think it's right to talk of such things. Cecily, are you sure your feet ain't damp? We ought to go in anyhow— it's too chilly out here for you."

"You girls had better go," said Dan, "but I ain't going in till old Isaac Frewen goes. I've no use for him."

"I hate him, too," said Felicity, agreeing with Dan for once in her life. "He chews tobacco all the time and spits on the floor—the horrid pig!"

"And yet his brother is an elder in the church," said Sara Ray wonderingly.

"I know a story about Isaac Frewen," said the Story Girl. "When he was young he went by the name of Oatmeal Frewen and he got it this way. He was noted for doing outlandish things. He lived at Markdale then and he was a great, over- grown, awkward fellow, six feet tall. He drove over to Baywater one Saturday to visit his uncle there and came home the next afternoon, and although it was Sunday he brought a big bag of oatmeal in the wagon with him. When he came to Carlisle church he saw that service was going on there, and he concluded to stop and go in. But he didn't like to leave his oatmeal outside for fear something would happen to it, because there were always mischievous boys around, so he hoisted the bag on his back and walked into church with it and right to the top of the aisle to Grandfather King's pew. Grandfather King used to say he would never forget it to his dying day. The minister was preaching and everything was quiet and solemn when he heard a snicker behind him. Grandfather King turned around with a terrible frown—for you know in those days it was thought a dreadful thing to laugh in church—to rebuke the offender; and what did he see but that great, hulking young Isaac stalking up the aisle, bending a little forward under the weight of a big bag of oatmeal? Grandfather King was so amazed he couldn't laugh, but almost everyone else in the church was laughing, and grandfather said he never blamed them, for no funnier sight was ever seen. Young Isaac turned into grandfather's pew and thumped the bag of oatmeal down on the seat with a thud that cracked it. Then he plumped down beside it, took off his hat, wiped his face, and settled back to listen to the sermon, just as if it was all a matter of course. When the service was over he hoisted his bag up again, marched out of church, and drove home. He could never understand why it made so much talk; but he was known by the name of Oatmeal Frewen for years."

Our laughter, as we separated, rang sweetly though the old orchard and across the far, dim meadows. Felicity and Cecily went into the house and Sara Ray and the Story Girl went home, but Peter decoyed me into the granary to ask advice.

"You know Felicity has a birthday next week," he said, "and I want to write her an ode."

"A—a what?" I gasped.

"An ode," repeated Peter, gravely. "It's poetry, you know. I'll put it in *Our Magazine*."

"But you can't write poetry, Peter," I protested.

"I'm going to try," said Peter stoutly. "That is, if you think she won't be offended at me."

"She ought to feel flattered," I replied.

"You never can tell how she'll take things," said Peter gloomily. "Of course I ain't going to sign my name, and if she ain't pleased I won't tell her I wrote it. Don't you let on."

I promised I wouldn't and Peter went off with a light heart. He said he meant to write two lines every day till he got it done.

Cupid was playing his world-old tricks with others than poor Peter that spring. Allusion has been made in these chronicles to one Cyrus Brisk, and to the fact that our brown-haired, soft-voiced Cecily had found favour in the eyes of the said Cyrus. Cecily did not regard her conquest with any pride. On the contrary, it annoyed her terribly to be teased about Cyrus. She declared she hated both him and his name. She was as uncivil to him as sweet Cecily could be to anyone, but the gallant Cyrus was nothing daunted. He laid determined siege to Cecily's young heart by all the methods known to love-lorn swains. He placed delicate tributes of spruce gum, molasses taffy, "conversation" candies and decorated slate pencils on her desk; he persistently "chose" her in all school games calling for a partner; he entreated to be allowed to carry her basket from school; he offered to work her sums for her; and rumour had it that he had made a wild statement to the effect that he meant to ask if he might see her home some night from prayer meeting. Cecily was quite frightened that he would; she confided to me that she would rather die than walk home with him, but that if he asked her she would be too bashful to say no. So far, however, Cyrus had not molested her out of school, nor had he as yet thumped Willy Fraser—who was reported to be very low in his spirits over the whole affair.

And now Cyrus had written Cecily a letter—a love letter, mark you. Moreover, he had sent it through the post-office, with a real stamp on it. Its arrival made a sensation among us. Dan brought it from the office and, recognizing the handwriting of Cyrus, gave Cecily no peace until she showed us the letter. It was a very sentimental and rather ill-spelled epistle in which the inflammable Cyrus reproached her in heart-rending words for her coldness, and begged her to answer his letter, saying that if she did he would keep the secret "in violets." Cyrus probably meant "inviolate" but Cecily thought it was intended for a poetical touch. He signed himself "your troo lover, Cyrus Brisk" and added in a postscript that he couldn't eat or sleep for thinking of her.

"Are you going to answer it?" asked Dan.

"Certainly not," said Cecily with dignity.

"Cyrus Brisk wants to be kicked," growled Felix, who never seemed to be any particular friend of Willy Fraser's either. "He'd better learn how to spell before he takes to writing love letters."

"Maybe Cyrus will starve to death if you don't," suggested Sara Ray.

"I hope he will," said Cecily cruelly. She was truly vexed over the letter; and yet, so contradictory a thing is the feminine heart, even at twelve years old, I think she was a little flattered by it also. It was her first love letter and she confided to me that it gives you a very queer feeling to get it. At all events—the letter, though unanswered, was not torn up. I feel sure Cecily preserved it. But she walked past Cyrus next morning at school with a frozen countenance, evincing not the slightest pity for his pangs of unrequited affection. Cecily winced when Pat caught a mouse, visited a school chum the day the pigs were killed that she might not hear their squealing, and would not have stepped on a caterpillar for anything; yet she did not care at all how much she made the brisk Cyrus suffer.

Then, suddenly, all our spring gladness and Maytime hopes were blighted as by a killing frost. Sorrow and anxiety pervaded our days and embittered our dreams by night. Grim tragedy held sway in our lives for the next fortnight.

Paddy disappeared. One night he lapped his new milk as usual at Uncle Roger's dairy door and then sat blandly on the flat stone before it, giving the world assurance of a cat, sleek sides glistening, plumy tail gracefully folded around his paws, brilliant eyes watching the stir and flicker of bare willow boughs in the twilight air above him. That was the last seen of him. In the morning he was not.

At first we were not seriously alarmed. Paddy was no roving Thomas, but occasionally he vanished for a day or so. But when two days passed without his return we became anxious, the third day worried us greatly, and the fourth found us distracted.

"Something has happened to Pat," the Story Girl declared miserably. "He never stayed away from home more than two days in his life."

"What could have happened to him?" asked Felix.

"He's been poisoned—or a dog has killed him," answered the Story Girl in tragic tones.

Cecily began to cry at this; but tears were of no avail. Neither was anything else, apparently. We searched every nook and cranny of barns and outbuildings and woods on both the King farms; we inquired far and wide; we roved over Carlisle meadows calling Paddy's name, until Aunt Janet grew exasperated and declared we must stop making such exhibitions of ourselves. But we found and heard no trace of our lost pet. The Story Girl moped and refused to be comforted; Cecily declared she could not sleep at night for thinking of poor Paddy dying miserably in some corner to which he had dragged his failing body, or lying somewhere mangled and torn by a dog. We hated every dog we saw on the ground that he might be the guilty one.

"It's the suspense that's so hard," sobbed the Story Girl. "If I just knew what had happened to him it wouldn't be *quite* so hard. But I don't know whether he's dead or alive. He may be living and suffering, and every night I dream that he has come home and when I wake up and find it's only a dream it just breaks my heart."

"It's ever so much worse than when he was so sick last fall," said Cecily drearily. "Then we knew that everything was done for him that could be done."

We could not appeal to Peg Bowen this time. In our desperation we would have done it, but Peg was far away. With the first breath of spring she was up and off, answering to the lure of the long road. She had not been seen in her accustomed haunts for many a day. Her pets were gaining their own living in the woods and her house was locked up.

CHAPTER XI

The
Witch's
Wishbone

WHEN a fortnight had elapsed we gave up all hope.

"Pat is dead," said the Story Girl hopelessly, as we returned one evening from a bootless quest to Andrew Cowan's where a strange gray cat had been reported—a cat which turned out to be a yellowish brown nondescript, with no tail to speak of.

"I'm afraid so," I acknowledged at last.

"If only Peg Bowen had been at home she could have found him for us," asserted Peter. "Her skull would have told her where he was."

"I wonder if the wishbone she gave me would have done any good," cried Cecily suddenly. "I'd forgotten all about it. Oh, do you suppose it's too late yet?"

"There's nothing in a wishbone," said Dan impatiently.

"You can't be sure. She *told* me I'd get the wish I made on it. I'm going to try whenever I get home."

"It can't do any harm, anyhow," said Peter, "but I'm afraid you've left it too late. If Pat is dead even a witch's wishbone can't bring him back to life."

"I'll never forgive myself for not thinking about it before," mourned Cecily.

As soon as we got home she flew to the little box upstairs where she kept her treasures, and brought therefrom the dry and brittle wishbone.

"Peg told me how it must be done. I'm to hold the wishbone with both hands, like this, and walk backward, repeating the wish nine times. And when I've finished the ninth time I'm to turn around nine times from right to left, and then the wish will come true right away."

"Do you expect to see Pat when you finish turning?" said Dan skeptically.

None of us had any faith in the incantation except Peter, and, by infection, Cecily. You never could tell what might happen. Cecily took the wishbone in her trembling little hands and began her backward pacing, repeating solemnly, "I wish that we may find Paddy alive, or else his body, so that we can bury him decently." By the time Cecily had repeated this nine times we were all slightly infected with the desperate hope that something might come of it; and when she had made her nine gyrations we looked eagerly down the sunset lane, half expecting to see our lost pet. But we saw only the Awkward Man turning in at the gate. This was almost as surprising as the sight of Pat himself would have been; but there was no sight of Pat and hope flickered out in every breast but Peter's.

"You've got to give the spell time to work," he expostulated. "If Pat was miles away when it was wished it wouldn't be reasonable to expect to see him right off."

But we of little faith had already lost that little, and it was a very disconsolate group which the Awkward Man presently joined.

He was smiling—his rare, beautiful smile which only children ever saw—and he lifted his hat to the girls with no trace of the shyness and awkwardness for which he was notorious.

"Good evening," he said. "Have you little peoples lost a cat lately?"

We stared. Peter said "I knew it!" in a triumphant pig's whisper. The Story Girl started eagerly forward.

"Oh, Mr. Dale, can you tell us anything of Paddy?" she cried.

"A silver gray cat with black points and very fine markings?"

"Yes, yes!"

"Well, he is over at Golden Milestone."

"Alive?"

"Yes."

"Well, doesn't that beat the Dutch!" muttered Dan.

But we were all crowding about the Awkward Man, demanding where and when he had found Paddy.

"You'd better come over to my place and make sure that it really is your cat," suggested the Awkward Man, "and I'll tell you all about finding him on the way. I must warn you that he is pretty thin—but I think he'll pull through."

We obtained permission to go without much difficulty,

although the spring evening was wearing late, for Aunt Janet said she supposed none of us would sleep a wink that night if we didn't. A joyful procession followed the Awkward Man and the Story Girl across the gray, star-litten meadows to his home and through his pine-guarded gate.

"You know that old barn of mine back in the woods?" said the Awkward Man. "I go to it only about once in a blue moon. There was an old barrel there, upside down, one side resting on a block of wood. This morning I went to the barn to see about having some hay hauled home, and I had occasion to move the barrel. I noticed that it seemed to have been moved slightly since my last visit, and it was now resting wholly on the floor. I lifted it up—and there was a cat lying on the floor under it. I had heard you had lost yours and I took it this was your pet. I was afraid he was dead at first. He was lying there with his eyes closed; but when I bent over him he opened them and gave a pitiful little mew; or rather his mouth made the motion of a mew, for he was too weak to utter a sound."

"Oh, poor, poor Paddy," said tender-hearted Cecily tearfully.

"He couldn't stand, so I carried him home and gave him just a little milk. Fortunately he was able to lap it. I gave him a little more at intervals all day, and when I left he was able to crawl around. I think he'll be all right, but you'll have to be careful how you feed him for a few days. Don't let your hearts run away with your judgment and kill him with kindness."

"Do you suppose any one put him under that barrel?" asked the Story Girl

"No. The barn was locked. Nothing but a cat could get in. I suppose he went under the barrel, perhaps in pursuit of a mouse, and somehow knocked it off the block and so imprisoned himself."

Paddy was sitting before the fire in the Awkward Man's clean, bare kitchen. Thin! Why, he was literally skin and bone, and his fur was dull and lustreless. It almost broke our hearts to see our beautiful Paddy brought so low.

"Oh, how he must have suffered!" moaned Cecily.

"He'll be as prosperous as ever in a week or two," said the Awkward Man kindly.

The Story Girl gathered Paddy up in her arms. Most mellifluously did he purr as we crowded around to stroke him; with friendly joy he licked our hands with his little red tongue;

poor Paddy was a thankful cat; he was no longer lost, starving, imprisoned, helpless; he was with his comrades once more and he was going home—home to his old familiar haunts of orchard and dairy and granary, to his daily rations of new milk and cream, to the cosy corner of his own fireside. We trooped home joyfully, the Story Girl in our midst carrying Paddy hugged against her shoulder. Never did April stars look down on a happier band of travellers on the golden road. There was a little gray wind out in the meadows that night, and it danced along beside us on viewless, fairy feet, and sang a delicate song of the lovely, waiting years, while the night laid her beautiful hands of blessing over the world

"You see what Peg's wishbone did," said Peter triumphantly.

"Now, look here, Peter, don't talk nonsense," expostulated Dan. "The Awkward Man found Paddy this morning and had started to bring us word before Cecily ever thought of the wishbone. Do you mean to say you believe he wouldn't have come walking up our lane just when he did if she had never thought of it?"

"I mean to say that I wouldn't mind if I had several wishbones of the same kind," retorted Peter stubbornly.

"Of course I don't think the wishbone had really anything to do with our getting Paddy back, but I'm glad I tried it, for all that," remarked Cecily in a tone of satisfaction.

"Well, anyhow, we've got Pat and that's the main thing," said Felix.

"And I hope it will be a lesson to him to stay home after this," commented Felicity.

"They say the barrens are full of mayflowers," said the Story Girl. "Let us have a mayflower picnic tomorrow to celebrate Paddy's safe return."

CHAPTER XII

Flowers o' May

ACCORDINGLY we went a-maying, following the lure of dancing winds to a certain westward sloping hill lying under the spirit-like blue of spring skies, feathered over with lisping young pines and firs, which cupped little hollows and corners where the sunshine got in and never got out again, but stayed there and grew mellow, coaxing dear things to bloom long before they would dream of waking up elsewhere.

'Twas there we found our mayflowers, after faithful seeking. Mayflowers, you must know, never flaunt themselves; they must be sought as becomes them, and then they will yield up their treasures to the seeker—clusters of star-white and dawn-pink that have in them the very soul of all the springs that ever were, re-incarnated in something it seems gross to call perfume, so exquisite and spiritual is it.

We wandered gaily over the hill, calling to each other with laughter and jest, getting parted and delightfully lost in that little pathless wilderness, and finding each other unexpectedly in nooks and dips and sunny silences, where the wind purred and gentled and went softly. When the sun began to hang low, sending great fan-like streamers of radiance up to the zenith, we foregathered in a tiny, sequestered valley, full of young green fern, lying in the shadow of a wooded hill. In it was a shallow pool—a glimmering green sheet of water on whose banks nymphs might dance as blithely as ever they did on Argive hill or in Cretan dale. There we sat and stripped the faded leaves and stems from our spoil, making up the blossoms into bouquets to fill our baskets with sweetness. The Story Girl twisted a spray of divinest pink in her brown curls, and told us an old legend of a beautiful Indian maiden who died of a broken heart when the first snows of winter were falling, because she believed her long-absent lover was false. But he came back in the spring time from his long captivity; and when he heard that she was dead he sought her grave to mourn her, and lo, under the dead leaves of the old year he found sweet sprays of a blossom never seen before, and knew that it was a message of love and remembrance from his dark-eyed sweetheart.

"Except in stories Indian girls are called squaws," remarked practical Dan, tying his mayflowers in one huge, solid, cabbage-like bunch. Not for Dan the bother of filling his basket with the loose sprays, mingled with feathery elephant's-ears and trails of creeping spruce, as the rest of us, following the Story Girl's example, did. Nor would he admit that ours looked any better than his.

"I like things of one kind together. I don't like them mixed," he said.

"You have no taste," said Felicity.

"Except in my mouth, best beloved," responded Dan.

"You do think you are so smart," retorted Felicity, flushing with anger.

"Don't quarrel this lovely day," implored Cecily.

"Nobody's quarrelling, Sis. I ain't a bit mad. It's Felicity. What on earth is that at the bottom of your basket, Cecily?"

"It's a History of the Reformation in France," confessed poor Cecily, "by a man named D-a-u-b-i-g-n-y. I can't pronounce it. I heard Mr. Marwood saying it was a book everyone ought to read, so I began it last Sunday. I brought it along today to read when I got tired picking flowers. I'd ever so much rather have brought *Ester Reid*. There's so much in the history I can't understand, and it is so dreadful to read of people being burned to death. But I felt I *ought* to read it."

"Do you really think your mind has improved any?" asked Sara Ray seriously, wreathing the handle of her basket with creeping spruce.

"No, I'm afraid it hasn't one bit," answered Cecily sadly. "I feel that I haven't succeeded very well in keeping my resolutions."

"I've kept mine," said Felicity complacently.

"It's easy to keep just one," retorted Cecily, rather resentfully.

"It's not so easy to think beautiful thoughts," answered Felicity.

"It's the easiest thing in the world," said the Story Girl, tiptoeing to the edge of the pool to peep at her own arch reflection, as some nymph left over from the golden age might do. "Beautiful thoughts just crowd into your mind at times."

"Oh, yes, *at times*. But that's different from thinking one *regularly* at a given hour. And mother is always calling up the stairs for me to hurry up and get dressed, and it's *very* hard sometimes."

"That's so," conceded the Story Girl. "There *are* times when I can't think anything but gray thoughts. Then, other days, I think pink and blue and gold and purple and rainbow thoughts all the time."

"The idea! As if thoughts were coloured," giggled Felicity.

"Oh, they are!" cried the Story Girl. "Why, I can always *see* the colour of any thought I think. Can't you?"

"I never heard of such a thing," declared Felicity, "and I don't believe it. I believe you are just making that up."

"Indeed I'm not. Why, I always supposed everyone thought in colours. It must be very tiresome if you don't."

"When you think of me what colour is it?" asked Peter curiously.

"Yellow," answered the Story Girl promptly. "And Cecily is a sweet pink, like those mayflowers, and Sara Ray is very pale blue, and Dan is red and Felix is yellow, like Peter, and Bev is striped."

"What colour am I?" asked Felicity, amid the laughter at my expense.

"You're—you're like a rainbow," answered the Story Girl rather reluctantly. She had to be honest, but she would rather not have complimented Felicity. "And you needn't laugh at Bev. His stripes are beautiful. It isn't *he* that is striped. It's just the *thought* of him. Peg Bowen is a queer sort of yellowish green and the Awkward Man is lilac. Aunt Olivia is pansy-purple mixed with gold, and Uncle Roger is navy blue."

"I never heard such nonsense," declared Felicity. The rest of us were rather inclined to agree with her for once. We thought the Story Girl was making fun of us. But I believe she really had a strange gift of thinking in colours. In later years, when we were grown up, she told me of it again. She said that everything had colour in her thought; the months of the year ran through all the tints of the spectrum, the days of the week were arrayed as Solomon in his glory, morning was golden, noon orange, evening crystal blue, and night violet. Every idea came to her mind robed in its own especial hue. Perhaps that was why her voice and words had such a charm, conveying to the listeners' perception such fine shadings of meaning and tint and music.

"Well, let's go and have something to eat," suggested Dan. "What colour is eating, Sara?"

"Golden brown, just the colour of a molasses cooky," laughed the Story Girl.

We sat on the ferny bank of the pool and ate of the generous basket Aunt Janet had provided, with appetites sharpened by the keen spring air and our wilderness rovings. Felicity had made some very nice sandwiches of ham which we all appreciated except Dan, who declared he didn't like things minced up and dug out of the basket a chunk of boiled pork which he proceeded to saw up with a jack-knife and devour with gusto.

"I told ma to put this in for me. There's some *chew* to it," he said.

"You are not a bit *refined*," commented Felicity.

"Not a morsel, my love," grinned Dan.

"You make me think of a story I heard Uncle Roger telling about Cousin Annetta King," said the Story Girl. "Great-uncle Jeremiah King used to live where Uncle Roger lives now, when Grandfather King was alive and Uncle Roger was a boy. In those days it was thought rather coarse for a young lady to have too hearty an appetite, and she was more admired if she was delicate about what she ate. Cousin Annetta set out to be very refined indeed. She pretended to have no appetite at all. One afternoon she was invited to tea at Grandfather King's when they had some special company—people from Charlottetown. Cousin Annetta said she could hardly eat anything. 'You know, Uncle Abraham,' she said, in a very affected, fine-young-lady voice, 'I really hardly eat enough to keep a bird alive. Mother says she wonders how I continue to exist.' And she picked and pecked until Grandfather King declared he would like to throw something at her. After tea Cousin Annetta went home, and just about dark Grandfather King went over to Uncle Jeremiah's on an errand. As he passed the open, lighted pantry window he happened to glance in, and what do you think he saw? Delicate Cousin Annetta standing at the dresser, with a big loaf of bread beside her and a big platterful of cold, boiled pork in front of her; and Annetta was hacking off great chunks, like Dan there, and gobbling them down as if she was starving. Grandfather King couldn't resist the temptation. He stepped up to the window and said, 'I'm glad your appetite has come back to you, Annetta. Your mother needn't worry about your continuing to exist as long as you can tuck away fat, salt pork in that fashion.'

"Cousin Annetta never forgave him, but she never pretended to be delicate again."

"The Jews don't believe in eating pork," said Peter.

"I'm glad I'm not a Jew and I guess Cousin Annettta was too," said Dan.

"I like bacon, but I can never look at a pig without wondering if they were ever intended to be eaten," remarked Cecily naively.

When we finished our lunch the barrens were already wrapping themselves in a dim, blue dusk and falling upon rest in dell and dingle. But out in the open there was still much light of a fine emerald-golden sort and the robins whistled us home in it. "Horns of Elfland" never sounded more sweetly around hoary castle and ruined fane than those vesper calls of the robins from the twilight spruce woods and across green pastures lying under the pale radiance of a young moon.

When we reached home we found that Miss Reade had been up to the hill farm on an errand and was just leaving. The Story Girl went for a walk with her and came back with an important expression on her face.

"You look as if you had a story to tell," said Felix.

"One is growing. It isn't a whole story yet," answered the Story Girl mysteriously.

"What is it?" asked Cecily.

"I can't tell you till it's fully grown," said the Story Girl. "But I'll tell you a pretty little story the Awkward Man told us—told me—tonight. He was walking in his garden as we went by, looking at his tulip beds. His tulips are up ever so much higher than ours, and I asked him how he managed to coax them along so early. And he said *he* didn't do it—it was all the work of the pixies who lived in the woods across the brook. There were more pixy babies than usual this spring, and the mothers were in a hurry for the cradles. The tulips are the pixy babies' cradles, it seems. The mother pixies come out of the woods at twilight and rock their tiny little brown babies to sleep in the tulip cups. That is the reason why tulip blooms last so much longer than other blossoms. The pixy babies must have a cradle until they are grown up. They grow very fast, you see, and the Awkward Man says on a spring evening, when the tulips are out, you can hear the sweetest, softest, clearest, fairy music in his garden, and it is the pixy folk singing as they rock the pixy babies to sleep."

"Then the Awkward Man says what isn't true," said Felicity severely.

CHAPTER XIII

A
Surprising
Announcement

"NOTHING exciting has happened for ever so long," said the Story Girl discontentedly, one late May evening, as we lingered under the wonderful white bloom of the cherry trees. There was a long row of them in the orchard, with a Lombardy poplar at either end, and a hedge of lilacs behind. When the wind blew over them all the spicy breezes of Ceylon's isle were never sweeter.

It was a time of wonder and marvel, of the soft touch of silver rain on greening fields, of the incredible delicacy of young leaves, of blossom in field and garden and wood. The whole world bloomed in a flush and tremor of maiden loveliness, instinct with all the evasive, fleeting charm of spring and girlhood and young morning. We felt and enjoyed it all without understanding or analyzing it. It was enough to be glad and young with spring on the golden road.

"I don't like excitement very much," said Cecily. "It makes one so tired. I'm sure it was exciting enough when Paddy was missing, but we didn't find that very pleasant."

"No, but it was interesting," returned the Story Girl thoughtfully. "After all, I believe I'd rather be miserable than dull."

"I wouldn't then," said Felicity decidedly. "And you need never be dull when you have work to do. 'Satan finds some mischief still for idle hands to do!'"

"Well, mischief is interesting," laughed the Story Girl. "And I thought you didn't think it lady-like to speak of that person, Felicity?"

"It's all right if you call him by his polite name," said Felicity stiffly.

"Why does the Lombardy poplar hold its branches straight

up in the air like that, when all the other poplars hold theirs out or hang them down?" interjected Peter, who had been gazing intently at the slender spire showing darkly against the fine blue eastern sky.

"Because it grows that way," said Felicity.

"Oh, I know a story about that," cried the Story Girl. "Once upon a time an old man found the pot of gold at the rainbow's end. There *is* a pot there, it is said, but it is very hard to find because you can never get to the rainbow's end before it vanishes from your sight. But this old man found it, just at sunset, when Iris, the guardian of the rainbow gold, happened to be absent. As he was a long way from home, and the pot was very big and heavy, he decided to hide it until morning and then get one of his sons to go with him and help him carry it. So he hid it under the boughs of the sleeping poplar tree.

"When Iris came back she missed the pot of gold and of course she was in a sad way about it. She sent Mercury, the messenger of the gods, to look for it, for she didn't dare leave the rainbow again, lest somebody should run off with that too. Mercury asked all the trees if they had seen the pot of gold, and the elm, oak and pine pointed to the poplar and said,

" 'The poplar can tell you where it is.'

" 'How can I tell you where it is?' cried the poplar, and she held up her branches in surprise, just as we hold up our hands—and down tumbled the pot of gold. The poplar was amazed and indignant, for she was a very honest tree. She stretched her boughs high above her head and declared that she would always hold them like that, so that nobody could hide stolen gold under them again. And she taught all the little poplars she knew to stand the same way, and that is why Lombardy poplars always do. But the aspen poplar leaves are always shaking, even on the very calmest day. And do you know why?"

And then she told us the old legend that the cross on which the Saviour of the world suffered was made of aspen poplar wood and so never again could its poor, shaken, shivering leaves know rest or peace. There was an aspen in the orchard, the very embodiment of youth and spring in its litheness and symmetry. Its little leaves were hanging tremulously, not yet so fully blown as to hide its development of bough and twig, making poetry against the spiritual tints of a spring sunset.

"It does look sad," said Peter, "but it is a pretty tree, and it wasn't its fault."

"There's a heavy dew and it's time we stopped talking nonsense and went in," decreed Felicity. "If we don't we'll all have a cold, and then we'll be miserable enough, but it won't be very exciting."

"All the same, I wish something exciting would happen," finished the Story Girl, as we walked up through the orchard, peopled with its nun-like shadows.

"There's a new moon tonight, so may be you'll get your wish," said Peter. "My Aunt Jane didn't believe there was anything in the moon business, but you never can tell."

The Story Girl did get her wish. Something happened the very next day. She joined us in the afternoon with a quite indescribable expression on her face, compounded of triumph, anticipation, and regret. Her eyes betrayed that she had been crying, but in them shone a chastened exultation. Whatever the Story Girl mourned over it was evident she was not without hope.

"I have some news to tell you," she said importantly. "Can you guess what it is?"

We couldn't and wouldn't try.

"Tell us right off," implored Felix. "You look as if it was something tremendous."

"So it is. Listen——Aunt Olivia is going to be married."

We stared in blank amazement. Peg Bowen's hint had faded from our minds and we had never put much faith in it.

"Aunt Olivia! I don't believe it," cried Felicity flatly. "Who told you?"

"Aunt Olivia herself. So it is perfectly true. I'm awfully sorry in one way——but oh, won't it be splendid to have a real wedding in the family? She's going to have a big wedding——and I am to be bridesmaid."

"I shouldn't think you were old enough to be a bridesmaid," said Felicity sharply.

"I'm nearly fifteen. Anyway, Aunt Olivia says I have to be."

"Who's she going to marry?" asked Cecily, gathering herself together after the shock, and finding that the world was going on just the same.

"His name is Dr. Seton and he is a Halifax man. She met him when she was at Uncle Edward's last summer. They've been engaged ever since. The wedding is to be the third week in June."

"And our school concert comes off the next week," complained Felicity. "Why do things always come together like that? And what are you going to do if Aunt Olivia is going away?"

"I'm coming to live at your house," answered the Story Girl rather timidly. She did not know how Felicity might like that. But Felicity took it rather well.

"You've been here most of the time anyhow, so it'll just be that you'll sleep and eat here, too. But what's to become of Uncle Roger?"

"Aunt Olivia says he'll have to get married, too. But Uncle Roger says he'd rather hire a housekeeper than marry one, because in the first case he could turn her off if he didn't like her, but in the second case he couldn't."

"There'll be a lot of cooking to do for the wedding," reflected Felicity in a tone of satisfaction.

"I s'pose Aunt Olivia will want some rusks made. I hope she has plenty of tooth-powder laid in," said Dan.

"It's a pity you don't use some of that tooth-powder you're so fond of talking about yourself," retorted Felicity. "When anyone has a mouth the size of yours the teeth show so plain."

"I brush my teeth every Sunday," asseverated Dan.

"Every Sunday! You ought to brush them every *day*."

"Did anyone ever hear such nonsense?" demanded Dan sincerely.

"Well, you know, it really does say so in the *Family Guide*," said Cecily quietly.

"Then the *Family Guide* people must have lots more spare time than I have," retorted Dan contemptuously.

"Just think, the Story Girl will have her name in the papers if she's bridesmaid," marvelled Sara Ray.

"In the Halifax papers, too," added Felix, "since Dr. Seton is a Halifax man. What is his first name?"

"Robert."

"And will we have to call him Uncle Robert?"

"Not until he's married to her. Then we will, of course."

"I hope your Aunt Olivia won't disappear before the ceremony," remarked Sara Ray, who was surreptitiously reading "*The Vanished Bride*," by Valeria H. Montague in the *Family Guide*.

"I hope Dr. Seton won't fail to show up, like your cousin Rachel Ward's beau," said Peter.

"That makes me think of another story I read the other day about Great-uncle Andrew King and Aunt Georgina," laughed the Story Girl. "It happened eighty years ago. It was a very stormy winter and the roads were bad. Uncle Andrew lived in Carlisle, and Aunt Georgina—she was Miss Georgina Matheson then—lived away up west, so he couldn't get to see her very often. They agreed to be married that winter, but Georgina couldn't set the day exactly because her brother, who lived in Ontario, was coming home for a visit, and she wanted to be married while he was home. So it was arranged that she was to write Uncle Andrew and tell him what day to come. She did, and she told him to come on a Tuesday. But her writing wasn't very good and poor Uncle Andrew thought she wrote Thursday. So on Thursday he drove all the way to Georgina's home to be married. It was forty miles and a bitter cold day. But it wasn't any colder than the reception he got from Georgina. She was out in the porch, with her head tied up in a towel, picking geese. She had been all ready Tuesday, and her friends and the minister were there, and the wedding supper prepared. But there was no bridegroom and Georgina was furious. Nothing Uncle Andrew could say would appease her. She wouldn't listen to a word of explanation, but told him to go, and never show his nose there again. So poor Uncle Andrew had to go ruefully home, hoping that she would relent later on, because he was really very much in love with her."

"And did she?" queried Felicity.

"She did. Thirteen years exactly from that day they were married. It took her just that long to forgive him."

"It took her just that long to find out she couldn't get anybody else," said Dan, cynically.

CHAPTER XIV

A Prodigal Returns

Aunt Olivia and the Story Girl lived in a whirlwind of dressmaking after that, and enjoyed it hugely. Cecily and Felicity also had to have new dresses for the great event, and they talked of little else for a fortnight. Cecily declared that she hated to go to sleep because she was sure to dream that she was at Aunt Olivia's wedding in her old faded gingham dress and a ragged apron.

"And no shoes or stockings," she added, "and I can't move, and everyone walks past and looks at my feet."

"That's only in a dream," mourned Sara Ray, "but I may have to wear my last summer's white dress to the wedding. It's too short, but ma says it's plenty good for this summer. I'll be so mortified if I have to wear it."

"I'd rather not go at all than wear a dress that wasn't nice," said Felicity pleasantly.

"I'd go to the wedding if I had to go in my school dress," cried Sara Ray. "I've never been to anything. I wouldn't miss it for the world."

"My Aunt Jane always said that if you were neat and tidy it didn't matter whether you were dressed fine or not," said Peter.

"I'm sick and tired of hearing about your Aunt Jane," said Felicity crossly.

Peter looked grieved but held his peace. Felicity was very hard on him that spring, but his loyalty never wavered. Everything she said or did was right in Peter's eyes.

"It's all very well to be neat and tidy," said Sara Ray, "but I like a little style too."

"I think you'll find your mother will get you a new dress after all," comforted Cecily. "Anyway, nobody will notice you because everyone will be looking at the bride. Aunt Olivia will make a lovely bride. Just think how sweet she'll look in a white silk dress and a floating veil."

"She says she is going to have the ceremony performed out here in the orchard under her own tree," said the Story Girl. "Won't that be romantic? It almost makes me feel like getting married myself."

"What a way to talk," rebuked Felicity, "and you only fifteen."

"Lots of people have been married at fifteen," laughed the Story Girl. "Lady Jane Gray was."

"But you are always saying that Valeria H. Montague's stories are silly and not true to life, so that is no argument," retorted Felicity, who knew more about cooking than about history, and evidently imagined that the Lady Jane Gray was one of Valeria's titled heroines.

The wedding was a perennial source of conversation among us in those days; but presently its interest palled for a time in the light of another quite tremendous happening. One Saturday night Peter's mother called to take him home with her for Sunday. She had been working at Mr. James Frewen's, and Mr. Frewen was driving her home. We had never seen Peter's mother before, and we looked at her with discreet curiosity. She was a plump, black-eyed little woman, neat as a pin, but with a rather tired and care-worn face that looked as if it should have been rosy and jolly. Life had been a hard battle for her, and I rather think that her curly-headed little lad was all that had kept heart and spirit in her. Peter went home with her and returned Sunday evening. We were in the orchard sitting around the Pulpit Stone, where we had, according to the custom of the households of King, been learning our golden texts and memory verses for the next Sunday School lesson. Paddy, grown sleek and handsome again, was sitting on the stone itself, washing his jowls.

Peter joined us with a very queer expression on his face. He seemed bursting with some news which he wanted to tell and yet hardly liked to.

"Why are you looking so mysterious, Peter?" demanded the Story Girl.

"What do you think has happened?" asked Peter solemnly.

"What has?"

"My father has come home," answered Peter.

The announcement produced all the sensation he could have wished. We crowded around him in excitement.

"Peter! When did he come back?"

"Saturday night. He was there when ma and I got home. It give her an awful turn. I didn't know him at first, of course."

"Peter Craig, I believe you are glad your father has come back," cried the Story Girl.

" 'Course I'm glad," retorted Peter.

"And after you saying you didn't want ever to see him again," said Felicity.

"You just wait. You haven't heard my story yet. I wouldn't have been glad to see father if he'd come back the same as he went away. But he is a changed man. He happened to go into a revival meeting one night this spring and he got converted. And he's come home to stay, and he says he's never going to drink another drop, but he's going to look after his family. Ma isn't to do any more washing for nobody but him and me, and I'm not to be a hired boy any longer. He says I can stay with your Uncle Roger till the fall 'cause I promised I would, but after that I'm to stay home and go to school right along and learn to be whatever I'd like to be. I tell you it made me feel queer. Everything seemed to be upset. But he gave ma forty dollars— every cent he had—so I guess he really is converted."

"I hope it will last, I'm sure," said Felicity. She did not say it nastily, however. We were all glad for Peter's sake, though a little dizzy over the unexpectedness of it all.

"This is what I'd like to know," said Peter. "How did Peg Bowen know my father was coming home? Don't you tell me she isn't a witch after that."

"And she knew about your Aunt Olivia's wedding, too," added Sara Ray.

"Oh, well, she likely heard that from some one. Grown up folks talk things over long before they tell them to children," said Cecily.

"Well, she couldn't have heard father was coming home from any one," answered Peter. "He was converted up in Maine, where nobody knew him, and he never told a soul he was coming till he got here. No, you can believe what you like, but I'm satisfied at last that Peg is a witch and that skull of hers does tell her things. She told me father was coming home and he come!"

"How happy you must be," sighed Sara Ray romantically.

"It's just like that story in the *Family Guide*, where the missing earl comes home to his family just as the Countess and Lady Violetta are going to be turned out by the cruel heir."

Felicity sniffed.

"There's some difference, I guess. The earl had been imprisoned for years in a loathsome dungeon."

Perhaps Peter's father had too, if we but realized it—imprisoned in the dungeon of his own evil appetites and habits, than which none could be more loathsome. But a Power, mightier than the forces of evil, had struck off his fetters and led him back to his long-forfeited liberty and light. And no countess or lady of high degree could have welcomed a long-lost earl home more joyfully than the tired little washerwoman had welcomed the erring husband of her youth.

But in Peter's ointment of joy there was a fly or two. So very, very few things are flawless in this world, even on the golden road.

"Of course I'm awful glad that father has come back and that ma won't have to wash any more," he said with a sigh, "but there are two things that kind of worry me. My Aunt Jane always said that it didn't do any good to worry, and I s'pose it don't, but it's kind of a relief."

"What's worrying you?" asked Felix.

"Well, for one thing I'll feel awful bad to go away from you all. I'll miss you just dreadful, and I won't even be able to go to the same school. I'll have to go to Markdale school."

"But you must come and see us often," said Felicity graciously. "Markdale isn't so far away, and you could spend every other Saturday afternoon with us anyway."

Peter's black eyes filled with adoring gratitude.

"That's so kind of you, Felicity. I'll come as often as I can, of course; but it won't be the same as being around with you all the time. The other things is even worse. You see, it was a Methodist revival father got converted in, and so of course he joined the Methodist church. He wasn't anything before. He used to say he was a Nothingarian and lived up to it—kind of bragging like. But he's a strong Methodist now, and is going to go to Markdale Methodist church and pay to the salary. Now what'll he say when I tell him I'm a Presbyterian?"

"You haven't told him, yet?" asked the Story Girl.

"No, I didn't dare. I was scared he'd say I'd have to be a Methodist."

"Well, Methodists are pretty near as good as Presbyterians," said Felicity, with the air of one making a great concession.

"I guess they're every bit as good," retorted Peter. "But that ain't the point. I've got to be a Presbyterian, 'cause I stick to a thing when I once decide it. But I expect father will be mad when he finds out."

"If he's converted he oughtn't to get mad," said Dan.

"Well, lots o' people do. But if he isn't mad he'll be sorry, and that'll be even worse, for a Presbyterian I'm bound to be. But I expect it will make things unpleasant."

"You needn't tell him anything about it," advised Felicity. "Just keep quiet and go to the Methodist church until you get big, and then you can go where you please."

"No, that wouldn't be honest," said Peter sturdily. "My Aunt Jane always said it was best to be open and above board in everything, and especially in religion. So I'll tell father right out, but I'll wait a few weeks so as not to spoil things for ma too soon if he acts up."

Peter was not the only one who had secret cares. Sara Ray was beginning to feel worried over her looks. I heard her and Cecily talking over their troubles one evening while I was weeding the onion bed and they were behind the hedge knitting lace. I did not mean to eavesdrop. I supposed they knew I was there until Cecily overwhelmed me with indignation later on.

"I'm so afraid, Cecily, that I'm going to be homely all my life," said poor Sara with a tremble in her voice. "You can stand being ugly when you are young if you have any hope of being better looking when you grow up. But I'm getting worse. Aunt Mary says I'm going to be the very image of Aunt Matilda. And Aunt Matilda is as homely as she can be. It isn't"—and poor Sara sighed—"a very cheerful prospect. If I am ugly nobody will ever want to marry me, and," concluded Sara candidly, "I don't want to be an old maid."

"But plenty of girls get married who aren't a bit pretty," comforted Cecily. "Besides, you are real nice looking at times, Sara. I think you are going to have a nice figure."

"But just look at my hands," moaned Sara. "They're simply covered with warts."

"Oh, the warts will all disappear before you grow up," said Cecily.

"But they won't disappear before the school concert. How am I to get up there and recite? You know there is one line in my recitation, 'She waved her lily-white hand,' and I have to wave mine when I say it. Fancy waving a lily-white hand all covered with warts. I've tried every remedy I ever heard of, but nothing does any good. Judy Pineau said if I rubbed them with toad-spit it would take them away for sure. But how am I to get any toad-spit?"

"It doesn't sound like a very nice remedy, anyhow," shuddered Cecily. "I'd rather have the warts. But do you know, I believe if you didn't cry so much over every little thing, you'd be ever so much better looking. Crying spoils your eyes and makes the end of your nose red."

"I can't help crying," protested Sara. "My feelings are so very sensitive. I've given up trying to keep *that* resolution."

"Well, men don't like cry-babies," said Cecily sagely. Cecily had a good deal of Mother Eve's wisdom tucked away in that smooth, brown head of hers.

"Cecily, do you ever intend to be married?" asked Sara in a confidential tone.

"Goodness!" cried Cecily, quite shocked. "It will be time enough when I grow up to think of that, Sara."

"I should think you'd have to think of it now, with Cyrus Brisk as crazy after you as he is."

"I wish Cyrus Brisk was at the bottom of the Red Sea," exclaimed Cecily, goaded into a spurt of temper by mention of the detested name.

"What has Cyrus been doing now?" asked Felicity, coming around the corner of the hedge.

"Doing *now*! It's *all* the time. He just worries me to death," returned Cecily angrily. "He keeps writing me letters and putting them in my desk or in my reader. I never answer one of them, but he keeps on. And in the last one, mind you, he said he'd do something desperate right off if I wouldn't promise to marry him when we grew up."

"Just think, Cecily, you've had a proposal already," said Sara Ray in an awe-struck tone.

"But he hasn't done anything desperate yet, and that was last week," commented Felicity, with a toss of her head.

"He sent me a lock of his hair and wanted one of mine in exchange," continued Cecily indignantly. "I tell you I sent his back to him pretty quick."

"Did you never answer any of his letters?" asked Sara Ray.

"No, indeed! I guess not!"

"Do you know," said Felicity, "I believe if you wrote him just once and told him your exact opinion of him in good plain English it would cure him of his nonsense."

"I couldn't do that. I haven't enough spunk," confessed Cecily with a blush. "But I'll tell you what I did do once. He wrote me a long letter last week. It was just awfully *soft,* and every other word was spelled wrong. He even spelled baking soda, 'bacon soda'!"

"What on earth had he to say about baking soda in a love-letter?" asked Felicity.

"Oh, he said his mother sent him to the store for some and he forgot it because he was thinking about me. Well, I just took his letter and wrote in all the words, spelled right, above the wrong ones, in red ink, just as Mr. Perkins makes us do with our dictation exercises, and sent it back to him. I thought maybe he'd feel insulted and stop writing to me."

"And did he?"

"No, he didn't. It is *my* opinion you can't insult Cyrus Brisk. He is too thick-skinned. He wrote another letter, and thanked me for correcting my mistakes, and said it made him feel glad because it showed I was beginning to take an interest in him when I wanted him to spell better. Did you ever? Miss Marwood says it is wrong to hate anyone, but I don't care, I hate Cyrus Brisk."

"Mrs. Cyrus Brisk *would* be an awful name," giggled Felicity.

"Flossie Brisk says Cyrus is ruining all the trees on his father's place cutting your name on them," said Sara Ray. "His father told him he would whip him if he didn't stop, but Cyrus keeps right on. He told Flossie it relieved his feelings. Flossie says he cut yours and his together on the birch tree in front of the parlour window, and a row of hearts around them."

"Just where every visitor can see them, I suppose," lamented Cecily. "He just worries my life out. And what I mind most of all is, he sits and looks at me in school with such melancholy, reproachful eyes when he ought to be working sums. I won't look at him, but I *feel* him staring at me, and it makes me so nervous."

"They say his mother was out of her mind at one time," said Felicity.

I do not think Felicity was quite well pleased that Cyrus should have passed over her rose-red prettiness to set his affections on that demure elf of a Cecily. She did not want the allegiance of Cyrus in the least, but it was something of a slight that he had not wanted her to want it.

"And he sends me pieces of poetry he cuts out of the papers," Cecily went on, "with lots of the lines marked with a lead pencil. Yesterday he put one in his letter, and this is what he marked:

> " 'If you will not relent to me
> Then must I learn to know
> Darkness alone till life be flown.'

Here—I have the piece in my sewing-bag—I'll read it all to you."

Those three graceless girls read the sentimental rhyme and giggled over it. Poor Cyrus! His young affections were sadly misplaced. But after all, though Cecily never relented towards him, he did not condemn himself to darkness alone till life was flown. Quite early in life he wedded a stout, rosy, buxom lass, the very antithesis of his first love; he prospered in his undertakings, raised a large and respectable family, and was eventually appointed a Justice of the Peace. Which was all very sensible of Cyrus.

CHAPTER XV

The Rape of the Lock

JUNE was crowded full of interest that year. We gathered in with its sheaf of fragrant days the choicest harvest of childhood. Things happened right along. Cecily declared she hated to go to sleep for fear she might miss something. There were so many dear delights along the golden road to give us pleasure—the earth dappled with new blossom, the dance of shadows in the fields, the rustling, rain-wet ways of the woods, the faint fragrance in meadow lanes, liltings of birds and croon of bees in the old orchard, windy pipings on the hills, sunset behind the pines, limpid dews filling primrose cups, crescent moons through darkling boughs, soft nights alight with blinking stars. We enjoyed all these boons, unthinkingly and light-heartedly, as children do. And besides these, there was the absorbing little drama of human life which was being enacted all around us, and in which each of us played a satisfying part—the gay preparations for Aunt Olivia's mid-June wedding, the excitement of practising for the concert with which our school-teacher, Mr. Perkins, had elected to close the school year, and Cecily's troubles with Cyrus Brisk, which furnished unholy mirth for the rest of us, though Cecily could not see the funny side of it at all.

Matters went from bad to worse in the case of the irrepressible Cyrus. He continued to shower Cecily with notes, the spelling of which showed no improvement; he worried the life out of her by constantly threatening to fight Willy Fraser—although, as Felicity sarcastically pointed out, he never did it.

"But I'm always afraid he will," said Cecily, "and it would be such a *disgrace* to have two boys fighting over me in school."

"You *must* have encouraged Cyrus a little in the beginning or he'd never have been so persevering," said Felicity unjustly.

"I never did!" cried outraged Cecily. "You know very well,

Felicity King, that I hated Cyrus Brisk ever since the very first time I saw his big, fat, red face. So there!"

"Felicity is just jealous because Cyrus didn't take a notion to her instead of you, Sis," said Dan.

"Talk sense!" snapped Felicity.

"If I did you wouldn't understand me, sweet little sister," rejoined aggravating Dan.

Finally Cyrus crowned his iniquities by stealing the denied lock of Cecily's hair. One sunny afternoon in school, Cecily and Kitty Marr asked and received permission to sit out on the side bench before the open window, where the cool breeze swept in from the green fields beyond. To sit on this bench was always considered a treat, and was only allowed as a reward of merit; but Cecily and Kitty had another reason for wishing to sit there. Kitty had read in a magazine that sunbaths were good for the hair; so both she and Cecily tossed their long braids over the window-sill and let them hang there in the broiling sunshine. And while Cecily sat thus, diligently working a fraction sum on her slate, that base Cyrus asked permission to go out, having previously borrowed a pair of scissors from one of the big girls who did fancy work at the noon recess. Outside, Cyrus sneaked up close to the window and cut off a piece of Cecily's hair.

This rape of the lock did not produce quite such terrible consequences as the more famous one in Pope's poem, but Cecily's soul was no less agitated than Belinda's. She cried all the way home from school about it, and only checked her tears when Dan declared he'd fight Cyrus and make him give it up.

"Oh, no, you mustn't," said Cecily, struggling with her sobs. "I won't have you fighting on my account for anything. And besides, he'd likely lick you—he's so big and rough. And the folks at home might find out all about it, and Uncle Roger would never give me any peace, and mother would be cross, for she'd never believe it wasn't my fault. It wouldn't be so bad if he'd only taken a little, but he cut a great big chunk right off the end of one of the braids. Just look at it. I'll have to cut the other to make them fair—and they'll look so awful stubby."

But Cyrus' acquirement of the chunk of hair was his last triumph. His downfall was near; and, although it involved Cecily in a most humiliating experience, over which she cried half the following night, in the end she confessed it was worth undergoing just to get rid of Cyrus.

Mr. Perkins was an exceedingly strict disciplinarian. No communication of any sort was permitted between his pupils during school hours. Anyone caught violating this rule was promptly punished by the infliction of one of the weird penances for which Mr. Perkins was famous, and which were generally far worse than ordinary whipping.

One day in school Cyrus sent a letter across to Cecily. Usually he left his effusions in her desk, or between the leaves of her books; but this time it was passed over to her under cover of the desk through the hands of two or three scholars. Just as Em Frewen held it over the aisle Mr. Perkins wheeled around from his station before the blackboard and caught her in the act.

"Bring that here, Emmeline," he commanded.

Cyrus turned quite pale. Em carried the note to Mr. Perkins. He took it, held it up, and scrutinized the address.

"Did you write this to Cecily, Emmeline?" he asked.

"No, sir."

"Who wrote it then?"

Em said quite shamelessly that she didn't know—it had just been passed over from the next row.

"And I suppose you have no idea where it came from?" said Mr. Perkins, with his frightful, sardonic grin. "Well, perhaps Cecily can tell us. You may take your seat, Emmeline, and you will remain at the foot of your spelling class for a week as punishment for passing the note. Cecily, come here."

Indignant Em sat down and poor, innocent Cecily was haled forth to public ignominy. She went with a crimson face.

"Cecily," said her tormentor, "do you know who wrote this letter to you?"

Cecily, like a certain renowned personage, could not tell a lie.

"I—I think so, sir," she murmured faintly.

"Who was it?"

"I can't tell you that," stammered Cecily, on the verge of tears.

"Ah!" said Mr. Perkins politely. "Well, I suppose I could easily find out by opening it. But it is very impolite to open other people's letters. I think I have a better plan. Since you refuse to tell me who wrote it, open it yourself, take this chalk, and copy the contents on the blackboard that we may all enjoy them. And sign the writer's name at the bottom."

"Oh," gasped Cecily, choosing the lesser of two evils, "I'll tell you who wrote it—it was—"

"Hush!" Mr. Perkins checked her with a gentle motion of his hand. He was always most gentle when most inexorable. "You did not obey me when I first ordered you to tell me the writer. You cannot have the privilege of doing so now. Open the note, take the chalk, and do as I command you."

Worms will turn, and even meek, mild, obedient little souls like Cecily may be goaded to the point of wild, sheer rebellion.

"I—I won't!" she cried passionately.

Mr. Perkins, martinet though he was, would hardly, I think, have inflicted such a punishment on Cecily, who was a favourite of his, had he known the real nature of that luckless missive. But, as he afterwards admitted, he thought it was merely a note from some other girl, of such trifling sort as school-girls are wont to write; and moreover, he had already committed himself to the decree, which, like those of Mede and Persian, must not alter. To let Cecily off, after her mad defiance, would be to establish a revolutionary precedent.

"So you really think you won't?" he queried smilingly. "Well, on second thoughts, you may take your choice. Either you will do as I have bidden you, or you will sit for three days with"—Mr. Perkins' eye skimmed over the school-room to find a boy who was sitting alone—"with Cyrus Brisk."

This choice of Mr. Perkins, who knew nothing of the little drama of emotions that went on under the routine of lessons and exercises in his domain, was purely accidental, but we took it at the time as a stroke of diabolical genius. It left Cecily no choice. She would have done almost anything before she would have sat with Cyrus Brisk. With flashing eyes she tore open the letter, snatched up the chalk, and dashed at the blackboard.

In a few minutes the contents of that letter graced the expanse usually sacred to more prosaic compositions. I cannot reproduce it verbatim, for I had no after opportunity of refreshing my memory. But I remember that it was exceedingly sentimental and exceedingly ill-spelled—for Cecily mercilessly copied down poor Cyrus' mistakes. He wrote her that he wore her hare over his hart—"and he stole it," Cecily threw passionately over her shoulder at Mr. Perkins—that her eyes were so sweet and lovely that he couldn't find words nice enuf to describ them, that he could never forget how butiful she had looked in prar meeting the evening before, and that some meels he couldn't eat for thinking of her, with more to the same effect and he signed it "yours till deth us do part, Cyrus Brisk."

As the writing proceeded we scholars exploded into smothered laughter, despite our awe of Mr. Perkins. Mr. Perkins himself could not keep a straight face. He turned abruptly away and looked out of the window, but we could see his shoulders shaking. When Cecily had finished and had thrown down the chalk with bitter vehemence, he turned around with a very red face.

"That will do. You may sit down. Cyrus, since it seems you are the guilty person, take the eraser and wipe that off the board. Then go stand in the corner, facing the room, and hold your arms straight above your head until I tell you to take them down."

Cyrus obeyed and Cecily fled to her seat and wept, nor did Mr. Perkins meddle with her more that day. She bore her burden of humiliation bitterly for several days, until she was suddenly comforted by a realization that Cyrus had ceased to persecute her. He wrote no more letters, he gazed no longer in rapt adoration, he brought no more votive offerings of gum and pencils to her shrine. At first we thought he had been cured by the unmerciful chaffing he had to undergo from his mates, but eventually his sister told Cecily the true reason. Cyrus had at last been driven to believe that Cecily's aversion to him was real, and not merely the defence of maiden coyness. If she hated him so intensely that she would rather write that note on the blackboard than sit with him, what use was it to sigh like a furnace longer for her? Mr. Perkins had blighted love's young dream for Cyrus with a killing frost. Thenceforth sweet Cecily kept the noiseless tenor of her way unvexed by the attentions of enamoured swains.

CHAPTER XVI

Aunt Una's Story

FELICITY, and Cecily, Dan, Felix, Sara Ray and I were sitting one evening on the mossy stones in Uncle Roger's hill pasture, where we had sat the morning the Story Girl told us the tale of the Wedding Veil of the Proud Princess. But it was evening now and the valley beneath us was brimmed up with the glow of the afterlight. Behind us, two tall, shapely spruce trees rose up against the sunset, and through the dark oriel of their sundered branches an evening star looked down. We sat on a little strip of emerald grassland and before us was a sloping meadow all white with daisies.

We were waiting for Peter and the Story Girl. Peter had gone to Markdale after dinner to spend the afternoon with his re-united parents because it was his birthday. He had left us grimly determined to confess to his father the dark secret of his Presbyterianism, and we were anxious to know what the result had been. The Story Girl had gone that morning with Miss Reade to visit the latter's home near Charlottetown, and we expected soon to see her coming gaily along over the fields from the Armstrong place.

Presently Peter came jauntily stepping along the field path up the hill.

"Hasn't Peter got tall?" said Cecily.

"Peter is growing to be a very fine looking boy," decreed Felicity.

"I notice he's got ever so much handsomer since his father came home," said Dan, with a killing sarcasm that was wholly lost on Felicity, who gravely responded that she supposed it was because Peter felt so much freer from care and responsibility.

"What luck, Peter?" yelled Dan, as soon as Peter was within earshot.

"Everything's all right," he shouted jubilantly. "I told father right off, licketty-split, as soon as I got home," he added when he reached us. "I was anxious to have it over with. I says, solemn-like, 'Dad, there's something I've got to tell you, and I don't know how you'll take it, but it can't be helped,' I says. Dad looked pretty sober, and he says, says he, 'What have you been up to, Peter? Don't be afraid to tell me. I've been forgiven to seventy times seven, so surely I can forgive a little, too?' 'Well,' I says, desperate-like, 'the truth is, father, I'm a Presbyterian. I made up my mind last summer, the time of the Judgment Day, that I'd be a Presbyterian, and I've got to stick to it. I'm sorry I can't be a Methodist, like you and mother and Aunt Jane, but I can't and that's all there is to it,' I says. Then I waited, scared-like. But father, he just looked relieved and he says, says he, 'Goodness, boy, you can be a Presbyterian or anything else you like, so long as it's Protestant. I'm not caring,' he says. 'The main thing is that you must be good and do what's right.' I tell you," concluded Peter emphatically, "father is a Christian all right."

"Well, I suppose your mind will be at rest now," said Felicity. "What's that you have in your buttonhole?"

"That's a four-leaved clover," answered Peter exultantly. "That means good luck for the summer. I found it in Markdale. There ain't much clover in Carlisle this year of any kind of leaf. The crop is going to be a failure. Your Uncle Roger says it's because there ain't enough old maids in Carlisle. There's lots of them in Markdale, and that's the reason, he says, why they always have such good clover crops there."

"What on earth have old maids to do with it?" cried Cecily.

"I don't believe they've a single thing to do with it, but Mr. Roger says they have, and he says a man called Darwin proved it. This is the rigmarole he got off to me the other day. The clover crop depends on there being plenty of bumble-bees, because they are the only insects with tongues long enough to—to—fer—fertilize—I think he called it—the blossoms. But mice eat bumble-bees and cats eat mice and old maids keep cats. So your Uncle Roger says the more old maids the more cats, and the more cats the fewer field-mice, and the fewer field-mice the more bumble-bees, and the more bumble-bees the better clover crops."

"So don't worry if you do get to be old maids, girls," said Dan. "Remember, you'll be helping the clover crops."

"I never heard such stuff as you boys talk," said Felicity, "and Uncle Roger is no better."

"There comes the Story Girl," cried Cecily eagerly. "Now we'll hear all about Beautiful Alice's home."

The Story Girl was bombarded with eager questions as soon as she arrived. Miss Reade's home was a dream of a place, it appeared. The house was just covered with ivy and there was a most delightful old garden—"and," added the Story Girl, with the joy of a connoisseur who has found a rare gem, "the sweetest little story connected with it. And I saw the hero of the story too."

"Where was the heroine?" queried Cecily.

"She is dead."

"Oh, of course she'd have to die," exclaimed Dan in disgust. "I'd like a story where somebody lived once in awhile."

"I've told you heaps of stories where people lived," retorted the Story Girl. "If this heroine hadn't died there wouldn't have been any story. She was Miss Reade's aunt and her name was Una, and I believe she must have been just like Miss Reade herself. Miss Reade told me all about her. When we went into the garden I saw in one corner of it an old stone bench arched over by a couple of pear trees and all grown about with grass and violets. And an old man was sitting on it—a bent old man with long, snow-white hair and beautiful sad blue eyes. He seemed very lonely and sorrowful and I wondered that Miss Reade didn't speak to him. But she never let on she saw him and took me away to another part of the garden. After awhile he got up and went away and then Miss Reade said, 'Come over to Aunt Una's seat and I will tell you about her and her lover—that man who has just gone out.'

" 'Oh, isn't he too old for a lover?' I said.

"Beautiful Alice laughed and said it was forty years since he had been her Aunt Una's lover. He had been a tall, handsome young man then, and her Aunt Una was a beautiful girl of nineteen.

"We went over and sat down and Miss Reade told me all about her. She said that when she was a child she had heard much of her Aunt Una—that she seemed to have been one of those people who are not soon forgotten, whose personality seems to linger about the scenes of their lives long after they have passed away."

"What is a personality? Is it another word for ghost?" asked Peter.

"No," said the Story Girl shortly. "I can't stop in a story to explain words."

"I don't believe you know what it is yourself," said Felicity.

The Story Girl picked up her hat, which she had thrown down on the grass, and placed it defiantly on her brown curls.

"I'm going in," she announced. "I have to help Aunt Olivia ice a cake tonight, and you all seem more interested in dictionaries than stories."

"That's not fair," I exclaimed. "Dan and Felix and Sara Ray and Cecily and I have never said a word. It's mean to punish us for what Peter and Felicity did. We want to hear the rest of the story. Never mind what a personality is but go on—and, Peter, you young ass, keep still."

"I only wanted to know," muttered Peter sulkily.

"I *do* know what personality is, but it's hard to explain," said the Story Girl, relenting. "It's what makes you different from Dan, Peter, and me different from Felicity or Cecily. Miss Reade's Aunt Una had a personality that was very uncommon. And she was beautiful, too, with white skin and night-black eyes and hair—a 'moonlight beauty,' Miss Reade called it. She used to keep a kind of a diary, and Miss Reade's mother used to read parts of it to her. She wrote verses in it and they were lovely; and she wrote descriptions of the old garden which she loved very much. Miss Reade said that everything in the garden, plot or shrub or tree, recalled to her mind some phrase or verse of her Aunt Una's, so that the whole place seemed full of her, and her memory haunted the walks like a faint, sweet perfume.

"Una had, as I've told you, a lover; and they were to have been married on her twentieth birthday. Her wedding dress was to have been a gown of white brocade with purple violets in it. But a little while before it she took ill with fever and died; and she was buried on her birthday instead of being married. It was just in the time of opening roses. Her lover has been faithful to her ever since; he has never married, and every June, on her birthday, he makes a pilgrimage to the old garden and sits for a long time in silence on the bench where he used to woo her on crimson eves and moonlight nights of long ago. Miss Reade says she always loves to see him sitting there because it gives her such a deep and lasting sense of the beauty and strength of love which can thus outlive time and death. And sometimes, she says, it gives her a little eerie feeling, too, as if her Aunt Una were really sitting there beside him, keeping tryst, although she has been in her grave for forty years."

"It would be real romantic to die young and have your lover make a pilgrimage to your garden every year," reflected Sara Ray.

"It would be more comfortable to go on living and get married to him," said Felicity. "Mother says all those sentimental ideas are bosh and I expect they are. It's a wonder Beautiful Alice hasn't a beau herself. She is so pretty and ladylike."

"The Carlisle fellows all say she is too stuck up," said Dan.

"There's nobody in Carlisle half good enough for her," cried the Story Girl, "except—except—"

"Except who?" asked Felix.

"Never mind," said the Story Girl mysteriously.

CHAPTER XVII

Aunt Olivia's Wedding

W HAT a delightful, old-fashioned, wholesome excitement there was about Aunt Olivia's wedding! The Monday and Tuesday preceding it we did not go to school at all, but were all kept home to do chores and run errands. The cooking and decorating and arranging that went on those two days was amazing, and Felicity was so happy over it all that she did not even quarrel with Dan—though she narrowly escaped it when he told her that the Governor's wife was coming to the wedding.

"Mind you have some of her favourite rusks for her," he said.

"I guess," said Felicity with dignity, "that Aunt Olivia's wedding supper will be good enough for even a Governor's wife."

"I s'pose none of us except the Story Girl will get to the first table," said Felix, rather gloomily.

"Never mind," comforted Felicity. "There's a whole turkey to be kept for us, and a freezerful of ice cream. Cecily and I are going to wait on the tables, and we'll put away a little of everything that's extra nice for our suppers."

"I do so want to have my supper with you," sighed Sara Ray, "but I s'pose ma will drag me with her wherever she goes. She won't trust me out of her sight a minute the whole evening—I know she won't."

"I'll get Aunt Olivia to ask her to let you have your supper with us," said Cecily. "She can't refuse the bride's request."

"You don't know all ma can do," returned Sara darkly. "No, I feel that I'll have to eat my supper with her. But I suppose I ought to be very thankful I'm to get to the wedding at all, and that ma did get me a new white dress for it. Even yet I'm so scared something will happen to prevent me from getting to it."

Monday evening shrouded itself in clouds, and all night long the voice of the wind answered to the voice of the rain. Tuesday the downpour continued. We were quite frantic about it. Suppose it kept on raining over Wednesday! Aunt Olivia couldn't be married in the orchard then. That would be too bad, especially when the late apple tree had most obligingly kept its store of blossom until after all the other trees had faded and then burst lavishly into bloom for Aunt Olivia's wedding. That apple tree was always very late in blooming, and this year it was a week later than usual. It was a sight to see—a great tree-pyramid with high, far-spreading boughs, over which a wealth of rosy snow seemed to have been flung. Never had bride a more magnificent canopy.

To our rapture, however, it cleared up beautifully Tuesday evening, and the sun, before setting in purple pomp, poured a flood of wonderful radiance over the whole great, green, diamond-dripping world, promising a fair morrow. Uncle Alec drove off to the station through it to bring home the bridegroom and his best man. Dan was full of a wild idea that we should all meet them at the gate, armed with cowbells and tin-pans, and "charivari" them up the lane. Peter sided with him, but the rest of us voted down the suggestion.

"Do you want Dr. Seton to think we are a pack of wild Indians?" asked Felicity severely. "A nice opinion he'd have of our manners!"

"Well, it's the only chance we'll have to chivaree them," grumbled Dan. "Aunt Olivia wouldn't mind. *She* can take a joke."

"Ma would kill you if you did such a thing," warned Felicity. "Dr. Seton lives in Halifax and they *never* chivaree people there. He would think it very vulgar."

"Then he should have stayed in Halifax and got married there," retorted Dan, sulkily.

We were very curious to see our uncle-elect. When he came and Uncle Alec took him into the parlour, we were all crowded into the dark corner behind the stairs to peep at him. Then we fled to the moonlight world outside and discussed him at the dairy.

"He's bald," said Cecily disappointedly.

"And *rather* short and stout," said Felicity.

"He's forty, if he's a day," said Dan.

"Never you mind," cried the Story Girl loyally, "Aunt Olivia loves him with all her heart."

"And more than that, he's got lots of money," added Felicity.

"Well, he may be all right," said Peter, "but it's my opinion that your Aunt Olivia could have done just as well on the Island."

"*Your* opinion doesn't matter very much to *our* family," said Felicity crushingly.

But when we made the acquaintance of Dr. Seton next morning we liked him enormously, and voted him a jolly good fellow. Even Peter remarked aside to me that he guessed Miss Olivia hadn't made much of a mistake after all, though it was plain he thought she was running a risk in not sticking to the Island. The girls had not much time to discuss him with us. They were all exceedingly busy and whisked about at such a rate that they seemed to possess the power of being in half a dozen places at once. The importance of Felicity was quite terrible. But after dinner came a lull.

"Thank goodness, everything is ready at last," breathed Felicity devoutly, as we foregathered for a brief space in the fir wood. "We've nothing more to do now but get dressed. It's really a serious thing to have a wedding in the family."

"I have a note from Sara Ray," said Cecily. "Judy Pineau brought it up when she brought Mrs. Ray's spoons. Just let me read it to you:—

" 'DEAREST CECILY:—A *dreadful misfortune* has happened to me. Last night I went with Judy to water the cows and in the spruce bush we found a *wasps' nest* and Judy thought it was *an old one* and she *poked it with a stick*. And it was a *new one*, full of wasps, and they all flew out and *stung us terribly*, on the face and hands. My face is all swelled up and I can *hardly see* out of one eye. The *suffering* was awful but I didn't mind that as much as being scared ma wouldn't take me to the wedding. But she says I can go and I'm going. I know that I am a *hard-looking sight*, but it isn't anything catching. I am writing this so that you won't get a shock when you see me. Isn't it *so strange* to think your dear Aunt Olivia is going away? How you will miss her! But your loss will be her gain.

" '*Au revoir*,

" 'Your loving chum,

" 'SARA RAY.' "

"That poor child," said the Story Girl.

"Well, all I hope is that strangers won't take her for one of the family," remarked Felicity in a disgusted tone.

Aunt Olivia was married at five o'clock in the orchard under the late apple tree. It was a pretty scene. The air was full of the perfume of apple bloom, and the bees blundered foolishly and delightfully from one blossom to another, half drunken with perfume. The old orchard was full of smiling guests in wedding garments. Aunt Olivia was most beautiful amid the frost of her bridal veil, and the Story Girl, in an unusually long white dress, with her brown curls clubbed up behind, looked so tall and grown-up that we hardly recognized her. After the ceremony— during which Sara Ray cried all the time—there was a royal wedding supper, and Sara Ray was permitted to eat her share of the feast with us.

"I'm glad I was stung by the wasps after all," she said delightedly. "If I hadn't been ma would never have let me eat with you. She just got tired explaining to people what was the matter with my face, and so she was glad to get rid of me. I know I look awful, but, oh, wasn't the bride a dream?"

We missed the Story Girl, who, of course, had to have her supper at the bridal table; but we were a hilarious little crew and the girls had nobly kept their promise to save tid-bits for us. By the time the last table was cleared away Aunt Olivia and our new uncle were ready to go. There was an orgy of tears and leavetakings, and then they drove away into the odorous moonlight night. Dan and Peter pursued them down the lane with a fiendish din of bells and pans, much to Felicity's wrath. But Aunt Olivia and Uncle Robert took it in good part and waved their hands back to us with peals of laughter.

"They're just that pleased with themselves that they wouldn't mind if there was an earthquake," said Felix, grinning.

"It's been splendid and exciting, and everything went off well," sighed Cecily, "but, oh dear, it's going to be so queer and lonesome without Aunt Olivia. I just believe I'll cry all night."

"You're tired to death, that's what's the matter with you," said Dan, returning. "You girls have worked like slaves today."

"Tomorrow will be even harder," said Felicity comfortingly. "Everything will have to be cleaned up and put away."

Peg Bowen paid us a call the next day and was regaled with a feast of fat things left over from the supper.

"Well, I've had all I can eat," she said, when she had finished and brought out her pipe. "And that doesn't happen to me every day. There ain't been as much marrying as there used to be, and half the time they just sneak off to the minister, as if they were ashamed of it, and get married without any wedding or supper. That ain't the King way, though. And so Olivia's gone off at last. She weren't in any hurry but they tell me she's done well. Time'll show."

"Why don't you get married yourself, Peg?" queried Uncle Roger teasingly. We held our breath over his temerity.

"Because I'm not so easy to please as your wife will be," retorted Peg.

She departed in high good humour over her repartee. Meeting Sara Ray on the doorstep she stopped and asked her what was the matter with her face.

"Wasps," stammered Sara Ray, laconic from terror.

"Humph! And your hands?"

"Warts."

"I'll tell you what'll take *them* away. You get a pertater and go out under the full moon, cut the pertater in two, rub your warts with one half and say, 'One, two, three, warts, go away from me.' Then rub them with the other half and say, 'One, two, three, four, warts, never trouble me more.' Then bury the pertater and never tell a living soul where you buried it. You won't have no more warts. Mind you bury the pertater, though. If you don't, and anyone picks it up, she'll get your warts."

CHAPTER XVIII

Sara Ray Helps Out

WE all missed Aunt Olivia greatly; she had been so merry and companionable, and had possessed such a knack of understanding small fry. But youth quickly adapts itself to changed conditions; in a few weeks it seemed as if the Story Girl had always been living at Uncle Alec's, and as if Uncle Roger had always had a fat, jolly housekeeper with a double chin and little, twinkling blue eyes. I don't think Aunt Janet ever quite got over missing Aunt Olivia, or looked upon Mrs. Hawkins as anything but a necessary evil; but life resumed its even tenor on the King farm, broken only by the ripples of excitement over the school concert and letters from Aunt Olivia describing her trip through the land of Evangeline. We incorporated the letters in *Our Magazine* under the heading "From Our Special Correspondent" and were very proud of them.

At the end of June our school concert came off and was a great event in our young lives. It was the first appearance of most of us on any platform, and some of us were very nervous. We all had recitations, except Dan, who had refused flatly to take any part and was consequently care-free.

"I'm sure I shall die when I find myself up on that platform, facing people," sighed Sara Ray, as we talked the affair over in Uncle Stephen's Walk the night before the concert.

"I'm afraid I'll faint," was Cecily's more moderate foreboding.

"I'm not one single bit nervous," said Felicity complacently.

"I'm not nervous this time," said the Story Girl, "but the first time I recited I was."

"My Aunt Jane," remarked Peter, "used to say that an old teacher of hers told her that when she was going to recite or speak in public she must just get it firmly into her mind that it was only a lot of cabbage heads she had before her, and she wouldn't be nervous."

"One mightn't be nervous, but I don't think there would be much inspiration in reciting to cabbage heads," said the Story Girl decidedly. "I want to recite to *people,* and see them looking interested and thrilled."

"If I can only get through my piece without breaking down I don't care whether I thrill people or not," said Sara Ray.

"I'm afraid I'll forget mine and get stuck," foreboded Felix. "Some of you fellows be sure and prompt me if I do—and do it quick, so's I won't get worse rattled."

"I know one thing," said Cecily resolutely, "and that is, I'm going to curl my hair for tomorrow night. I've never curled it since Peter almost died, but I simply must tomorrow night, for all the other girls are going to have theirs in curls."

"The dew and heat will take all the curl out of yours and then you'll look like a scarecrow," warned Felicity.

"No, I won't. I'm going to put my hair up in paper tonight and wet it with a curling-fluid that Judy Pineau uses. Sara brought me up a bottle of it. Judy says it is great stuff—your hair will keep in curl for days, no matter how damp the weather is. I'll leave my hair in the papers till tomorrow evening, and then I'll have beautiful curls."

"You'd better leave your hair alone," said Dan gruffly. "Smooth hair is better than a lot of fly-away curls."

But Cecily was not to be persuaded. Curls she craved and curls she meant to have.

"I'm thankful my warts have all gone, anyway," said Sara Ray.

"So they have," exclaimed Felicity. "Did you try Peg's recipe?"

"Yes. I didn't believe in it but I tried it. For the first few days afterwards I kept watching my warts, but they didn't go away, and then I gave up and forgot them. But one day last week I just happened to look at my hands and there wasn't a wart to be seen. It was the most amazing thing."

"And yet you'll say Peg Bowen isn't a witch," said Peter.

"Pshaw, it was just the potato juice," scoffed Dan.

"It was a dry old potato I had, and there wasn't much juice in it," said Sara Ray. "One hardly knows what to believe. But one thing is certain—my warts are gone."

Cecily put her hair up in curl-papers that night, thoroughly soaked in Judy Pineau's curling-fluid. It was a nasty job, for the fluid was very sticky, but Cecily persevered and got it done. Then she went to bed with a towel tied over her head to protect the pillow. She did not sleep well and had uncanny dreams, but she came down to breakfast with an expression of triumph. The Story Girl examined her head critically and said,

"Cecily, if I were you I'd take those papers out this morning."

"Oh, no; if I do my hair will be straight again by night. I mean to leave them in till the last minute."

"I wouldn't do that—I really wouldn't," persisted the Story Girl. "If you do your hair will be too curly and all bushy and fuzzy."

Cecily finally yielded and went upstairs with the Story Girl. Presently we heard a little shriek—then two little shrieks—then three. Then Felicity came flying down and called her mother. Aunt Janet went up and presently came down again with a grim mouth. She filled a large pan with warm water and carried it upstairs. We dared ask her no questions, but when Felicity came down to wash the dishes we bombarded her.

"What on earth is the matter with Cecily?" demanded Dan. "Is she sick?"

"No, she isn't. I warned her not to put her hair in curls but she wouldn't listen to me. I guess she wishes she had now. When people haven't natural curly hair they shouldn't try to make it curly. They get punished if they do."

"Look here, Felicity, never mind all that. Just tell us what has happened, Sis."

"Well, this is what has happened to her. That ninny of a Sara Ray brought up a bottle of mucilage instead of Judy's curling-fluid, and Cecily put her hair up with *that*. It's in an awful state."

"Good gracious!" exclaimed Dan. "Look here, will she ever get it out?"

"Goodness knows. She's got her head in soak now. Her hair is just matted together hard as a board. That's what comes of vanity," said Felicity, than whom no vainer girl existed.

Poor Cecily paid dearly enough for *her* vanity. She spent a bad forenoon, made no easier by her mother's severe rebukes. For an hour she "soaked" her head; that is, she stood over a panful of warm water and kept dipping her head in with tightly shut eyes. Finally her hair softened sufficiently to be disentangled from the curl papers; and then Aunt Janet subjected it to a merciless shampoo. Eventually they got all the mucilage washed out of it and Cecily spent the remainder of the forenoon sitting before the open oven door in the hot kitchen drying her ill-used tresses. She felt very down-hearted; her hair was of that order which, glossy and smooth normally, is dry and harsh and lustreless for several days after being shampooed.

"I'll look like a fright tonight," said the poor child to me with trembling voice. "The ends will be sticking out all over my head."

"Sara Ray is a perfect idiot," I said wrathfully.

"Oh, don't be hard on poor Sara. She didn't mean to bring me mucilage. It's really all my own fault, I know. I made a solemn vow when Peter was dying that I would never curl my hair again, and I should have kept it. It isn't right to break solemn vows. But my hair will look like dried hay tonight."

Poor Sara Ray was quite overwhelmed when she came up and found what she had done. Felicity was very hard on her, and Aunt Janet was coldly disapproving, but sweet Cecily forgave her unreservedly, and they walked to the school that night with their arms about each other's waists as usual.

The school-room was crowded with friends and neighbours. Mr. Perkins was flying about, getting things into readiness, and Miss Reade, who was the organist of the evening, was sitting on the platform, looking her sweetest and prettiest. She wore a delightful white lace hat with a fetching little wreath of tiny forget-me-nots around the brim, a white muslin dress with sprays of blue violets scattered over it, and a black lace scarf.

"Doesn't she look angelic?" said Cecily rapturously.

"Mind you," said Sara Ray, "the Awkward Man is here—in the corner behind the door. I never remember seeing him at a concert before."

"I suppose he came to hear the Story Girl recite," said Felicity. "He is such a friend of hers."

The concert went off very well. Dialogues, choruses and recitations followed each other in rapid succession. Felix got through his without "getting stuck," and Peter did excellently, though he stuffed his hands in his trousers pockets—a habit of which Mr. Perkins had vainly tried to break him. Peter's recitation was one greatly in vogue at that time, beginning,

> "My name is Norval; on the Grampian hills
> My father feeds his flocks."

At our first practice Peter had started gaily in, rushing through the first line with no thought whatever of punctuation— "My name is Norval on the Grampian Hills."

"Stop, stop, Peter," quoth Mr. Perkins, sarcastically, "your name might be Norval if you were never on the Grampian Hills. There's a semi-colon in that line, I wish you to remember."

Peter did remember it. Cecily neither fainted nor failed when it came her turn. She recited her little piece very well, though somewhat mechanically. I think she really did much better than if she had had her desired curls. The miserable conviction that her hair, alone among that glossy-tressed bevy, was looking badly, quite blotted out all nervousness and self-consciousness from her mind. Her hair apart, she looked very pretty. The prevailing excitement had made bright her eye and flushed her cheeks rosily—too rosily, perhaps. I heard a Carlisle woman behind me whisper that Cecily King looked consumptive, just like her Aunt Felicity; and I hated her fiercely for it.

Sara Ray also managed to get through respectably, although she was pitiably nervous. Her bow was naught but a short nod—"as if her head worked on wires," whispered Felicity uncharitably—and the wave of her lily-white hand more nearly resembled an agonized jerk than a wave. We all felt relieved when she finished. She was, in a sense, one of "our crowd," and we had been afraid she would disgrace us by breaking down.

Felicity followed her and recited her selection without haste, without rest, and absolutely without any expression whatever. But what mattered it how she recited? To look at her was sufficient. What with her splendid fleece of golden curls, her great, brilliant blue eyes, her exquisitely tinted face, her dimpled hands and arms, every member of the audience must have felt it was worth the ten cents he had paid merely to see her.

The Story Girl followed. An expectant silence fell over the room, and Mr. Perkins' face lost the look of tense anxiety it had worn all the evening. Here was a performer who could be depended on. No need to fear stage fright or forgetfulness on her part. The Story Girl was not looking her best that night. White never became her, and her face was pale, though her eyes were splendid. But nobody thought about her appearance when the power and magic of her voice caught and held her listeners spellbound.

Her recitation was an old one, figuring in one of the School Readers, and we scholars all knew it off by heart. Sara Ray alone had not heard the Story Girl recite it. The latter had not been drilled at practices as had the other pupils, Mr. Perkins choosing not to waste time teaching her what she already knew far better than he did. The only time she had recited it had been at the "dress rehearsal" two nights before, at which Sara Ray had not been present.

In the poem a Florentine lady of old time, wedded to a cold and cruel husband, had died, or was supposed to have died, and had been carried to "the rich, the beautiful, the dreadful tomb" of her proud family. In the night she wakened from her trance and made her escape. Chilled and terrified, she had made her way to her husband's door, only to be driven away brutally as a restless ghost by the horror-stricken inmates. A similar reception awaited her at her father's. Then she had wandered blindly through the streets of Florence until she had fallen exhausted at the door of the lover of her girlhood. He, unafraid, had taken her in and cared for her. On the morrow, the husband and father, having discovered the empty tomb, came to claim her. She refused to return to them and the case was carried to the court of law. The verdict given was that a woman who had been "to burial borne" and left for dead, who had been driven from her husband's door and from her childhood home, "must be adjudged as dead in law and fact," was no more daughter or wife, but was set free to form what new ties she would. The climax of the whole selection came in the line,

"The court pronounces the defendant—*Dead*!" and the Story Girl was wont to render it with such dramatic intensity and power that the veriest dullard among her listeners could not have missed its force and significance.

She swept along through the poem royally, playing on the emotions of her audience as she had so often played on ours in the old orchard. Pity, terror, indignation, suspense, possessed her hearers in turn. In the court scene she surpassed herself. She was, in very truth, the Florentine judge, stern, stately, impassive. Her voice dropped into the solemnity of the all-important line,

" 'The court pronounces the defendant—' "

She paused for a breathless moment, the better to bring out the tragic import of the last word.

"Dead," piped up Sara Ray in her shrill, plaintive little voice.

The effect, to use a hackneyed but convenient phrase, can better be imagined than described. Instead of the sigh of relieved tension that should have swept over the audience at the conclusion of the line, a burst of laughter greeted it. The Story Girl's performance was completely spoiled. She dealt the luckless Sara a glance that would have slain her on the spot could glances kill, stumbled lamely and impotently through the few remaining lines of her recitation, and fled with crimson cheeks to hide her mortification in the little corner that had been curtained off for a dressing-room. Mr. Perkins looked things not lawful to be uttered, and the audience tittered at intervals for the rest of the performance.

Sara Ray alone remained serenely satisfied until the close of the concert, when we surrounded her with a whirlwind of reproaches.

"Why," she stammered aghast, "what did I do? I—I thought she was stuck and that I ought to prompt her quick."

"You little fool, she just paused for effect," cried Felicity angrily. Felicity might be rather jealous of the Story Girl's gift, but she was furious at beholding "one of our family" made ridiculous in such a fashion. "You have less sense than anyone I ever heard of, Sara Ray."

Poor Sara dissolved in tears.

"I didn't know. I thought she was stuck," she wailed again.

She cried all the way home, but we did not try to comfort her. We felt quite out of patience with her. Even Cecily was seriously annoyed. This second blunder of Sara's was too much even for her loyalty. We saw her turn in at her own gate and go sobbing up her lane with no relenting.

The Story Girl was home before us, having fled from the schoolhouse as soon as the programme was over. We tried to sympathize with her but she would not be sympathized with.

"Please don't ever mention it to me again," she said, with compressed lips. "I never want to be reminded of it. Oh, that little *idiot!*"

"She spoiled Peter's sermon last summer and now she's spoiled your recitation," said Felicity. "*I* think it's time we gave up associating with Sara Ray."

"Oh, don't be quite so hard on her," pleaded Cecily. "Think of the life the poor child has to live at home. I know she'll cry all night."

"Oh, let's go to bed," growled Dan. "I'm good and ready for it. I've had enough of school concerts."

CHAPTER XIX

By Way
of the
Stars

Bᴜᴛ for two of us the adventures of the night were not yet over. Silence settled down over the old house—the eerie, whisperful, creeping silence of night. Felix and Dan were already sound asleep; I was drifting near the coast o' dreams when I was aroused by a light tap on the door.

"Bev, are you asleep?" came in the Story Girl's whisper.

"No, what is it?"

"S-s-h. Get up and dress and come out. I want you."

With a good deal of curiosity and some misgiving I obeyed. What was in the wind now? Outside in the hall I found the Story Girl, with a candle in her hand, and her hat and jacket.

"Where are you going?" I whispered in amazement.

"Hush. I've got to go to the school and you must come with me. I left my coral necklace there. The clasp came loose and I was so afraid I'd lose it that I took it off and put it in the bookcase. I was feeling so upset when the concert was over that I forgot all about it."

The coral necklace was a very handsome one which had belonged to the Story Girl's mother. She had never been permitted to wear it before, and it had only been by dint of much coaxing that she had induced Aunt Janet to let her wear it to the concert.

"But there's no sense in going for it in the dead of night," I objected. "It will be quite safe. You can go for it in the morning."

"Lizzie Paxton and her daughter are going to clean the school tomorrow, and I heard Lizzie say tonight she meant to be at it by five o'clock to get through before the heat of the day. You know perfectly well what Liz Paxton's reputation is. If she finds that necklace I'll never see it again. Besides, if I wait till the morning, Aunt Janet may find out that I left it there and she'd never let me wear it again. No, I'm going for it now. If you're afraid," added the Story Girl with delicate scorn, "of course you needn't come."

Afraid! I'd show her!

"Come on," I said.

We slipped out of the house noiselessly and found ourselves in the unutterable solemnity and strangeness of a dark night. It was a new experience, and our hearts thrilled and our nerves tingled to the charm of it. Never had we been abroad before at such an hour. The world around us was not the world of daylight. 'Twas an alien place, full of weird, evasive enchantment and magicry.

Only in the country can one become truly acquainted with the night. There it has the solemn calm of the infinite. The dim wide fields lie in silence, wrapped in the holy mystery of darkness. A wind, loosened from wild places far away, steals out to blow over dewy, star-lit, immemorial hills. The air in the pastures is sweet with the hush of dreams, and one may rest here like a child on its mother's breast.

"Isn't it wonderful?" breathed the Story Girl as we went down the long hill. "Do you know, I can forgive Sara Ray now. I thought tonight I never could—but now it doesn't matter any more. I can even see how funny it was. Oh, wasn't it funny? *'Dead'* in that squeaky little voice of Sara's! I'll just behave to her tomorrow as if nothing had happened. It seems so long ago now, here in the night."

Neither of us ever forgot the subtle delight of that stolen walk. A spell of glamour was over us. The breezes whispered strange secrets of elf-haunted glens, and the hollows where the ferns grew were brimmed with mystery and romance. Ghostlike scents crept out of the meadows to meet us, and the fir wood before we came to the church was a living sweetness of Junebells growing in abundance.

Junebells have another and more scientific name, of course. But who could desire a better name than Junebells? They are so perfect in their way that they seem to epitomize the very scent and charm of the forest, as if the old wood's daintiest thoughts had material-ized in blossom; and not all the roses by Bendameer's stream are as fragrant as a shallow sheet of Junebells under the boughs of fir.

There were fireflies abroad that night, too, increasing the gramarye of it. There is certainly something a little supernatural about fireflies. Nobody pretends to understand them. They are akin to the tribes of fairy, survivals of the elder time when the woods and hills swarmed with the little green folk. It is still very easy to believe in fairies when you see those goblin lanterns glimmering among the fir tassels.

"Isn't it beautiful?" said the Story Girl in rapture. "I wouldn't have missed it for anything. I'm glad I left my necklace. And I am glad you are with me, Bev. The others wouldn't understand so well. I like you because I don't have to talk to you all the time. It's so nice to walk with someone you don't have to talk to. Here is the graveyard. Are you frightened to pass it, Bev?"

"No, I don't think I'm frightened," I answered slowly, "but I have a queer feeling."

"So have I. But it isn't fear. I don't know what it is. I feel as if something was reaching out of the graveyard to hold me— something that wanted life—I don't like it—let's hurry. But isn't it strange to think of all the dead people in there who were once alive like you and me. I don't feel as if I could *ever* die. Do you?"

"No, but everybody must. Of course we go on living afterwards, just the same. Don't let's talk of such things here," I said hurriedly.

When we reached the school I contrived to open a window. We scrambled in, lighted a lamp and found the missing necklace. The Story Girl stood on the platform and gave an imitation of the catastrophe of the evening that made me shout with laughter. We prowled around for sheer delight over being there at an unearthly hour when everybody supposed we were sound asleep in our beds. It was with regret that we left, and we walked home as slowly as we could to prolong the adventure.

"Let's never tell anyone," said the Story Girl, as we reached home. "Let's just have it as a secret between us for ever and ever—something that nobody else knows a thing about but you and me."

"We'd better keep it a secret from Aunt Janet anyhow," I whispered, laughing. "She'd think we were both crazy."

"It's real jolly to be crazy once in a while," said the Story Girl.

CHAPTER XX

Extracts from Our Magazine

As will be seen there is no Honour Roll in this number. Even Felicity has thought all the beautiful thoughts that can be thought and cannot think any more. Peter has never got drunk but, under existing circumstances, that is not greatly to his credit. As for our written resolutions they have silently disappeared from our chamber walls and the place that once knew them knows them no more for ever. (*Peter, perplexedly:* "Seems to me I've heard something like that before.") It is very sad but we will all make some new resolutions next year and maybe it will be easier to keep those.

THE STORY OF THE LOCKET THAT WAS BAKED

This was a story my Aunt Jane told me about her granma when she was a little girl. Its funny to think of baking a locket, but it wasn't to eat. She was my great granma but Ill call her granma for short. It happened when she was ten years old. Of course she wasent anybodys granma then. Her father and mother and her were living in a new settlement called Brinsley. Their nearest naybor was a mile away. One day her Aunt Hannah from Charlottetown came and wanted her ma to go visiting with her. At first granma's ma thought she couldent go because it was baking day and granma's pa was away. But granma wasent afraid to stay alone and she knew how to bake the bread so she made her ma go and her Aunt Hannah took off the handsome gold locket and chain she was waring round her neck and hung it on granmas and told her she could ware it all day. Granma was awful pleased for she had never had any jewelry. She did all the chores and then was needing the loaves when she looked up and saw a tramp coming in and he was an awful villenus looking tramp. He dident even pass the time of day but just set down on a chair. Poor granma was awful fritened and she turned her back on him and went on needing the loaf cold and trembling—that is, granma was trembling not the loaf. She was worried about the locket. She didn't know how she could hide it for to get anywhere she would have to turn round and pass him.

All of a suddent she thought she would hide it in the bread. She put her hand up and pulled it hard and quick and broke the fastening and needed it right into the loaf. Then she put the loaf in the pan and set it in the oven.

The tramp hadent seen her do it and then he asked for something to eat. Granma got him up a meal and when hed et it he began prowling about the kitchen looking into everything and opening the cubbord doors. Then he went into granma's mas room and turned the buro drawers and trunk inside out and threw the things in them all about. All he found was a purse with a dollar in it and he swore about it and took it and went away. When granma was sure he was really gone she broke down and cried. She forgot all about the bread and it burned as black as coal. When she smelled it burning granma run and pulled it out. She was awful scared the locket was spoiled but she sawed open the loaf and it was there safe and sound. When her Aunt Hannah came back she said granma deserved the locket because she had saved it so clever and she gave it to her and grandma always wore it and was very proud of it. And granma used to say that was the only loaf of bread she ever spoiled in her life.

PETER CRAIG.

(*Felicity:* "Those stories are all very well but they are only true stories. It's easy enough to write true stories. *I* thought Peter was appointed fiction editor, but he has never written any fiction since the paper started. That's not *my* idea of a fiction editor. He ought to make up stories out of his own head." *Peter, spunkily:* "I can do it, too, and I will next time. And it ain't easier to write true stories. It's harder, 'cause you have to stick to facts." *Felicity:* "I don't believe you could make up a story." *Peter:* "I'll show you!")

MY MOST EXCITING ADVENTURE

It's my turn to write it but I'm *so nervous*. My worst adventure happened *two years ago*. It was an awful one. I had a striped ribbon, striped brown and yellow and *I lost it*. I was very sorry for it was a handsome ribbon and all the girls in school were jealous of it. (*Felicity:* "*I* wasn't. I didn't think it one bit pretty." *Cecily:* "Hush!") I hunted everywhere but I couldn't find it. Next day was Sunday and I was running into the house by the front door and I saw *something lying on the step* and I thought it was my ribbon and I made a grab at it as I passed. But, oh, it was a *snake*! Oh, I can never describe how I felt when that awful thing *wriggling in my hand*. I let it go and *screamed and screamed*, and ma was cross at me for yelling on Sunday and made me read seven chapters in the Bible but I didn't mind that much after what I had come through. I would rather *die* than have *such an experience* again.

SARA RAY.

TO FELICITY ON HER BIRTHDAY

Oh maiden fair with golden hair
And brow of purest white,
Id fight for you I'd die for you
Let me be your faithful knite.

This is your berthday blessed day
You are thirteen years old today
May you be happy and fair as you are now
Until your hair is gray.

I gaze into your shining eyes,
They are so blue and bright.
Id fight for you Id die for you
Let me be your faithful knite

A FRIEND.

(*Dan:* "Great snakes, who got that up? I'll bet it was Peter." *Felicity, with dignity:* "Well, it's more than *you* could do. *You* couldn't write poetry to save your life." *Peter, aside to Beverley:* "She seems quite pleased. I'm glad I wrote it, but it was awful hard work.")

PERSONALS

Patrick Grayfur, Esq., caused his friends great anxiety recently by a prolonged absence from home. When found he was very thin but is now as fat and conceited as ever.

On Wednesday, June 20th, Miss Olivia King was united in the bonds of holy matrimony to Dr. Robert Seton of Halifax. Miss Sara Stanley was bridesmaid, and Mr. Andrew Seton attended the groom. The young couple received many handsome presents. Rev. Mr. Marwood tied the nuptial knot. After the ceremony a substantial repast was served in Mrs. Alex King's well-known style and the happy couple left for their new home in Nova Scotia. Their many friends join in wishing them a very happy and prosperous journey through life.

> A precious one from us is gone,
> A voice we loved is stilled.
> A place is vacant in our home
> That never can be filled.

(*The Story Girl:* "Goodness, that sounds as if somebody had died. I've seen that verse on a tombstone. *Who* wrote that notice?" *Felicity, who wrote it:* "I think it is just as appropriate to a wedding as to a funeral!")

Our school concert came off on the evening of June 29th and was a great success. We made ten dollars for the library.

We regret to chronicle that Miss Sara Ray met with a misfortune while taking some violent exercise with a wasps' nest recently. The moral is that it is better not to monkey with a wasps' nest, new or old.

Mrs. C. B. Hawkins of Baywater is keeping house for Uncle Roger. She is a very large woman. Uncle Roger says he has to spend too much time walking round her, but otherwise she is an excellent housekeeper.

It is reported that the school is haunted. A mysterious light was seen there at two o'clock one night recently.

(The Story Girl and I exchange knowing smiles behind the others' backs.)

Dan and Felicity had a fight last Tuesday—not with fists but with tongues. Dan came off best—as usual. *(Felicity laughs sarcastically.)*

Mr. Newton Craig of Markdale returned home recently after a somewhat prolonged visit in foreign parts. We are glad to welcome Mr. Craig back to our midst.

Billy Robinson was hurt last week. A cow kicked him. I suppose it is wicked of us to feel glad but we all do feel glad because of the way he cheated us with the magic seed last summer.

On April 1st Uncle Roger sent Mr. Peter Craig to the manse to borrow the biography of Adam's grandfather. Mr. Marwood told Peter he didn't think Adam had any grandfather and advised him to go home and look at the almanac. *(Peter, sourly:* "Your Uncle Roger thought he was pretty smart." *Felicity, severely:* "Uncle Roger *is* smart. It was so easy to fool you.")

A pair of blue birds have built a nest in a hole in the sides of the well, just under the ferns. We can see the eggs when we look down. They are so cunning.

Felix sat down on a tack one day in May. Felix thinks house-cleaning is great foolishness.

Flossie tells me. He says he means to keep it always for a remembrance though he has given up hope." *Dan:* "I'll steal it out of his Bible in Sunday School." *Cecily, blushing:* "Oh, let him keep it if it is any comfort to him. Besides, it isn't right to steal." *Dan:* "He stole it." *Cecily:* "But Mr. Marwood says two wrongs never make a right.")

HOUSEHOLD DEPARTMENT

Aunt Olivia's wedding cake was said to be the best one of its kind ever tasted in Carlisle. Me and mother made it.

ANXIOUS INQUIRER:—It is not advisable to curl your hair with mucilage if you can get anything else. Quince juice is better. (*Cecily, bitterly:* "I suppose I'll never hear the last of that mucilage." *Dan:* "Ask her who used toothpowder to raise biscuits?")

We had rhubarb pies for the first time this spring last week. They were fine but hard on the cream.

FELICITY KING.

ETIQUETTE DEPARTMENT

PATIENT SUFFERER:—What will I do when a young man steals a lock of my hair? Ans.:—Grow some more.

No, F-l-x, a little caterpillar is not called a kittenpillar. (*Felix, enraged:* "I never asked that! Dan just makes that etiquette column up from beginning to end!" *Felicity:* "I don't see what that kind of a question has to do with etiquette anyhow.")

Yes, P-t-r, it is quite proper to treat a lady friend to ice cream twice if you can afford it.

No, F-l-c-t-y, it is not ladylike to chew tobacco. Better stick to spruce gum.

DAN KING.

FASHION NOTES

Frilled muslin aprons will be much worn this summer. It is no longer fashionable to trim them with knitted lace. One pocket is considered smart.

Clam-shells are fashionable keepsakes. You write your name

and the date inside one and your friend writes hers in the other and you exchange.

CECILY KING.

FUNNY PARAGRAPHS

Mr. Perkins:—"Peter, name the large islands of the world."

Peter:—"The Island, the British Isles and Australia." (*Peter, defiantly:* "Well, Mr. Perkins said he guessed I was right, so you needn't laugh.")

This is a true joke and really happened. It's about Mr. Samuel Clask again. He was once leading a prayer meeting and he looked through the window and saw the constable driving up and guessed he was after him because he was always in debt. So in a great hurry he called on Brother Casey to lead in prayer and while Brother Casey was praying with his eyes shut and everybody else had their heads bowed Mr. Clask got out of the window and got away before the constable got in because he didn't like to come in till the prayer was finished.

Uncle Roger says it was a smart trick on Mr. Clask's part, but I don't think there was much religion about it.

FELIX KING.

CHAPTER XXI

Peg Bowen Comes to Church

WHEN those of us who are still left of that band of children who played long years ago in the old orchard and walked the golden road together in joyous companionship, foregather now and again in our busy lives and talk over the events of those many merry moons—there are some of our adventures that gleam out more vividly in memory than the others, and are oftener discussed. The time we bought God's picture from Jerry Cowan—the time Dan ate the poison berries—the time we heard the ghostly bell ring—the bewitchment of Paddy—the visit of the Governor's wife—and the night we were lost in the storm—all awaken reminiscent jest and laughter; but none more than the recollection of the Sunday Peg Bowen came to church and sat in our pew. Though goodness knows, as Felicity would say, we did not think it any matter for laughter at the time—far from it.

It was one Sunday evening in July. Uncle Alec and Aunt Janet, having been out to the morning service, did not attend in the evening, and we small fry walked together down the long hill road, wearing Sunday attire and trying, more or less successfully, to wear Sunday faces also. Those walks to church, through the golden completeness of the summer evenings, were always very pleasant to us, and we never hurried, though, on the other hand, we were very careful not to be late.

This particular evening was particularly beautiful. It was cool after a hot day, and wheat fields all about us were ripening to their harvestry. The wind gossiped with the grasses along our way, and over them the buttercups danced, goldenly-glad. Waves of sinuous shadow went over the ripe hayfields, and plundering bees sang a freebooting lilt in wayside gardens.

"The world is so lovely tonight," said the Story Girl. "I just hate the thought of going into the church and shutting all the sunlight and music outside. I wish we could have the service outside in summer."

"I don't think that would be very religious," said Felicity.

"I'd feel ever so much more religious outside than in," retorted the Story Girl.

"If the service was outside we'd have to sit in the graveyard and that wouldn't be very cheerful," said Felix.

"Besides, the music isn't shut out," added Felicity. "The choir is inside."

" 'Music has charms to soothe a savage breast,' " quoted Peter, who was getting into the habit of adorning his conversation with similar gems. "That's in one of Shakespeare's plays. I'm reading them now, since I got through with the Bible. They're great."

"I don't see when you get time to read them," said Felicity.

"Oh, I read them Sunday afternoons when I'm home."

"I don't believe they're fit to read on Sundays," exclaimed Felicity. "Mother says Valeria Montague's stories ain't."

"But Shakespeare's different from Valeria," protested Peter.

"I don't see in what way. He wrote a lot of things that weren't true, just like Valeria, and he wrote swear words too. Valeria never does that. Her characters all talk in a very refined fashion."

"Well, I always skip the swear words," said Peter. "And Mr. Marwood said once that the Bible and Shakespeare would furnish any library well. So you see he put them together, but I'm sure that he would never say that the Bible and Valeria would make a library."

"Well, all I know is, I shall never read Shakespeare on Sunday," said Felicity loftily.

"I wonder what kind of a preacher young Mr. Davidson is," speculated Cecily.

"Well, we'll know when we hear him tonight," said the Story Girl. "He ought to be good, for his uncle before him was a fine preacher, though a very absent-minded man. But Uncle Roger says the supply in Mr. Marwood's vacation never amounts to much. I know an awfully funny story about old Mr. Davidson. He used to be the minister in Baywater, you know, and he had a large family and his children were very mischievous. One day his wife was ironing and she ironed a great big nightcap with a frill round it. One of the children too it when she wasn't looking and hid it in his father's best beaver hat—the one he wore on Sundays. When Mr. Davidson went to church next Sunday he put the hat on without ever looking into the crown. He walked to church in a brown study and at the door he took off his hat. The nightcap just slipped down on his head, as if it had been put on, and the frill stood out around his face and the string hung down his back. But he never noticed it, because his thoughts were far away, and he walked up the church aisle and into the pulpit, like that. One of his elders had to tiptoe up and tell him what he had on his head. He plucked it off in a dazed fashion, held it up, and looked at it. 'Bless me, it is Sally's nightcap!' he exclaimed mildly. 'I do not know how I could have got it on.' Then he just stuffed it into his pocket calmly and went on with the service, and the long strings of the nightcap hung down out of his pocket all the time."

"It seems to me," said Peter, amid the laughter with which we greeted the tale, "that a funny story is funnier when it is about a minister than it is about any other man. I wonder why."

"Sometimes I don't think it is right to tell funny stories about ministers," said Felicity. "It certainly isn't respectful."

"A good story is a good story—no matter who it's about," said the Story Girl with ungrammatical relish.

There was as yet no one in the church when we reached it, so we took our accustomed ramble through the graveyard surrounding it. The Story Girl had brought flowers for her mother's grave as usual, and while she arranged them on it the rest of us read for the hundredth time the epitaph on Great-Grandfather King's tombstone, which had been composed by Great-Grandmother King. That epitaph was quite famous among the little family traditions that entwine every household with mingled mirth and sorrow, smiles and tears. It had a perennial fascination for us and we read it over every Sunday. Cut deeply in the upright slab of red Island sandstone, the epitaph ran as follows:—

SWEET DEPARTED SPIRIT

Do receive the vows a grateful widow pays,

Each future day and night shall hear her speak her Isaac's
      praise.
Though thy beloved form must in the grave decay
Yet from her heart thy memory no time, no change shall
      steal away.
Do thou from mansions of eternal bliss
Remember thy distressed relict.
Look on her with an angel's love—
Soothe her sad life and cheer her end
Through this world's dangers and its griefs.
Then meet her with thy well-known smiles and welcome
At the last great day.

"Well, I can't make out what the old lady was driving at,"
said Dan.

"That's a nice way to speak of your great-grandmother," said
Felicity severely.

"How does The Family Guide say you ought to speak of your
great-grandma, sweet one?" asked Dan.

"There is one thing about it that puzzles me," remarked
Cecily. "She calls herself a grateful widow. Now, what was she
grateful for?"

"Because she was rid of him at last," said graceless Dan.

"Oh, it couldn't have been that," protested Cecily seriously.
"I've always heard that Great-Grandfather and Great-Grandmother
were very much attached to each other."

"Maybe, then, it means she was grateful that she'd had him
as long as she did," suggested Peter.

"She was grateful to him because he had been so kind to her
in life, I think," said Felicity.

"What is a 'distressed relict'?" asked Felix.

" 'Relict' is a word I hate," said the Story Girl. "It sounds so
much like relic. Relict means just the same as widow, only a
man can be a relict, too."

"Great-Grandmother seemed to run short of rhymes at the
last of the epitaph," commented Dan.

"Finding rhymes isn't as easy as you might think," avowed
Peter, out of his own experience.

"I think Grandmother King intended the last of the epitaph
to be in blank verse," said Felicity with dignity.

There was still only a sprinkling of people in the church when we went in and took our places in the old-fashioned, square King pew. We had just got comfortably settled when Felicity said in an agitated whisper, "Here is Peg Bowen!"

We all stared at Peg, who was pacing composedly up the aisle. We might be excused for so doing, for seldom were the decorous aisles of Carlisle church invaded by such a figure. Peg was dressed in her usual short drugget skirt, rather worn and frayed around the bottom, and a waist of brilliant turkey red calico. She wore no hat, and her grizzled black hair streamed in elf locks over her shoulders. Face, arms and feet were bare—and face, arms and feet were liberally powdered with *flour*. Certainly no one who saw Peg that night could ever forget the apparition.

Peg's black eyes, in which shone a more than usually wild and fitful light, roved scrutinizingly over the church, then settled on our pew.

"She's coming here," whispered Felicity in horror. "Can't we spread out and make her think the pew is full?"

But the manoeuvre was too late. The only result was that Felicity and the Story Girl in moving over left a vacant space between them and Peg promptly plumped down in it.

"Well, I'm here," she remarked aloud. "I did say once I'd never darken the door of Carlisle church again, but what that boy there"—nodding at Peter—"said last winter set me thinking, and I concluded maybe I'd better come once in a while, to be on the safe side."

Those poor girls were in an agony. Everybody in the church was looking at our pew and smiling. We all felt that we were terribly disgraced; but we could do nothing. Peg was enjoying herself hugely, beyond all doubt. From where she sat she could see the whole church, including pulpit and gallery, and her black eyes darted over it with restless glances.

"Bless me, there's Sam Kinnaird," she exclaimed, still aloud. "He's the man that dunned Jacob Marr for four cents on the church steps one Sunday. I heard him. 'I think, Jacob, you owe me four cents on that cow you bought last fall. Rec'llect you couldn't make the change?' Well, you know, 'twould a-made a cat laugh. The Kinnairds were all mighty close, I can tell you. That's how they got rich."

What Sam Kinnaird felt or thought during this speech, which everyone in the church must have heard, I know not.

Gossip had it that he changed colour. We wretched occupants of the King pew were concerned only with our own outraged feelings.

"And there's Melita Ross," went on Peg. "She's got the same bonnet on she had last time I was in Carlisle church six years ago. Some folks has the knack of making things last. But look at the style Mrs. Elmer Brewer wears, will yez? Yez wouldn't think her mother died in the poorhouse, would yez, now?"

Poor Mrs. Brewer! From the tip of her smart kid shoes to the dainty cluster of ostrich tips in her bonnet—she was most immaculately and handsomely arrayed; but I venture to think she could have taken small pleasure in her fashionable attire that evening. Some of the unregenerate, including Dan, were shaking with suppressed laughter, but most of the people looked as if they were afraid to smile, lest their turn should come next.

"There's old Stephen Grant coming in," exclaimed Peg viciously, shaking her floury fist at him, "and looking as if butter wouldn't melt in his mouth. He may be an elder, but he's a scoundrel just the same. He set fire to his house to get the insurance and then blamed *me* for doing it. But I got even with him for it. Oh, yes! He knows that, and so do I! He, he!"

Peg chuckled quite fiendishly and Stephen Grant tried to look as if nothing had been said.

"Oh, will the minister never come?" moaned Felicity in my ear. "Surely she'll have to stop then."

But the minister did not come and Peg had no intention of stopping.

"There's Maria Dean," she resumed. "I haven't seen Maria for years. I never call there for she never seems to have anything to eat in the house. She was a Clayton and the Claytons never could cook. Maria sorter looks as if she'd shrunk in the wash, now, don't she? And there's Douglas Nicholson. His brother put rat poison in the family pancakes. Nice little trick that, wasn't it? They say it was by mistake. I hope it *was* a mistake. His wife is all rigged out in silk. Yez wouldn't think to look at her she was married in cotton—and mighty thankful to get married in anything, it's my opinion. There's Timothy Patterson. He's the meanest man alive—meaner'n Sam Kinnaird even. Timothy pays his children five cents apiece to go without their suppers, and then steals the cents out of their pockets after they've gone to bed. It's a fact. And when his old father died he wouldn't let his wife put his best shirt on him. He said his second best was plenty good to be buried in. That's another fact."

"I can't stand much more of this," wailed Felicity.

"See here, Miss Bowen, you really oughtn't to talk like that about people," expostulated Peter in a low tone, goaded thereto, despite his awe of Peg, by Felicity's anguish.

"Bless you, boy," said Peg good-humouredly, "the only difference between me and other folks is that I say these things out loud and they just think them. If I told yez all the things I know about the people in this congregation you'd be amazed. Have a peppermint?"

To our horror Peg produced a handful of peppermint lozenges from the pocket of her skirt and offered us one each. We did not dare refuse but we each held our lozenge very gingerly in our hands.

"Eat them," commanded Peg rather fiercely.

"Mother doesn't allow us to eat candy in church," faltered Felicity.

"Well, I've seen just as fine ladies as your ma give their children lozenges in church," said Peg loftily. She put a peppermint in her own mouth and sucked it with gusto. We were relieved, for she did not talk during the process; but our relief was of short duration. A bevy of three very smartly dressed young ladies, sweeping past our pew, started Peg off again.

"Yez needn't be so stuck up," she said, loudly and derisively. "Yez was all of yez rocked in a flour barrel. And there's old Henry Frewen, still above ground. I called my parrot after him because their noses were exactly alike. Look at Caroline Marr, will yez? That's a woman who'd like pretty well to get married. And there's Alexander Marr. He's a real Christian, anyhow, and so's his dog. I can always size up what a man's religion amounts to by the kind of dog he keeps. Alexander Marr is a good man."

It was a relief to hear Peg speak well of somebody; but that was the only exception she made.

"Look at Dave Fraser strutting in," she went on. "That man has thanked God so often that he isn't like other people that it's come to be true. He isn't! And there's Susan Frewen. She's jealous of everybody. She's even jealous of Old Man Rogers because he's buried in the best spot in the graveyard. Seth Erskine has the same look he was born with. They say the Lord made everybody but *I* believe the devil made all the Erskines."

"She's getting worse all the time. What *will* she say next?" whispered poor Felicity.

But her martyrdom was over at last. The minister appeared in the pulpit and Peg subsided into silence. She folded her bare, floury arms over her breast and fastened her black eyes on the young preacher. Her behaviour for the next half-hour was decorum itself, save that when the minister prayed that we might all be charitable in judgment Peg ejaculated "Amen" several times, loudly and forcibly, somewhat to the discomfiture of the young man, to whom Peg was a stranger. He opened his eyes, glanced at our pew in a startled way, then collected himself and went on.

Peg listened to the sermon, silently and motionlessly, until Mr. Davidson was half through. Then she suddenly got on her feet.

"This is too dull for me," she exclaimed. "I want something more exciting."

Mr. Davidson stopped short and Peg marched down the aisle in the midst of complete silence. Half way down the aisle she turned around and faced the minister.

"There are so many hypocrites in this church that it isn't fit for decent people to come to," she said. "Rather than be such hypocrites as most of you are it would be better for you to go miles into the woods and commit suicide."

Wheeling about, she strode to the door. Then she turned for a Parthian shot.

"I've felt kind of worried for God sometimes, seeing He has so much to attend to," she said, "but I see I needn't be, so long's there's plenty of ministers to tell Him what to do."

With that Peg shook the dust of Carlisle church from her feet. Poor Mr. Davidson resumed his discourse. Old Elder Bayley, whose attention an earthquake could not have distracted from the sermon, afterwards declared that it was an excellent and edifying exhortation, but I doubt if anyone else in Carlisle church tasted it much or gained much good therefrom. Certainly we of the King household did not. We could not even remember the text when we reached home. Felicity was comfortless.

"Mr. Davidson would be sure to think she belonged to our family when she was in our pew," she said bitterly. "Oh, I feel as if I could never get over such a mortification! Peter, I do wish you wouldn't go telling people they ought to go to church. It's all your fault that this happened."

"Never mind, it will be a good story to tell sometime," remarked the Story Girl with relish.

CHAPTER XXII

The
Yankee
Storm

IN an August orchard six children and a grown-up were sitting around the pulpit stone. The grown-up was Miss Reade, who had been up to give the girls their music lesson and had consented to stay to tea, much to the rapture of the said girls, who continued to worship her with unabated and romantic ardour. To us, over the golden grasses, came the Story Girl, carrying in her hand a single large poppy, like a blood-red chalice filled with the wine of August wizardry. She proffered it to Miss Reade and, as the latter took it into her singularly slender, beautiful hand, I saw a ring on her third finger. I noticed it, because I had heard the girls say that Miss Reade never wore rings, not liking them. It was not a new ring; it was handsome, but of an old-fashioned design and setting, with a glint of diamonds about a central sapphire. Later on, when Miss Reade had gone, I asked the Story Girl if she had noticed the ring. She nodded, but seemed disinclined to say more about it.

"Look here, Sara," I said, "there's something about that ring—something you know."

"I told you once there was a story growing but you would have to wait until it was fully grown," she answered.

"Is Miss Reade going to marry anybody—anybody we know?" I persisted.

"Curiosity killed a cat," observed the Story Girl coolly. "Miss Reade hasn't told me that she was going to marry anybody. You will find out all that is good for you to know in due time."

When the Story Girl put on grown-up airs I did not like her so well, and I dropped the subject with a dignity that seemed to amuse her mightily.

She had been away for a week, visiting cousins in Markdale,

and she had come home with a new treasure-trove of stories, most of which she had heard from the old sailors of Markdale Harbour. She had promised that morning to tell us of "the most tragic event that had ever been known on the north shore," and we now reminded her of her promise.

"Some call it the 'Yankee Storm,' and others the 'American Gale,'" she began, sitting down by Miss Reade and beaming, because the latter put her arm around her waist. "It happened nearly forty years ago, in October of 1851. Old Mr. Coles at the Harbour told me all about it. He was a young man then and he says he can never forget that dreadful time. You know in those days hundreds of American fishing schooners used to come down to the Gulf every summer to fish mackerel. On one beautiful Saturday night in this October of 1851, more than one hundred of these vessels could be counted from Markdale Capes. By Monday night more than seventy of them had been destroyed. Those which had escaped were mostly those which went into harbour Saturday night, to keep Sunday. Mr. Coles says the rest stayed outside and fished all day Sunday, same as through the week, and *he* says the storm was a judgment on them for doing it. But he admits that even some of them got into harbour later on and escaped, so it's hard to know what to think. But it is certain that on Sunday night there came up a sudden and terrible storm—the worst, Mr. Coles says, that has ever been known on the north shore. It lasted for two days and scores of vessels were driven ashore and completely wrecked. The crews of most of the vessels that went ashore on the sand beaches were saved, but those that struck on the rocks went to pieces and all hands were lost. For weeks after the storm the north shore was strewn with the bodies of drowned men. Think of it! Many of them were unknown and unrecognizable, and they were buried in Markdale graveyard. Mr. Coles says the schoolmaster who was in Markdale then wrote a poem on the storm and Mr. Coles recited the first two verses to me.

> "'Here are the fishers' hillside graves,
>   The church beside, the woods around,
> Below, the hollow moaning waves
>   Where the poor fishermen were drowned.

> " 'A sudden tempest the blue welkin tore,
> The seamen tossed and torn apart
> Rolled with the seaweed to the shore
> While landsmen gazed with aching heart.' "

"Mr. Coles couldn't remember any more of it. But the saddest of all the stories of the Yankee Storm was the one about the *Franklin Dexter.* The *Franklin Dexter* went ashore on the Markdale Capes and all on board perished, the Captain and three of his brothers among them. These four young men were the sons of an old man who lived in Portland, Maine, and when he heard what had happened he came right down to the Island to see if he could find their bodies. They had all come ashore and had been buried in Markdale graveyard; but he was determined to take them up and carry them home for burial. He said he had promised their mother to take her boys home to her and he must do it. So they were taken up and put on board a sailing vessel at Markdale Harbour to be taken back to Maine, while the father himself went home on a passenger steamer. The name of the sailing vessel was the *Seth Hall,* and the captain's name was Seth Hall, too. Captain Hall was a dreadfully profane man and used to swear blood-curdling oaths. On the night he sailed out of Markdale Harbour the old sailors warned him that a storm was brewing and that it would catch him if he did not wait until it was over. The captain had become very impatient because of several delays he had already met with, and he was in a furious temper. He swore a wicked oath that he would sail out of Markdale Harbour that night and 'God Almighty Himself shouldn't catch him.' He did sail out of the harbour; and the storm did catch him, and the *Seth Hall* went down with all hands, the dead and the living finding a watery grave together. So the poor old mother up in Maine never had her boys brought back to her after all. Mr. Coles says it seems as if it were foreordained that they should not rest in a grave, but should lie beneath the waves until the day when the sea gives up its dead."

> " 'They sleep as well beneath that purple tide
> As others under turf,' "

quoted Miss Reade softly. "I am very thankful," she added,

"that I am not one of those whose dear ones 'go down to the sea in ships.' It seems to me that they have treble their share of this world's heartache."

"Uncle Stephen was a sailor and he was drowned," said Felicity, "and they say it broke Grandmother King's heart. I don't see why people can't be contented on dry land."

Cecily's tears had been dropping on the autograph quilt square she was faithfully embroidering. She had been diligently collecting names for it ever since the preceding autumn and had a goodly number; but Kitty Marr had one more and this was certainly a fly in Cecily's ointment.

"Besides, one I've got isn't paid for—Peg Bowen's," she lamented, "and I don't suppose it ever will be, for I'll never dare to ask her for it."

"I wouldn't put it on at all," said Felicity.

"Oh, I don't dare not to. She'd be sure to find out I didn't and then she'd be very angry. I wish I could get just one more name and then I'd be contented. But I don't know of a single person who hasn't been asked already."

"Except Mr. Campbell," said Dan.

"Oh, of course nobody would ask Mr. Campbell. We all know it would be of no use. He doesn't believe in missions at all—in fact, he says he detests the very mention of missions—and he never gives one cent to them."

"All the same, I think he ought to be asked, so that he wouldn't have the excuse that nobody *did* ask him," declared Dan.

"Do you really think so, Dan?" asked Cecily earnestly.

"Sure," said Dan, solemnly. Dan liked to tease even Cecily a wee bit now and then.

Cecily relapsed into anxious thought, and care sat visibly on her brow for the rest of the day. Next morning she came to me and said:

"Bev, would you like to go for a walk with me this afternoon?"

"Of course," I replied. "Any particular where?"

"I'm going to see Mr. Campbell and ask him for his name for my square," said Cecily resolutely. "I don't suppose it will do any good. He wouldn't give anything to the library last summer, you remember, till the Story Girl told him that story about his grandmother. She won't go with me this time—I don't know why. I can't tell a story and I'm frightened to death just to think of going to him. But I believe it is my duty; and besides I would love to get as many names on my square as Kitty Marr has. So if you'll go with me we'll go this afternoon. I simply *couldn't* go alone."

CHAPTER XXIII

A
Missionary
Heroine

ACCORDINGLY, that afternoon we bearded the lion in his den. The road we took was a beautiful one, for we went "cross lots," and we enjoyed it, in spite of the fact that we did not expect the interview with Mr. Campbell to be a very pleasant one. To be sure, he had been quite civil on the occasion of our last call upon him, but the Story Girl had been with us then and had beguiled him into good-humour and generosity by the magic of her voice and personality. We had no such ally now, and Mr. Campbell was known to be virulently opposed to missions in any shape or form.

"I don't know whether it would have been any better if I could have put on my good clothes," said Cecily, with a rueful glance at her print dress, which, though neat and clean, was undeniably faded and *rather* short and tight. "The Story Girl said it would, and I wanted to, but mother wouldn't let me. She said it was all nonsense, and Mr. Campbell would never notice what I had on."

"It's my opinion that Mr. Campbell notices a good deal more than you'd think for," I said sagely.

"Well, I wish our call was over," sighed Cecily. "I can't tell you how I dread it."

"Now, see here, Sis," I said cheerfully, "let's not think about it till we get there. It'll only spoil our walk and do no good. Let's just forget it and enjoy ourselves."

"I'll try," agreed Cecily, "but it's ever so much easier to preach than to practise."

Our way lay first over a hill top, gallantly plumed with golden rod, where cloud shadows drifted over us like a gypsying crew. Carlisle, in all its ripely tinted length and breadth, lay below us, basking in the August sunshine, that spilled over the brim of the valley to the far-off Markdale Harbour, cupped in its harvest-golden hills.

Then came a little valley overgrown with the pale purple bloom of thistles and elusively haunted with their perfume. You say that thistles have no perfume? Go you to a brook hollow where they grow some late summer twilight at dewfall; and on the still air that rises suddenly to meet you will come a waft of faint, aromatic fragrance, wondrously sweet and evasive, the distillation of that despised thistle bloom.

Beyond this the path wound through a forest of fir, where a wood wind wove its murmurous spell and a wood brook dimpled pellucidly among the shadows—the dear, companionable, elfin shadows—that lurked under the low growing boughs. Along the edges of that winding path grew banks of velvet green moss, starred with clusters of pigeon berries. Pigeon berries are not to be eaten. They are woolly, tasteless things. But they are to be looked at in their glowing scarlet. They are the jewels with which the forest of cone-bearers loves to deck its brown breast. Cecily gathered some and pinned them on hers, but they did not become her. I thought how witching the Story Girl's brown curls would have looked twined with those brilliant clusters. Perhaps Cecily was thinking of it, too, for she presently said,

"Bev, don't you think the Story Girl is changing somehow?"

"There are times—just times—when she seems to belong more among the grown-ups than among us," I said, reluctantly, "especially when she puts on her bridesmaid dress."

"Well, she's the oldest of us, and when you come to think of it, she's fifteen,—that's almost grown-up," sighed Cecily. Then she added, with sudden vehemence, "I hate the thought of any of us growing up. Felicity says she just longs to be grown-up, but I don't, not a bit. I wish I could just stay a little girl for ever—and have you and Felix and all the others for playmates right along. I don't know how it is—but whenever I think of being grown-up I seem to feel tired."

Something about Cecily's speech—or the wistful look that had crept into her sweet brown eyes—made me feel vaguely uncomfortable; I was glad that we were at the end of our journey, with Mr. Campbell's big house before us, and his dog sitting gravely at the veranda steps.

"Oh, dear," said Cecily, with a shiver, "I'd been hoping that dog wouldn't be around."

"He never bites," I assured her.

"Perhaps he doesn't, but he always looks as if he was going to," rejoined Cecily.

The dog continued to look, and, as we edged gingerly past him and up the veranda steps, he turned his head and kept on looking. What with Mr. Campbell before us and the dog behind, Cecily was trembling with nervousness; but perhaps it was as well that the dour brute was there, else I verily believe she would have turned and fled shamelessly when we heard steps in the hall.

It was Mr. Campbell's housekeeper who came to the door, however; she ushered us pleasantly into the sitting-room where Mr. Campbell was reading. He laid down his book with a slight frown and said nothing at all in response to our timid "good afternoon." But after we had sat for a few minutes in wretched silence, wishing ourselves a thousand miles away, he said, with a chuckle,

"Well, is it the school library again?"

Cecily had remarked as we were coming that what she dreaded most of all was introducing the subject; but Mr. Campbell had given her a splendid opening, and she plunged wildly in at once, rattling her explanation off nervously with trembling voice and flushed cheeks.

"No, it's our Mission Band autograph quilt, Mr. Campbell. There are to be as many squares in it as there are members in the Band. Each one has a square and is collecting names for it. If you want to have your name on the quilt you pay five cents, and if you want to have it right in the round spot in the middle of the square you must pay ten cents. Then when we have got all the names we can we will embroider them on the squares. The money is to go to the little girl our Band is supporting in Korea. I heard that nobody had asked you, so I thought perhaps you would give me your name for my square."

Mr. Campbell drew his black brows together in a scowl.

"Stuff and nonsense!" he exclaimed angrily. "I don't believe in Foreign Missions—don't believe in them at all. I never give a cent to them."

"Five cents isn't a very large sum," said Cecily earnestly.

Mr. Campbell's scowl disappeared and he laughed.

"It wouldn't break me," he admitted, "but it's the principle of the thing. And as for that Mission Band of yours, if it wasn't for the fun you get out of it, catch one of you belonging. You don't really care a rap more for the heathen than I do."

"Oh, we do," protested Cecily. "We do think of all the poor little children in Korea, and we like to think we are helping them, if it's ever so little. We *are* in earnest, Mr. Campbell—indeed we are."

"Don't believe it—don't believe a word of it," said Mr. Campbell impolitely. "You'll do things that are nice and interesting. You'll get up concerts, and chase people about for autographs and give money your parents give you and that doesn't cost you either time or labour. But you wouldn't do anything you disliked for the heathen children—you wouldn't make any real sacrifice for them—catch you!"

"Indeed we would," cried Cecily, forgetting her timidity in her zeal. "I just wish I had a chance to prove it to you."

"You do, eh? Come, now, I'll take you at your word. I'll test you. Tomorrow is Communion Sunday and the church will be full of folks and they'll all have their best clothes on. If you go to church tomorrow in the very costume you have on at present, without telling anyone why you do so, until it is all over, I'll give you—why, I vow I'll give you five dollars for that quilt of yours."

Poor Cecily! To go to church in a faded print dress, with a shabby little old sun-hat and worn shoes! It was very cruel of Mr. Campbell.

"I—I don't think mother would let me," she faltered.

Her tormentor smiled grimly.

"It's not hard to find some excuse," he said sarcastically.

Cecily crimsoned and sat up facing Mr. Campbell spunkily.

"It's *not* an excuse," she said. "If mother will let me go to church like this I'll go. But I'll have to tell *her* why, Mr. Campbell, because I'm certain she'd never let me if I didn't."

"Oh, you can tell all your own family," said Mr. Campbell, "but remember, none of them must tell it outside until Sunday is over. If they do, I'll be sure to find it out and then our bargain is off. If I see you in church tomorrow, dressed as you are now, I'll give you my name and five dollars. But I won't see you. You'll shrink when you've had time to think it over."

"I sha'n't," said Cecily resolutely.

"Well, we'll see. And now come out to the barn with me.

I've got the prettiest little drove of calves out there you ever saw. I want you to see them."

Mr. Campbell took us all over his barns and was very affable. He had beautiful horses, cows and sheep, and I enjoyed seeing them. I don't think Cecily did, however. She was very quiet and even Mr. Campbell's handsome new span of dappled grays failed to arouse any enthusiasm in her. She was already in bitter anticipation living over the martyrdom of the morrow. On the way home she asked me seriously if I thought Mr. Campbell would go to heaven when he died.

"Of course he will," I said. "Isn't he a member of the church?"

"Oh, yes, but I can't imagine him fitting into heaven. You know he isn't really fond of anything but live stock."

"He's fond of teasing people, I guess," I responded. "Are you really going to church tomorrow in that dress, Sis?"

"If mother'll let me I'll have to," said poor Cecily. "I won't let Mr. Campbell triumph over me. And I *do* want to have as many names as Kitty has. And I *do* want to help the poor little Korean children. But it will be simply dreadful. I don't know whether I hope mother will or not."

I did not believe she would, but Aunt Janet sometimes could be depended on for the unexpected. She laughed and told Cecily she could please herself. Felicity was in a rage over it, and declared *she* wouldn't go to church if Cecily went in such a rig. Dan sarcastically inquired if all she went to church for was to show off her fine clothes and look at other people's; then they quarrelled and didn't speak to each other for two days, much to Cecily's distress.

I suspect poor Sis wished devoutly that it might rain the next day; but it was gloriously fine. We were all waiting in the orchard for the Story Girl who had not begun to dress for church until Cecily and Felicity were ready. Felicity was her prettiest in flower-trimmed hat, crisp muslin, floating ribbons and trim black slippers. Poor Cecily stood beside her mute and pale, in her faded school garb and heavy copper-toed boots. But her face, if pale, was very determined. Cecily, having put her hand to the plough, was not of those who turn back.

"You do look just awful," said Felicity. "I don't care—I'm going to sit in Uncle James' pew. I *won't* sit with you. There will be so many strangers there, and all the Markdale people, and what will they think of you? Some of them will never know the reason, either."

"I wish the Story Girl would hurry," was all poor Cecily said. "We're going to be late. It wouldn't have been quite so hard if I could have got there before anyone and slipped quietly into our pew."

"Here she comes at last," said Dan. "Why—what's she got on?"

The Story Girl joined us with a quizzical smile on her face. Dan whistled. Cecily's pale cheeks flushed with understanding and gratitude. The Story Girl wore her school print dress and hat also, and was gloveless and heavy shod.

"You're not going to have to go through this all alone, Cecily," she said.

"Oh, it won't be half so hard now," said Cecily, with a long breath of relief.

I fancy it was hard enough even then. The Story Girl did not care a whit, but Cecily rather squirmed under the curious glances that were cast at her. She afterwards told me that she really did not think she could have endured it if she had been alone.

Mr. Campbell met us under the elms in the churchyard, with a twinkle in his eye.

"Well, you did it, Miss," he said to Cecily, "but you should have been alone. That was what I meant. I suppose you think you've cheated me nicely."

"No, she doesn't," spoke up the Story Girl undauntedly. "She was all dressed and ready to come before she knew I was going to dress the same way. So she kept her bargain faithfully, Mr. Campbell, and I think you were cruel to make her do it."

"You do, eh? Well, well, I hope you'll forgive me. I didn't think she'd do it—I was sure feminine vanity would win the day over missionary zeal. It seems it didn't—though how much was pure missionary zeal and how much just plain King spunk I'm doubtful. I'll keep my promise, Miss. You shall have your five dollars, and mind you put my name in the round space. No five-cent corners for me."

CHAPTER XXIV

A
Tantalizing
Revelation

"I SHALL have something to tell you in the orchard this evening," said the Story Girl at breakfast one morning. Her eyes were very bright and excited. She looked as if she had not slept a great deal. She had spent the previous evening with Miss Reade and had not returned until the rest of us were in bed. Miss Reade had finished giving music lessons and was going home in a few days. Cecily and Felicity were in despair over this and mourned as those without comfort. But the Story Girl, who had been even more devoted to Miss Reade than either of them, had not, as I noticed, expressed any regret and seemed to be very cheerful over the whole matter.

"Why can't you tell it now?" asked Felicity.

"Because the evening is the nicest time to tell things in. I only mentioned it now so that you would have something interesting to look forward to all day."

"Is it about Miss Reade?" asked Cecily.

"Never mind."

"I'll bet she's going to be married," I exclaimed, remembering the ring.

"Is she?" cried Felicity and Cecily together.

The Story Girl threw an annoyed glance at me. She did not like to have her dramatic announcements forestalled.

"I don't say that it is about Miss Reade or that it isn't. You must just wait till the evening."

"I wonder what it is," speculated Cecily, as the Story Girl left the room.

"I don't believe it's much of anything," said Felicity, beginning to clear away the breakfast dishes. "The Story Girl always likes to make so much out of so little. Anyhow, I don't believe Miss Reade is going to be married. She hasn't any beaus around here and Mrs. Armstrong says she's sure she doesn't correspond with anybody. Besides, if she was she wouldn't be likely to tell the Story Girl."

"Oh, she might. They're such friends, you know," said Cecily.

"Miss Reade is no better friends with her than she is with me and you," retorted Felicity.

"No, but sometimes it seems to me that she's a different kind of friend with the Story Girl than she is with me and you," reflected Cecily. "I can't just explain what I mean."

"No wonder. Such nonsense," sniffed Felicity.

"It's only some girl's secret, anyway," said Dan, loftily. "I don't feel much interest in it."

But he was on hand with the rest of us that evening, interest or no interest, in Uncle Stephen's Walk, where the ripening apples were beginning to glow like jewels among the boughs.

"Now, are you going to tell us your news?" asked Felicity impatiently.

"Miss Reade *is* going to be married," said the Story Girl. "She told me so last night. She is going to be married in a fortnight's time."

"Who to?" exclaimed the girls.

"To"—the Story Girl threw a defiant glance at me as if to say, "You can't spoil the surprise of *this,* anyway,"—"to—the Awkward Man."

For a few moments amazement literally held us dumb.

"You're not in earnest, Sara Stanley?" gasped Felicity at last.

"Indeed I am. I thought you'd be astonished. But I wasn't. I've suspected it all summer, from little things I've noticed. Don't you remember that evening last spring when I went a piece with Miss Reade and told you when I came back that a story was growing? I guessed it from the way the Awkward Man looked at her when I stopped to speak to him over his garden fence."

"But—the Awkward Man!" said Felicity helplessly. "It doesn't seem possible. Did Miss Reade tell you *herself?*"

"Yes."

"I suppose it must be true then. But how did it ever come about? He's *so* shy and awkward. How did he ever manage to get up enough spunk to ask her to marry him?"

"Maybe she asked him," suggested Dan.

The Story Girl looked as if she might tell if she would.

"I believe that *was* the way of it," I said, to draw her on.

"Not exactly," she said reluctantly. "I know all about it but I can't tell you. I guessed part from things I've seen—and Miss Reade told me a good deal—and the Awkward Man himself told me his side of it as we came home last night. I met him just as I left Mr. Armstrong's and we were together as far as his house. It was dark and he just talked on as if he were talking to himself—I think he forgot I was there at all, once he got started. He has never been shy or awkward with me, but he never talked as he did last night."

"You might tell us what he said," urged Cecily. "We'd never tell."

The Story Girl shook her head.

"No, I can't. You wouldn't understand. Besides, I couldn't tell it just right. It's one of the things that are hardest to tell. I'd spoil it if I told it—now. Perhaps some day I'll be able to tell it properly. It's very beautiful—but it might sound very ridiculous if it wasn't told just exactly the right way."

"I don't know what you mean, and I don't believe you know yourself," said Felicity pettishly. "All that I can make out is that Miss Reade is going to marry Jasper Dale, and I don't like the idea one bit. She is so beautiful and sweet. I thought she'd marry some dashing young man. Jasper Dale must be nearly twenty years older than her—and he's so queer and shy—and such a hermit."

"Miss Reade is perfectly happy," said the Story Girl. "She thinks the Awkward Man is lovely—and so he is. You don't know him, but I do."

"Well, you needn't put on such airs about it," sniffed Felicity.

"I am not putting on any airs. But it's true. Miss Reade and I are the only people in Carlisle who really know the Awkward Man. Nobody else ever got behind his shyness to find out just what sort of a man he is."

"When are they to be married?" asked Felicity.

"In a fortnight's time. And then they are coming right back to live at Golden Milestone. Won't it be lovely to have Miss Reade always so near us?"

"I wonder what she'll think about the mystery of Golden Milestone," remarked Felicity.

Golden Milestone was the beautiful name the Awkward Man had given his home; and there was a mystery about it, as readers of the first volume of these chronicles will recall.

"She knows all about the mystery and thinks it perfectly lovely—and so do I," said the Story Girl.

"Do *you* know the secret of the locked room?" cried Cecily.

"Yes, the Awkward Man told me all about it last night. I told you I'd find out the mystery some time."

"And what is it?"

"I can't tell you that either."

"I think you're hateful and mean," exclaimed Felicity. "It hasn't anything to do with Miss Reade, so I think you might tell us."

"It has something to do with Miss Reade. It's all about her."

"Well, I don't see how that can be when the Awkward Man never saw or heard of Miss Reade until she came to Carlisle in the spring," said Felicity incredulously, "and he's had that locked room for years."

"I can't explain it to you—but it's just as I've said," responded the Story Girl.

"Well, it's a very queer thing," retorted Felicity.

"The name in the books in the room was Alice—and Miss Reade's name is Alice," marvelled Cecily. "Did he know her before she came here?"

"Mrs. Griggs says that room has been locked for ten years. Ten years ago Miss Reade was just a little girl of ten. *She* couldn't be the Alice of the books," argued Felicity.

"I wonder if she'll wear the blue silk dress," said Sara Ray.

"And what will she do about the picture, if it isn't hers?" added Cecily.

"The picture couldn't be hers, or Mrs. Griggs would have known her for the same when she came to Carlisle," said Felix.

"I'm going to stop wondering about it," exclaimed Felicity crossly, aggravated by the amused smile with which the Story Girl was listening to the various speculations. "I think Sara is just as mean as mean when she won't tell us."

"I can't," repeated the Story Girl patiently.

"You said one time you had an idea who 'Alice' was," I said. "Was your idea anything like the truth?"

"Yes, I guessed pretty nearly right."

"Do you suppose they'll keep the room locked after they are married?" asked Cecily.

"Oh, no. I can tell you that much. It is to be Miss Reade's own particular sitting room."

"Why, then, perhaps we'll see it some time ourselves, when we go to see Miss Reade," cried Cecily.

"I'd be frightened to go into it," confessed Sara Ray. "I hate things with mysteries. They always make me nervous."

"I love them. They're so exciting," said the Story Girl.

"Just think, this will be the second wedding of people we know," reflected Cecily. "Isn't that interesting?"

"I only hope the next thing won't be a funeral," remarked Sara Ray gloomily. "There were three lighted lamps on our kitchen table last night, and Judy Pineau says that's a sure sign of a funeral."

"Well, there are funerals going on all the time," said Dan.

"But it means the funeral of somebody you know. *I* don't believe in it—*much*—but Judy says she's seen it come true time and again. I hope if it does it won't be anybody we know *very* well. But I hope it'll be somebody I know a *little,* because then I might get to the funeral. I'd just love to go to a funeral."

"That's a dreadful thing to say," commented Felicity in a shocked tone.

Sara Ray looked bewildered.

"I don't see what is dreadful in it," she protested.

"People don't go to funerals for the fun of it," said Felicity severely. "And you just as good as said you hoped somebody you knew would die so you'd get to the funeral."

"No, no, I didn't. I didn't mean that *at all,* Felicity. I don't want anybody to die; but what I meant was, if anybody I knew *had* to die there might be a chance to go to the funeral. I've never been to a single funeral yet, and it must be so interesting."

"Well, don't mix up talk about funerals with talk about weddings," said Felicity. "It isn't lucky. *I* think Miss Reade is simply throwing herself away, but I hope she'll be happy. And I hope the Awkward Man will manage to get married without making some awful blunder, but it's more than I expect."

"The ceremony is to be very private," said the Story Girl.

"I'd like to see them the day they appear out in church," chuckled Dan. "How'll he ever manage to bring her in and show her into the pew? I'll bet he'll go in first—or tramp on her dress—or fall over his feet."

"Maybe he won't go to church at all the first Sunday and she'll have to go alone," said Peter. "That happened in Markdale. A man was too bashful to go to church the first time after getting married, and his wife went alone till he got used to the idea."

"They may do things like that in Markdale but that is not the way people behave in Carlisle," said Felicity loftily.

Seeing the Story Girl slipping away with a disapproving face I joined her.

"What is the matter, Sara?" I asked.

"I hate to hear them talking like that about Miss Reade and Mr. Dale," she answered vehemently. "It's really all so beautiful— but they make it seem silly and absurd, somehow."

"You might tell me all about it, Sara," I insinuated. "I wouldn't tell—and I'd understand."

"Yes, I think you would," she said thoughtfully. "But I can't tell it even to you because I can't tell it well enough yet. I've a feeling that there's only one way to tell it—and I don't know the way yet. Some day I'll know it—and then I'll tell you, Bev."

Long, long after she kept her word. Forty years later I wrote to her, across the leagues of land and sea that divided us, and told her that Jasper Dale was dead; and I reminded her of her old promise and asked its fulfilment. In reply she sent me the written love story of Jasper Dale and Alice Reade. Now, when Alice sleeps under the whispering elms of the old Carlisle churchyard, beside the husband of her youth, that story may be given, in all its old-time sweetness, to the world.

CHAPTER XXV

The
Love Story
of the
Awkward Man

(Written by the Story Girl)

JASPER DALE lived alone in the old homestead which he had named Golden Milestone. In Carlisle this giving one's farm a name was looked upon as a piece of affectation; but if a place must be named why not give it a sensible name with some meaning to it? Why Golden Milestone, when Pinewood or Hillslope or, if you wanted to be very fanciful, Ivy Lodge, might be had for the taking?

He had lived alone at Golden Milestone since his mother's death; he had been twenty then and he was close upon forty now, though he did not look it. But neither could it be said that he looked young; he had never at any time looked young with common youth; there had always been something in his appearance that stamped him as different from the ordinary run of men, and, apart from his shyness, built up an intangible, invisible barrier between him and his kind. He had lived all his life in Carlisle; and all the Carlisle people knew of or about him—although they thought they knew everything—was that he was painfully, abnormally shy. He never went anywhere except to church; he never took part in Carlisle's simple social life; even with most men he was distant and reserved; as for women, he never spoke to or looked at them; if one spoke to him, even if she were a matronly old mother in Israel, he was at once in an agony of painful blushes. He had no friends in the sense of companions; to all outward appearance his life was solitary and devoid of any human interest.

He had no housekeeper; but his old house, furnished as it had been in his mother's lifetime, was cleanly and daintily kept.

The quaint rooms were as free from dust and disorder as a woman could have had them. This was known, because Jasper Dale occasionally had his hired man's wife, Mrs. Griggs, in to scrub for him. On the morning she was expected he betook himself to woods and fields, returning only at night-fall. During his absence Mrs. Griggs was frankly wont to explore the house from cellar to attic, and her report of its condition was always the same—"neat as wax." To be sure, there was one room that was always locked against her, the west gable, looking out on the garden and the hill of pines beyond. But Mrs. Griggs knew that in the lifetime of Jasper Dale's mother it had been unfurnished. She supposed it still remained so, and felt no especial curiosity concerning it, though she always tried the door.

Jasper Dale had a good farm, well cultivated; he had a large garden where he worked most of his spare time in summer; it was supposed that he read a great deal, since the postmistress declared that he was always getting books and magazines by mail. He seemed well contented with his existence and people let him alone, since that was the greatest kindness they could do him. It was unsupposable that he would ever marry; nobody ever had supposed it.

"Jasper Dale never so much as *thought* about a woman," Carlisle oracles declared. Oracles, however, are not always to be trusted.

One day Mrs. Griggs went away from the Dale place with a very curious story, which she diligently spread far and wide. It made a good deal of talk, but people, although they listened eagerly, and wondered and questioned, were rather incredulous about it. They thought Mrs. Griggs must be drawing considerably upon her imagination; there were not lacking those who declared that she had invented the whole account, since her reputation for strict veracity was not wholly unquestioned.

Mrs. Griggs's story was as follows:—

One day she found the door of the west gable unlocked. She went in, expecting to see bare walls and a collection of odds and ends. Instead she found herself in a finely furnished room. Delicate lace curtains hung before the small, square, broad-silled windows. The walls were adorned with pictures in much finer taste than Mrs. Griggs could appreciate. There was a bookcase between the windows filled with choicely bound books. Beside it stood a little table with a very dainty work-basket on it. By the basket Mrs. Griggs saw a pair of tiny scissors and a silver thimble. A wicker rocker, comfortable with silk cushions, was near it. Above the bookcase a woman's picture hung—a water-colour, if Mrs. Griggs had but known it—representing a pale, very sweet face, with large, dark eyes and a wistful expression under loose masses of black, lustrous hair. Just beneath the picture, on the top shelf of the bookcase, was a vaseful of flowers. Another vaseful stood on the table beside the basket.

All this was astonishing enough. But what puzzled Mrs. Griggs completely was the fact that a woman's dress was hanging over a chair before the mirror—a pale blue, silken affair. And on the floor beside it were two little blue satin slippers!

Good Mrs. Griggs did not leave the room until she had thoroughly explored it, even to shaking out the blue dress and discovering it to be a tea-gown—wrapper, she called it. But she found nothing to throw any light on the mystery. The fact that the simple name "Alice" was written on the fly-leaves of all the books only deepened it, for it was a name unknown in the Dale family. In this puzzled state she was obliged to depart, nor did she ever find the door unlocked again; and, discovering that people thought she was romancing when she talked about the mysterious west gable at Golden Milestone, she indignantly held her peace concerning the whole affair.

But Mrs. Griggs had told no more than the simple truth. Jasper Dale, under all his shyness and aloofness, possessed a nature full of delicate romance and poesy, which, denied expression in the common ways of life, bloomed out in the realm of fancy and imagination. Left alone, just when the boy's nature was deepening into the man's, he turned to this ideal kingdom for all he believed the real world could never give him. Love—a strange, almost mystical love—played its part here for him. He shadowed forth to himself the vision of a woman, loving and beloved; he cherished it until it became almost as real to him as his own personality and he gave this dream woman the name he liked best—Alice. In fancy he walked and talked with her, spoke words of love to her, and heard words of love in return. When he came from work at the close of day she met him at his threshold in the twilight—a strange, fair, starry shape, as elusive and spiritual as a blossom reflected in a pool by moonlight—with welcome on her lips and in her eyes.

One day, when he was in Charlottetown on business, he had been struck by a picture in the window of a store. It was strangely like the woman of his dream love. He went in, awkward and embarrassed, and bought it. When he took it home he did not know where to put it. It was out of place among the dim old engravings of bewigged portraits and conventional landscapes on the walls of Golden Milestone. As he pondered the matter in his garden that evening he had an inspiration. The sunset, flaming on the windows of the west gable, kindled them into burning rose. Amid the splendour he fancied Alice's fair face peeping archly down at him from the room. The inspiration came then. It should be her room; he would fit it up for her; and her picture should hang there.

He was all summer carrying out his plan. Nobody must know or suspect, so he must go slowly and secretly. One by one the furnishings were purchased and brought home under cover of darkness. He arranged them with his own hands. He bought the books he thought she would like best and wrote her name in them; he got the little feminine knick-knacks of basket and thimble. Finally he saw in a store a pale blue tea-gown and the satin slippers. He had always fancied her as dressed in blue. He bought them and took them home to her room. Thereafter it was sacred to her; he always knocked on its door before he entered; he kept it sweet with fresh flowers; he sat there in the purple summer evenings and talked aloud to her or read his favourite books to her. In his fancy she sat opposite to him in her rocker, clad in the trailing blue gown, with her head leaning on one slender hand, as white as a twilight star.

But Carlisle people knew nothing of this—would have thought him tinged with mild lunacy if they had known. To them, he was just the shy, simple farmer he appeared. They never knew or guessed at the real Jasper Dale.

One spring Alice Reade came to teach music in Carlisle. Her pupils worshipped her, but the grown people thought she was rather too distant and reserved. They had been used to merry, jolly girls who joined eagerly in the social life of the place. Alice Reade held herself aloof from it—not disdainfully, but as one to whom these things were of small importance. She was very fond of books and solitary rambles; she was not at all shy but she was as sensitive as a flower; and after a time Carlisle people were content to let her live her own life and no longer resented her unlikeness to themselves.

She boarded with the Armstrongs, who lived beyond Golden Milestone around the hill of pines. Until the snow disappeared she went out to the main road by the long Armstrong lane; but when spring came she was wont to take a shorter way, down the pine hill, across the brook, past Jasper Dale's garden, and out through his lane. And one day, as she went by, Jasper Dale was working in his garden.

He was on his knees in a corner, setting out a bunch of roots—an unsightly little tangle of rainbow possibilities. It was a still spring morning; the world was green with young leaves; a little wind blew down from the pines and lost itself willingly among the budding delights of the garden. The grass opened eyes of blue violets. The sky was high and cloudless, turquoise-blue, shading off into milkiness on the far horizons. Birds were singing along the brook valley. Rollicking robins were whistling joyously in the pines. Jasper Dale's heart was filled to overflowing with a realization of all the virgin loveliness around him; the feeling in his soul had the sacredness of a prayer. At this moment he looked up and saw Alice Reade.

She was standing outside the garden fence, in the shadow of a great pine tree, looking not at him, for she was unaware of his presence, but at the virginal bloom of the plum trees in a far corner, with all her delight in it outblossoming freely in her face. For a moment Jasper Dale believed that his dream love had taken visible form before him. She was like—so like; not in feature, perhaps, but in grace and colouring—the grace of a slender, lissome form and the colouring of cloudy hair and wistful, dark gray eyes, and curving red mouth; and more than all, she was like her in expression—in the subtle revelation of personality exhaling from her like perfume from a flower. It was as if his own had come to him at last and his whole soul suddenly leaped out to meet and welcome her.

Then her eyes fell upon him and the spell was broken. Jasper remained kneeling mutely there, shy man once more, crimson with blushes, a strange, almost pitiful creature in his abject confusion. A little smile flickered about the delicate corners of her mouth, but she turned and walked swiftly away down the lane.

Jasper looked after her with a new, painful sense of loss and loveliness. It had been agony to feel her conscious eyes upon him, but he realized now that there had been a strange sweetness in it, too. It was still greater pain to watch her going from him.

He thought she must be the new music teacher but he did not even know her name. She had been dressed in blue, too—a pale, dainty blue; but that was of course; he had known she must wear it; and he was sure her name must be Alice. When, later on, he discovered that it was, he felt no surprise.

He carried some mayflowers up to the west gable and put them under the picture. But the charm had gone out of the tribute; and looking at the picture, he thought how scant was the justice it did her. Her face was so much sweeter, her eyes so much softer, her hair so much more lustrous. The soul of his love had gone from the room and from the picture and from his dreams. When he tried to think of the Alice he loved he saw, not the shadowy spirit occupant of the west gable, but the young girl who had stood under the pine, beautiful with the beauty of moonlight, of starshine on still water, of white, wind-swayed flowers growing in silent, shadowy places. He did not then realize what this meant; had he realized it he would have suffered bitterly; as it was he felt only a vague discomfort—a curious sense of loss and gain commingled.

He saw her again that afternoon on her way home. She did not pause by the garden but walked swiftly past. Thereafter, every day for a week he watched unseen to see her pass his home. Once a little child was with her, clinging to her hand. No child had ever before had any part in the shy man's dream life. But that night in the twilight the vision of the rocking-chair was a girl in a blue print dress, with a little, golden-haired shape at her knee—a shape that lisped and prattled and called her "mother;" and both of them were his.

It was the next day that he failed for the first time to put flowers in the west gable. Instead, he cut a loose handful of daffodils and, looking furtively about him as if committing a crime, he laid them across the footpath under the pine. She must pass that way; her feet would crush them if she failed to see them. Then he slipped back into his garden, half exultant, half repentant. From a safe retreat he saw her pass by and stoop to lift his flowers. Thereafter he put some in the same place every day.

When Alice Reade saw the flowers she knew at once who had put them there, and divined that they were for her. She lifted them tenderly in much surprise and pleasure. She had heard all about Jasper Dale and his shyness; but before she had heard about him she had seen him in church and liked him. She thought his face and his dark blue eyes beautiful; she even liked the long brown hair that Carlisle people laughed at. That he was quite different from other people she had understood at once, but she thought the difference in his favour. Perhaps her sensitive nature divined and responded to the beauty in his. At least, in her eyes Jasper Dale was never a ridiculous figure.

When she heard the story of the west gable, which most people disbelieved, she believed it, although she did not understand it. It invested the shy man with interest and romance. She felt that she would have liked, out of no impertinent curiosity, to solve the mystery; she believed that it contained the key to his character.

Thereafter, every day she found flowers under the pine tree; she wished to see Jasper to thank him, unaware that he watched her daily from the screen of shrubbery in his garden; but it was some time before she found the opportunity. One evening she passed when he, not expecting her, was leaning against his garden fence with a book in his hand. She stopped under the pine.

"Mr. Dale," she said softly, "I want to thank you for your flowers."

Jasper, startled, wished that he might sink into the ground. His anguish of embarrassment made her smile a little. He could not speak, so she went on gently.

"It has been so good of you. They have given me so much pleasure—I wish you could know how much."

"It was nothing—nothing," stammered Jasper. His book had fallen on the ground at her feet, and she picked it up and held it out to him.

"So you like Ruskin," she said. "I do, too. But I haven't read this."

"If you—would care—to read it—you may have it," Jasper contrived to say.

She carried the book away with her. He did not again hide

when she passed, and when she brought the book back they talked a little about it over the fence. He lent her others, and got some from her in return; they fell into the habit of discussing them. Jasper did not find it hard to talk to her now; it seemed as if he were talking to his dream Alice, and it came strangely natural to him. He did not talk volubly, but Alice thought what he did say was worth while. His words lingered in her memory and made music. She always found his flowers under the pine, and she always wore some of them; but she did not know if he noticed this or not.

One evening Jasper walked shyly with her from his gate up the pine hill. After that he always walked that far with her. She would have missed him much if he had failed to do so; yet it did not occur to her that she was learning to love him. She would have laughed with girlish scorn at the idea. She liked him very much; she thought his nature beautiful in its simplicity and purity; in spite of his shyness she felt more delightfully at home in his society than in that of any other person she had ever met. He was one of those rare souls whose friendship is at once a pleasure and a benediction, showering light from their own crystal clearness into all the dark corners in the souls of others, until, for the time being at least, they reflected his own nobility. But she never thought of love. Like other girls she had her dreams of a possible Prince Charming, young and handsome and debonair. It never occurred to her that he might be found in the shy, dreamy recluse of Golden Milestone.

In August came a day of gold and blue. Alice Reade, coming through the trees, with the wind blowing her little dark love-locks tricksily about under her wide blue hat, found a fragrant heap of mignonette under the pine. She lifted it and buried her face in it, drinking in the wholesome, modest perfume.

She had hoped Jasper would be in his garden, since she wished to ask him for a book she greatly desired to read. But she saw him sitting on the rustic seat at the further side. His back was towards her, and he was partially screened by a copse of lilacs.

Alice, blushing slightly, unlatched the garden gate, and went down the path. She had never been in the garden before, and she found her heart beating in a strange fashion.

He did not hear her footsteps, and she was close behind him

when she heard his voice, and realized that he was talking to himself, in a low, dreamy tone. As the meaning of his words dawned on her consciousness she started and grew crimson. She could not move or speak; as one in a dream she stood and listened to the shy man's reverie, guiltless of any thought of eavesdropping.

"How much I love you, Alice," Jasper Dale was saying, unafraid, with no shyness in voice or manner. "I wonder what you would say if you knew. You would laugh at me—sweet as you are, you would laugh in mockery. I can never tell you. I can only dream of telling you. In my dream you are standing here by me, dear. I can see you very plainly, my sweet lady, so tall and gracious, with your dark hair and your maiden eyes. I can dream that I tell you my love; that—maddest, sweetest dream of all—that you love me in return. Everything is possible in dreams, you know, dear. My dreams are all I have, so I go far in them, even to dreaming that you are my wife. I dream how I shall fix up my dull old house for you. One room will need nothing more—it is your room, dear, and has been ready for you a long time—long before that day I saw you under the pine. Your books and your chair and your picture are there, dear— only the picture is not half lovely enough. But the other rooms of the house must be made to bloom out freshly for you. What a delight it is thus to dream of what I would do for you! Then I would bring you home, dear, and lead you through my garden and into my house as its mistress. I would see you standing beside me in the old mirror at the end of the hall—a bride, in your pale blue dress, with a blush on your face. I would lead you through all the rooms made ready for your coming, and then to your own. I would see you sitting in your own chair and all my dreams would find rich fulfilment in that royal moment. Oh, Alice, we would have a beautiful life together! It's sweet to make believe about it. You will sing to me in the twilight, and we will gather early flowers together in the spring days. When I come home from work, tired, you will put your arms about me and lay your head on my shoulder. I will stroke it—so—that bonny, glossy head of yours. Alice, my Alice—all mine in my dream—never to be mine in real life—how I love you!"

The Alice behind him could bear no more. She gave a little choking cry that betrayed her presence. Jasper Dale sprang up and gazed upon her. He saw her standing there, amid the languorous shadows of August, pale with feeling, wide-eyed, trembling.

For a moment shyness wrung him. Then every trace of it was banished by a sudden, strange, fierce anger that swept over him. He felt outraged and hurt to the death; he felt as if he had been cheated out of something incalculably precious—as if sacrilege had been done to his most holy sanctuary of emotion. White, tense with his anger, he looked at her and spoke, his lips as pale as if his fiery words scathed them.

"How dare you? You have spied on me—you have crept in and listened! How dare you? Do you know what you have done, girl? You have destroyed all that made life worth while to me. My dream is dead. It could not live when it was betrayed. And it was all I had. Oh, laugh at me—mock me! I know that I am ridiculous! What of it? It never could have hurt you! Why must you creep in like this to hear me and put me to shame? Oh, I love you—I will say it, laugh as you will. Is it such a strange thing that I should have a heart like other men? This will make sport for you! I, who love you better than my life, better than any other man in the world can love you, will be a jest to you all your life. I love you—and yet I think I could hate you—you have destroyed my dream—you have done me deadly wrong."

"Jasper! Jasper!" cried Alice, finding her voice. His anger hurt her with a pain she could not endure. It was unbearable that Jasper should be angry with her. In that moment she realized that she loved him—that the words he had spoken when unconscious of her presence were the sweetest she had ever heard, or ever could hear. Nothing mattered at all, save that he loved her and was angry with her.

"Don't say such dreadful things to me," she stammered, "I did not mean to listen. I could not help it. I shall never laugh at you. Oh, Jasper"—she looked bravely at him and the fine soul of her shone through the flesh like an illuminating lamp—"I am *glad* that you love me! and I am glad I chanced to overhear you, since you would never have had the courage to tell me otherwise. Glad—glad! Do you understand, Jasper?"

Jasper looked at her with the eyes of one who, looking through pain, sees rapture beyond.

"Is it possible?" he said, wonderingly. "Alice—I am so much older than you—and they call me the Awkward Man—they say I am unlike other people"—

"You *are* unlike other people," she said softly, "and that is why I love you. I know now that I must have loved you ever since I saw you."

"I loved you long before I saw you," said Jasper.

He came close to her and drew her into his arms, tenderly and reverently, all his shyness and awkwardness swallowed up in the grace of his great happiness. In the old garden he kissed her lips and Alice entered into her own.

CHAPTER XXVI

Uncle Blair
Comes Home

IT happened that the Story Girl and I both got up very early on the morning of the Awkward Man's wedding day. Uncle Alec was going to Charlottetown that day, and I, awakened at daybreak by the sounds in the kitchen beneath us, remembered that I had forgotten to ask him to bring me a certain school-book I wanted. So I hurriedly dressed and hastened down to tell him before he went. I was joined on the stairs by the Story Girl, who said she had wakened and, not feeling like going to sleep again, thought she might as well get up.

"I had such a funny dream last night," she said. "I dreamed that I heard a voice calling me from away down in Uncle Stephen's Walk—'Sara, Sara, Sara,' it kept calling. I didn't know whose it was, and yet it seemed like a voice I knew. I wakened up while it was calling, and it seemed so real I could hardly believe it was a dream. It was bright moonlight, and I felt just like getting up and going out to the orchard. But I knew that would be silly and of course I didn't go. But I kept on wanting to and I couldn't sleep any more. Wasn't it queer?"

When Uncle Alec had gone I proposed a saunter to the farther end of the orchard, where I had left a book the preceding evening. A young morn was walking rosily on the hills as we passed down Uncle Stephen's Walk, with Paddy trotting before us. High overhead was the spirit-like blue of paling skies; the east was a great arc of crystal, smitten through with auroral crimsonings; just above it was one milk-white star of morning, like a pearl on a silver sea. A light wind of dawn was weaving an orient spell.

"It's lovely to be up as early as this, isn't it?" said the Story Girl. "The world seems so different just at sunrise, doesn't it? It makes me feel just like getting up to see the sun rise every morning of my life after this. But I know I won't. I'll likely sleep later than ever tomorrow morning. But I wish I could."

"The Awkward Man and Miss Reade are going to have a lovely day for their wedding," I said.

"Yes, and I'm so glad. Beautiful Alice deserves everything good. Why, Bev—why, Bev! Who is that in the hammock?"

I looked. The hammock was swung under the two end trees of the Walk. In it a man was lying, asleep, his head pillowed on his overcoat. He was sleeping easily, lightly, and wholesomely. He had a pointed brown beard and thick wavy brown hair. His cheeks were a dusky red and th᷑ lashes of his closed eyes were as long and dark and silken as a girl's. He wore a light gray suit, and on the slender white hand that hung down over the hammock's edge was a spark of diamond fire.

It seemed to me that I knew his face, although assuredly I had never seen him before. While I groped among vague speculations the Story Girl gave a queer, choked little cry. The next moment she had sprung over the intervening space, dropped on her knees by the hammock, and flung her arms about the man's neck.

"Father! Father!" she cried, while I stood, rooted to the ground in my amazement.

The sleeper stirred and opened two large, exceedingly brilliant hazel eyes. For a moment he gazed rather blankly at the brown-curled young lady who was embracing him. Then a most delightful smile broke over his face; he sprang up and caught her to his heart.

"Sara—Sara—my little Sara! To think I didn't know you at first glance! But you are almost a woman. And when I saw you last you were just a little girl of eight. My own little Sara!"

"Father—father—sometimes I've wondered if you were ever coming back to me," I heard the Story Girl say, as I turned and scuttled up the Walk, realizing that I was not wanted there just then and would be little missed. Various emotions and speculations possessed my mind in my retreat; but chiefly did I feel a sense of triumph in being the bearer of exciting news.

"Aunt Janet, Uncle Blair is here," I announced breathlessly at the kitchen door.

Aunt Janet, who was kneading her bread, turned round and lifted floury hands. Felicity and Cecily, who were just entering the kitchen, rosy from slumber, stopped still and stared at me.

"Uncle who?" exclaimed Aunt Janet.

"Uncle Blair—the Story Girl's father, you know. He's here."

"*Where?*"

"Down in the orchard. He was asleep in the hammock. We found him there."

"Dear me!" said Aunt Janet, sitting down helplessly. "If that isn't like Blair! Of course he couldn't come like anybody else. I wonder," she added in a tone unheard by anyone else save myself, "I wonder if he has come to take the child away."

My elation went out like a snuffed candle. I had never thought of this. If Uncle Blair took the Story Girl away would not life become rather savourless on the hill farm? I turned and followed Felicity and Cecily out in a very subdued mood.

Uncle Blair and the Story Girl were just coming out of the orchard. His arm was about her and hers was on his shoulder. Laughter and tears were contending in her eyes. Only once before—when Peter had come back from the Valley of the Shadow—had I seen the Story Girl cry. Emotion had to go very deep with her ere it touched the source of tears. I had always known that she loved her father passionately, though she rarely talked of him, understanding that her uncles and aunts were not whole-heartedly his friends.

But Aunt Janet's welcome was cordial enough, though a trifle flustered. Whatever thrifty, hard-working farmer folk might think of gay, Bohemian Blair Stanley in his absence, in his presence even they liked him, by the grace of some winsome, lovable quality in the soul of him. He had "a way with him"—revealed even in the manner with which he caught staid Aunt Janet in his arms, swung her matronly form around as though she had been a slim schoolgirl, and kissed her rosy cheek.

"Sister o' mine, are you never going to grow old?" he said. "Here you are at forty-five with the roses of sixteen—and not a gray hair, I'll wager."

"Blair, Blair, it is you who are always young," laughed Aunt Janet, not ill pleased. "Where in the world did you come from? And what is this I hear of your sleeping all night in the hammock?"

"I've been painting in the Lake District all summer, as you know," answered Uncle Blair, "and one day I just got homesick to see my little girl. So I sailed for Montreal without further delay. I got here at eleven last night—the station-master's son drove me down. Nice boy. The old house was in darkness and I thought it would be a shame to rouse you all out of bed after a hard day's work. So I decided that I would spend the night in the orchard. It was moonlight, you know, and moonlight in an old orchard is one of the few things left over from the Golden Age."

"It was very foolish of you," said practical Aunt Janet. "These September nights are real chilly. You might have caught your death of cold—or a bad dose of rheumatism."

"So I might. No doubt it was foolish of me," agreed Uncle Blair gaily. "It must have been the fault of the moonlight. Moonlight, you know, Sister Janet, has an intoxicating quality. It is a fine, airy, silver wine, such as fairies may drink at their revels, unharmed of it; but when a mere mortal sips of it, it mounts straightway to his brain, to the undoing of his daylight common sense. However, I have got neither cold nor rheumatism, as a sensible person would have done had he ever been lured into doing such a nonsensible thing; there is a special Providence for us foolish folk. I enjoyed my night in the orchard; for a time I was companioned by sweet old memories; and then I fell asleep listening to the murmurs of the wind in those old trees yonder. And I had a beautiful dream, Janet. I dreamed that the old orchard blossomed again, as it did that spring eighteen years ago. I dreamed that its sunshine was the sunshine of spring, not autumn. There was newness of life in my dream, Janet, and the sweetness of forgotten words."

"Wasn't it strange about *my* dream?" whispered the Story Girl to me.

"Well, you'd better come in and have some breakfast," said Aunt Janet. "These are my little girls—Felicity and Cecily."

"I remember them as two most adorable tots," said Uncle Blair, shaking hands. "They haven't changed quite so much as my own baby-child. Why, she's a woman, Janet—she's a woman."

"She's child enough still," said Aunt Janet hastily.

The Story Girl shook her long brown curls.

"I'm fifteen," she said. "And you ought to see me in my long dress, father."

"We must not be separated any longer, dear heart," I heard Uncle Blair say tenderly. I hoped that he meant he would stay in Canada—not that he would take the Story Girl away.

Apart from this we had a gay day with Uncle Blair. He evidently liked our society better than that of the grown-ups, for he was a child himself at heart, gay, irresponsible, always acting on the impulse of the moment. We all found him a delightful companion. There was no school that day, as Mr. Perkins was absent, attending a meeting of the Teachers' Convention, so we spent most of its golden hours in the orchard with Uncle Blair, listening to his fascinating accounts of foreign wanderings. He also drew all our pictures for us, and this was especially delightful, for the day of the camera was only just dawning and none of us had ever had even our photographs taken. Sara Ray's pleasure was, as usual, quite spoiled by wondering what her mother would say of it, for Mrs. Ray had, so it appeared, some very peculiar prejudices against the taking or making of any kind of picture whatsoever, owing to an exceedingly strict interpretation of the second commandment. Dan suggested that she need not tell her mother anything about it; but Sara shook her head.

"I'll have to tell her. I've made it a rule to tell ma everything I do ever since the Judgment Day."

"Besides," added Cecily seriously, "the *Family Guide* says one ought to tell one's mother everything."

"It's pretty hard sometimes, though," sighed Sara. "Ma scolds so much when I do tell her things, that it sort of discourages me. But when I think of how dreadful I felt the time of the Judgment Day over deceiving her in some things it nerves me up. I'd do almost anything rather than feel like that the next time the Judgment Day comes."

"Fe, fi, fo, fum, I smell a story," said Uncle Blair. "What do you mean by speaking of the Judgment Day in the past tense?"

The Story Girl told him the tale of that dreadful Sunday in the preceding summer and we all laughed with him at ourselves.

"All the same," muttered Peter, "I don't want to have another experience like that. I hope I'll be dead the next time the Judgment Day comes."

"But you'll be raised up for it," said Felix.

"Oh, that'll be all right. I won't mind that. I won't know anything about it till it really happens. It's the expecting it that's the worst."

"I don't think you ought to talk of such things," said Felicity.

When evening came we all went to Golden Milestone. We knew the Awkward Man and his bride were expected home at sunset, and we meant to scatter flowers on the path by which she must enter her new home. It was the Story Girl's idea, but I don't think Aunt Janet would have let us go if Uncle Blair had not pleaded for us. He asked to be taken along, too, and we agreed, if he would stand out of sight when the newly married pair came home.

"You see, father, the Awkward Man won't mind us, because we're only children and he knows us well," explained the Story Girl, "but if he sees you, a stranger, it might confuse him and we might spoil the home-coming, and that would be such a pity."

So we went to Golden Milestone, laden with all the flowery spoil we could plunder from both gardens. It was a clear amber-tinted September evening and far away, over Markdale Harbour, a great round red moon was rising as we waited. Uncle Blair was hidden behind the wind-blown tassels of the pines at the gate, but he and the Story Girl kept waving their hands at each other and calling out gay, mirthful jests.

"Do you really feel acquainted with your father?" whispered Sara Ray wonderingly. "It's long since you saw him."

"If I hadn't seen him for a hundred years it wouldn't make any difference that way," laughed the Story Girl.

"S-s-h-s-s-h—they're coming," whispered Felicity excitedly.

And then they came—Beautiful Alice blushing and lovely, in the prettiest of pretty blue dresses, and the Awkward Man, so fervently happy that he quite forgot to be awkward. He lifted her out of the buggy gallantly and led her forward to us, smiling. We retreated before them, scattering our flowers lavishly on the path, and Alice Dale walked to the very doorstep of her new home over a carpet of blossoms. On the step they both paused and turned towards us, and we shyly did the proper thing in the way of congratulations and good wishes.

"It was so sweet of you to do this," said the smiling bride.

"It was lovely to be able to do it for you, dearest," whispered the Story Girl, "and oh, Miss Reade—Mrs. Dale, I mean—we all hope you'll be so, so happy for ever."

"I am sure I shall," said Alice Dale, turning to her husband. He looked down into her eyes—and we were quite forgotten by

both of them. We saw it, and slipped away, while Jasper Dale
drew his wife into their home and shut the world out.

We scampered joyously away through the moonlit dusk.
Uncle Blair joined us at the gate and the Story Girl asked him
what he thought of the bride.

"When she dies white violets will grow out of her dust," he
answered.

"Uncle Blair says even queerer things than the Story Girl,"
Felicity whispered to me.

And so that beautiful day went away from us, slipping
through our fingers as we tried to hold it. It hooded itself in
shadows and fared forth on the road that is lighted by the white
stars of evening. It had been a gift of Paradise. Its hours had all
been fair and beloved. From dawn flush to fall of night there had
been naught to mar it. It took with it its smiles and laughter.
But it left the boon of memory.

CHAPTER XXVII

The Old Order Changeth

"I AM going away with father when he goes. He is going to spend the winter in Paris, and I am to go to school there."

The Story Girl told us this one day in the orchard. There was a little elation in her tone, but more regret. The news was not a great surprise to us. We had felt it in the air ever since Uncle Blair's arrival. Aunt Janet had been very unwilling to let the Story Girl go. But Uncle Blair was inexorable. It was time, he said, that she should go to a better school than the little country one in Carlisle; and besides, he did not want her to grow into womanhood a stranger to him. So it was finally decided that she was to go.

"Just think, you are going to Europe," said Sara Ray in an awe-struck tone. "Won't that be splendid!"

"I suppose I'll like it after a while," said the Story Girl slowly, "but I know I'll be dreadfully homesick at first. Of course, it will be lovely to be with father, but oh, I'll miss the rest of you so much!"

"Just think how *we'll* miss *you*," sighed Cecily. "It will be so lonesome here this winter, with you and Peter both gone. Oh, dear, I do wish things didn't have to change."

Felicity said nothing. She kept looking down at the grass on which she sat, absently pulling at the slender blades. Presently we saw two big tears roll down over her cheeks. The Story Girl looked surprised.

"Are you crying because I'm going away, Felicity?" she asked.

"Of course I am," answered Felicity, with a big sob. "Do you think I've no f-f-eeling?"

"I didn't think you'd care much," said the Story Girl frankly. "You've never seemed to like me very much."

"I d-don't wear my h-heart on my sleeve," said poor Felicity, with an attempt at dignity. "I think you m-might stay. Your father would let you s-stay if you c-coaxed him."

"Well, you see I'd have to go some time," sighed the Story Girl, "and the longer it was put off the harder it would be. But I do feel dreadfully about it. I can't even take poor Paddy. I'll have to leave him behind, and oh, I want you all to promise to be kind to him for my sake."

We all solemnly assured her that we would.

"I'll g-give him cream every m-morning and n-night," sobbed Felicity, "but I'll never be able to look at him without crying. He'll make me think of you."

"Well, I'm not going right away," said the Story Girl, more cheerfully. "Not till the last of October. So we have over a month yet to have a good time in. Let's all just determine to make it a splendid month for the last. We won't think about my going at all till we have to, and we won't have any quarrels among us, and we'll just enjoy ourselves all we possibly can. So don't cry any more, Felicity. I'm awfully glad you do like me and am sorry I'm going away, but let's all forget it for a month."

Felicity sighed, and tucked away her damp handkerchief.

"It isn't so easy for me to forget things, but I'll try," she said disconsolately, "and if you want any more cooking lessons before you go I'll be real glad to teach you anything I know."

This was a high plane of self-sacrifice for Felicity to attain. But the Story Girl shook her head.

"No, I'm not going to bother my head about cooking lessons this last month. It's too vexing."

"Do you remember the time you made the pudding—" began Peter, and suddenly stopped.

"Out of sawdust?" finished the Story Girl cheerfully. "You needn't be afraid to mention it to me after this. I don't mind any more. I begin to see the fun of it now. I should think I do remember it—and the time I baked the bread before it was raised enough."

"People have made worse mistakes than that," said Felicity kindly.

"Such as using tooth-powd—" but here Dan stopped abruptly, remembering the Story Girl's plea for a beautiful month. Felicity coloured, but said nothing—did not even *look* anything.

"We *have* had lots of fun together one way or another," said Cecily, retrospectively.

"Just think how much we've laughed this last year or so," said the Story Girl. "We've had good times together; but I think we'll have lots more splendid years ahead."

"Eden is always behind us—Paradise always before," said Uncle Blair, coming up in time to hear her. He said it with a sigh that was immediately lost in one of his delightful smiles.

"I like Uncle Blair so much better than I expected to," Felicity confided to me. "Mother says he's a rolling stone, but there really is something very nice about him, although he says a great many things I don't understand. I suppose the Story Girl will have a very gay time in Paris."

"She's going to school and she'll have to study hard," I said.

"She says she's going to study for the stage," said Felicity. "Uncle Roger thinks it is all right, and says she'll be very famous some day. But mother thinks it's dreadful, and so do I."

"Aunt Julia is a concert singer," I said.

"Oh, that's very different. But I hope poor Sara will get on all right," sighed Felicity. "You never know what may happen to a person in those foreign countries. And everybody says Paris is such a wicked place. But we must hope for the best," she concluded in a resigned tone.

That evening the Story Girl and I drove the cows to pasture after milking, and when we came home we sought out Uncle Blair in the orchard. He was sauntering up and down Uncle Stephen's Walk, his hands clasped behind him and his beautiful, youthful face uplifted to the western sky where waves of night were breaking on a dim primrose shore of sunset.

"See that star over there in the south-west?" he said, as we joined him. "The one just above that pine? An evening star shining over a dark pine tree is the whitest thing in the universe—because it is *living* whiteness—whiteness possessing a soul. How full this old orchard is of twilight! Do you know, I have been trysting here with ghosts."

"The Family Ghost?" I asked, very stupidly.

"No, not the Family Ghost. I never saw beautiful, broken-hearted Emily yet. Your mother saw her once, Sara—that was a strange thing," he added absently, as if to himself.

"Did mother really see her?" whispered the Story Girl.

"Well, she always believed she did. Who knows?"

"Do you think there are such things as ghosts, Uncle Blair?" I asked curiously.

"I never saw any, Beverley."

"But you said you were trysting with ghosts here this evening," said the Story Girl.

"Oh, yes—the ghosts of the old years. I love this orchard because of its many ghosts. We are good comrades, those ghosts and I; we walk and talk—we even laugh together—sorrowful laughter that has sorrow's own sweetness. And always there comes to me one dear phantom and wanders hand in hand with me—a lost lady of the old years."

"My mother?" said the Story Girl very softly.

"Yes, your mother. Here, in her old haunts, it is impossible for me to believe that she can be dead—that her *laughter* can be dead. She was the gayest, sweetest thing—and so young—only three years older than you, Sara. Yonder old house had been glad because of her for eighteen years when I met her first."

"I wish I could remember her," said the Story Girl, with a little sigh. "I haven't even a picture of her. Why didn't you paint one, father?"

"She would never let me. She had some queer, funny, half-playful, half-earnest superstition about it. But I always meant to when she would become willing to let me. And then—she died. Her twin brother Felix died the same day. There was something strange about that, too. I was holding her in my arms and she was looking up at me; suddenly she looked past me and gave a little start. 'Felix!' she said. For a moment she trembled and then she smiled and looked up at me again a little beseechingly. 'Felix has come for me, dear,' she said. 'We were always together before you came—you must not mind— you must be glad I do not have to go alone.' Well, who knows? But she left me, Sara—she left me."

There was that in Uncle Blair's voice that kept us silent for a time. Then the Story Girl said, still very softly:

"What did mother look like, father? I don't look the least little bit like her, do I?"

"No, I wish you did, you brown thing. Your mother's face was as white as a wood-lily, with only a faint dream of rose in her cheeks. She had the eyes of one who always had a song in her heart—blue as a mist, those eyes were. She had dark lashes, and a little red mouth that quivered when she was very sad or very happy like a crimson rose too rudely shaken by the wind. She was as slim and lithe as a young, white-stemmed birch tree. How I loved her! How happy we were! But he who accepts human love must bind it to his soul with pain, and she is not lost to me. Nothing is ever really lost to us as long as we remember it."

Uncle Blair looked up at the evening star. We saw that he had forgotten us, and we slipped away, hand in hand, leaving him alone in the memory-haunted shadows of the old orchard.

CHAPTER XXVIII

The Path to Arcady

OCTOBER that year gathered up all the spilled sunshine of the summer and clad herself in it as in a garment. The Story Girl had asked us to try to make the last month together beautiful, and Nature seconded our efforts, giving us that most beautiful of beautiful things—a gracious and perfect moon of falling leaves. There was not in all that vanished October one day that did not come in with auroral splendour and go out attended by a fair galaxy of evening stars—not a day when there were not golden lights in the wide pastures and purple hazes in the ripened distances. Never was anything so gorgeous as the maple trees that year. Maples are trees that have primeval fire in their souls. It glows out a little in their early youth, before the leaves open, in the redness and rosy-yellowness of their blossoms, but in summer it is carefully hidden under a demure, silver-lined greenness. Then when autumn comes, the maples give up trying to be sober and flame out in all the barbaric splendour and gorgeousness of their real nature, making of the hills things out of an Arabian Nights dream in the golden prime of good Haroun Alraschid.

You may never know what scarlet and crimson really are until you see them in their perfection on an October hillside, under the unfathomable blue of an autumn sky. All the glow and radiance and joy at earth's heart seem to have broken loose in a splendid determination to express itself for once before the frost of winter chills her beating pulses. It is the year's carnival ere the dull Lenten days of leafless valleys and penitential mists come.

The time of apple-picking had come around once more and we worked joyously. Uncle Blair picked apples with us, and between him and the Story Girl it was an October never to be forgotten.

"Will you go far afield for a walk with me today?" he said to her and me, one idle afternoon of opal skies, pied meadows and misty hills.

It was Saturday and Peter had gone home; Felix and Dan were helping Uncle Alec top turnips; Cecily and Felicity were making cookies for Sunday, so the Story Girl and I were alone in Uncle Stephen's Walk.

We liked to be alone together that last month, to think the long, long thoughts of youth and talk about our futures. There had grown up between us that summer a bond of sympathy that did not exist between us and the others. We were older than they—the Story Girl was fifteen and I was nearly that; and all at once it seemed as if we were immeasurably older than the rest, and possessed of dreams and visions and forward-reaching hopes which they could not possibly share or understand. At times we were still children, still interested in childish things. But there came hours when we seemed to our two selves very grown up and old, and in those hours we talked our dreams and visions and hopes, vague and splendid, as all such are, over together, and so began to build up, out of the rainbow fragments of our childhood's companionship, that rare and beautiful friendship which was to last all our lives, enriching and enstarring them. For there is no bond more lasting than that formed by the mutual confidences of that magic time when youth is slipping from the sheath of childhood and beginning to wonder what lies for it beyond those misty hills that bound the golden road.

"Where are you going?" asked the Story Girl.

"To 'the woods that belt the gray hillside'—ay, and overflow beyond it into many a valley purple-folded in immemorial peace," answered Uncle Blair. "I have a fancy for one more ramble in Prince Edward Island woods before I leave Canada again. But I would not go alone. So come, you two gay youthful things to whom all life is yet fair and good, and we will seek the path to Arcady. There will be many little things along our way to make us glad. Joyful sounds will 'come ringing down the wind;' a wealth of gypsy gold will be ours for the gathering; we will learn the potent, unutterable charm of a dim spruce wood and the grace of flexile mountain ashes fringing a lonely glen; we will tryst with the folk of fur and feather; we'll hearken to the music of gray old firs. Come, and you'll have a ramble and an afternoon that you will both remember all your lives."

We did have it; never has its remembrance faded; that idyllic afternoon of roving in the old Carlisle woods with the Story Girl and Uncle Blair gleams in my book of years, a page of living beauty. Yet it was but a few hours of simplest pleasure; we wandered pathlessly through the sylvan calm of those dear places which seemed that day to be full of a great friendliness; Uncle Blair sauntered along behind us, whistling softly; sometimes he talked to himself; we delighted in those brief reveries of his; Uncle Blair was the only man I have ever known who could, when he so willed, "talk like a book," and do it without seeming ridiculous; perhaps it was because he had the knack of choosing "fit audience, though few," and the proper time to appeal to that audience.

We went across the fields, intending to skirt the woods at the back of Uncle Alec's farm and find a lane that cut through Uncle Roger's woods; but before we came to it we stumbled on a sly, winding little path quite by accident—if, indeed, there can be such a thing as accident in the woods, where I am tempted to think we are led by the Good People along such of their fairy ways as they have a mind for us to walk in.

"Go to, let us explore this," said Uncle Blair. "It always drags terribly at my heart to go past a wood lane if I can make any excuse at all for traversing it: for it is the by-ways that lead to the heart of the woods and we must follow them if we would know the forest and be known of it. When we can really feel its wild heart beating against ours its subtle life will steal into our veins and make us its own for ever, so that no matter where we go or how wide we wander in the noisy ways of cities or over the lone ways of the sea, we shall yet be drawn back to the forest to find our most enduring kinship."

"I always feel so *satisfied* in the woods," said the Story Girl dreamily, as we turned in under the low-swinging fir boughs. "Trees seem such friendly things."

"They are the most friendly things in God's good creation," said Uncle Blair emphatically. "And it is so easy to live with them. To hold converse with pines, to whisper secrets with the poplars, to listen to the tales of old romance that beeches have to tell, to walk in eloquent silence with self-contained firs, is to learn what real companionship is. Besides, trees are the same all over the world. A beech tree on the slopes of the Pyrenees is just what a beech tree here in these Carlisle woods is; and there used to be an old pine hereabouts whose twin brother I was well acquainted with in a dell among the Apennines. Listen to those squirrels, will you, chattering over yonder. Did you ever hear such a fuss over nothing? Squirrels are the gossips and busybodies of the woods; they haven't learned the fine reserve of its other denizens. But after all, there is a certain shrill friendliness in their greeting."

"They seem to be scolding us," I said, laughing.

"Oh, they are not half such scolds as they sound," answered Uncle Blair gaily. "If they would but 'tak a thought and mend' their shrew-like ways they would be dear, lovable creatures enough."

"If I had to be an animal I think I'd like to be a squirrel," said the Story Girl. "It must be next best thing to flying."

"Just see what a spring that fellow gave," laughed Uncle Blair. "And now listen to his song of triumph! I suppose that chasm he cleared seemed as wide and deep to him as Niagara Gorge would to us if we leaped over it. Well, the wood people are a happy folk and very well satisfied with themselves."

Those who have followed a dim, winding, balsamic path to the unexpected hollow where a wood-spring lies have found the rarest secret the forest can reveal. Such was our good fortune that day. At the end of our path we found it, under the pines, a crystal-clear thing with lips unkissed by so much as a stray sunbeam.

"It is easy to dream that this is one of the haunted springs of old romance," said Uncle Blair. "'Tis an enchanted spot this, I am very sure, and we should go softly, speaking low, lest we disturb the rest of a white, wet naiad, or break some spell that has cost long years of mystic weaving."

"It's so easy to believe things in the woods," said the Story Girl, shaping a cup from a bit of golden-brown birch bark and filling it at the spring.

"Drink a toast in that water, Sara," said Uncle Blair. "There's not a doubt that it has some potent quality of magic in it and the wish you wish over it will come true."

The Story Girl lifted her golden-hued flagon to her red lips. Her hazel eyes laughed at us over the brim.

"Here's to our futures," she cried, "I wish that every day of our lives may be better than the one that went before."

"An extravagant wish—a very wish of youth," commented

Uncle Blair, "and yet in spite of its extravagance, a wish that will come true if you are true to yourselves. In that case, every day *will* be better than all that went before—but there will be many days, dear lad and lass, when you will not believe it."

We did not understand him, but we knew Uncle Blair never explained his meaning. When asked it he was wont to answer with a smile, "Some day you'll grow to it. Wait for that." So we addressed ourselves to follow the brook that stole away from the spring in its windings and doublings and tricky surprises.

"A brook," quoth Uncle Blair, "is the most changeful, bewitching, lovable thing in the world. It is never in the same mind or mood two minutes. Here it is sighing and murmuring as if its heart were broken. But listen—yonder by the birches it is laughing as if it were enjoying some capital joke all by itself."

It was indeed a changeful brook; here it would make a pool, dark and brooding and still, where we bent to look at our mirrored faces; then it grew communicative and gossiped shallowly over a broken pebble bed where there was a diamond dance of sunbeams and no troutling or minnow could glide through without being seen. Sometimes its banks were high and steep, hung with slender ashes and birches; again they were mere, low margins, green with delicate mosses, shelving out of the wood. Once it came to a little precipice and flung itself over undauntedly in an indignation of foam, gathering itself up rather dizzily among the mossy stones below. It was some time before it got over its vexation; it went boiling and muttering along, fighting with the rotten logs that lie across it, and making far more fuss than was necessary over every root that interfered with it. We were getting tired of its ill-humour and talked of leaving it, when it suddenly grew sweet-tempered again, swooped around a curve—and presto, we were in fairyland.

It was a little dell far in the heart of the woods. A row of birches fringed the brook, and each birch seemed more exquisitely graceful and golden than her sisters. The woods receded from it on every hand, leaving it lying in a pool of amber sunshine. The yellow trees were mirrored in the placid stream, with now and then a leaf falling on the water, mayhap to drift away and be used, as Uncle Blair suggested, by some adventurous wood sprite who had it in mind to fare forth to some far-off, legendary region where all the brooks ran into the sea.

"Oh, what a lovely place!" I exclaimed, looking around me with delight.

"A spell of eternity is woven over it, surely," murmured Uncle Blair. "Winter may not touch it, or spring ever revisit it. It should be like this for ever."

"Let us never come here again," said the Story Girl softly, "never, no matter how often we may be in Carlisle. Then we will never see it changed or different. We can always remember it just as we see it now, and it will be like this for ever for us."

"I'm going to sketch it," said Uncle Blair.

While he sketched it the Story Girl and I sat on the banks of the brook and she told me the story of the Sighing Reed. It was a very simple little story, that of the slender brown reed which grew by the forest pool and always was sad and sighing because it could not utter music like the brook and the birds and the winds. All the bright, beautiful things around it mocked it and laughed at it for its folly. Who would ever look for music in it, a plain, brown, unbeautiful thing? But one day a youth came through the wood; he was as beautiful as the spring; he cut the brown reed and fashioned it according to his liking; and then he put it to his lips and breathed on it; and, oh, the music that floated through the forest! It was so entrancing that everything— brooks and birds and winds—grew silent to listen to it. Never had anything so lovely been heard; it was the music that had for so long been shut up in the soul of the sighing reed and was set free at last through its pain and suffering.

I had heard the Story Girl tell many a more dramatic tale; but that one stands out for me in memory above them all, partly, perhaps, because of the spot in which she told it, partly because it was the last one I was to hear her tell for many years—the last one she was ever to tell me on the golden road.

When Uncle Blair had finished his sketch the shafts of sunshine were turning crimson and growing more and more remote; the early autumn twilight was falling over the woods. We left our dell, saying good-bye to it for ever, as the Story Girl had suggested, and we went slowly homeward through the fir woods, where a haunting, indescribable odour stole out to meet us.

"There is magic in the scent of dying fir," Uncle Blair was saying aloud to himself, as if forgetting he was not quite alone. "It gets into our blood like some rare, subtly-compounded wine, and thrills us with unutterable sweetnesses, as of recollections from some other fairer life, lived in some happier star. Compared to it, all other scents seem heavy and earth-born, luring to the valleys instead of the heights. But the tang of the fir summons onward and upward to some 'far-off, divine event'—some spiritual peak of attainment whence we shall see with unfaltering, unclouded vision the spires of some aerial City Beautiful, or the fulfilment of some fair, fadeless land of promise."

He was silent for a moment, then added in a lower tone,

"Felicity, you loved the scent of dying fir. If you were here tonight with me—Felicity—Felicity!"

Something in his voice made me suddenly sad. I was comforted when I felt the Story Girl slip her hand into mine. So we walked out of the woods into the autumn dusk.

We were in a little valley. Half-way up the opposite slope a brush fire was burning clearly and steadily in a maple grove. There was something indescribably alluring in that fire, glowing so redly against the dark background of forest and twilit hill.

"Let us go to it," cried Uncle Blair, gaily, casting aside his sorrowful mood and catching our hands. "A wood fire at night has a fascination not to be resisted by those of mortal race. Hasten—we must not lose time."

"Oh, it will burn a long time yet," I gasped, for Uncle Blair was whisking us up the hill at a merciless rate.

"You can't be sure. It *may* have been lighted by some good, honest farmer-man, bent on tidying up his sugar orchard, but it may also, for anything we know, have been kindled by no earthly woodman as a beacon or summons to the tribes of fairyland, and may vanish away if we tarry."

It did not vanish and presently we found ourselves in the grove. It was very beautiful; the fire burned with a clear, steady glow and a soft crackle; the long arcades beneath the trees were illuminated with a rosy radiance, beyond which lurked companies of gray and purple shadows. Everything was very still and dreamy and remote.

"It is impossible that out there, just over the hill, lies a village of men, where tame household lamps are shining," said Uncle Blair.

"I feel as if we must be thousands of miles away from everything we've ever known," murmured the Story Girl.

"So you are!" said Uncle Blair emphatically. "You're back in the youth of the race—back in the beguilement of the young world. Everything is in this hour—the beauty of classic myths, the primal charm of the silent and the open, the lure of mystery. Why, it's a time and place when and where everything might come true—when the men in green might creep out to join hands and dance around the fire, or dryads steal from their trees to warm their white limbs, grown chilly in October frosts, by the blaze. I wouldn't be much surprised if we should see something of the kind. Isn't that the flash of an ivory shoulder through yonder gloom? And didn't you see a queer little elfin face peering at us around that twisted gray trunk? But one can't be sure. Mortal eyesight is too slow and clumsy a thing to match against the flicker of a pixy-litten fire."

Hand in hand we wandered through that enchanted place, seeking the folk of elf-land, "and heard their mystic voices calling, from fairy knoll and haunted hill." Not till the fire died down into ashes did we leave the grove. Then we found that the full moon was gleaming lustrously from a cloudless sky across the valley. Between us and her stretched up a tall pine, wondrously straight and slender and branchless to its very top, where it overflowed in a crest of dark boughs against the silvery splendour behind it. Beyond, the hill farms were lying in a suave, white radiance.

"Doesn't it seem a long, long time to you since we left home this afternoon?" asked the Story Girl. "And yet it is only a few hours."

Only a few hours—true; yet such hours were worth a cycle of common years untouched by the glory and the dream.

CHAPTER XXIX

We Lose a Friend

OUR beautiful October was marred by one day of black tragedy—the day Paddy died. For Paddy, after seven years of as happy a life as ever a cat lived, died suddenly—of poison, as was supposed. Where he had wandered in the darkness to meet his doom we did not know, but in the frosty dawnlight he dragged himself home to die. We found him lying on the doorstep when we got up, and it did not need Aunt Janet's curt announcement, or Uncle Blair's reluctant shake of the head, to tell us that there was no chance of our pet recovering this time. We felt that nothing could be done. Lard and sulphur on his paws would be of no use, nor would any visit to Peg Bowen avail. We stood around in mournful silence; the Story Girl sat down on the step and took poor Paddy upon her lap.

"I s'pose there's no use even in praying now," said Cecily desperately.

"It wouldn't do any harm to try," sobbed Felicity.

"You needn't waste your prayers," said Dan mournfully, "Pat is beyond human aid. You can tell that by his eyes. Besides, I don't believe it was the praying cured him last time."

"No, it was Peg Bowen," declared Peter, "but she couldn't have bewitched him this time for she's been away for months, nobody knows where."

"If he could only *tell* us where he feels the worst!" said Cecily piteously. "It's so dreadful to see him suffering and not be able to do a single thing to help him!"

"I don't think he's suffering much now," I said comfortingly.

The Story Girl said nothing. She passed and repassed her long brown hand gently over her pet's glossy fur. Pat lifted his head and essayed to creep a little nearer to his beloved mistress. The Story Girl drew his limp body close in her arms. There was a plaintive little mew—a long quiver—and Paddy's friendly soul had fared forth to wherever it is that good cats go.

"Well, he's gone," said Dan, turning his back abruptly to us.

"It doesn't seem as if it can be true," sobbed Cecily. "This time yesterday morning he was full of life."

"He drank two full saucers of cream," moaned Felicity, "and I saw him catch a mouse in the evening. Maybe it was the last one he ever caught."

"He did for many a mouse in his day," said Peter, anxious to pay his tribute to the departed.

"'He was a cat—take him for all in all. We shall not look upon his like again,'" quoted Uncle Blair.

Felicity and Cecily and Sara Ray cried so much that Aunt Janet lost patience completely and told them sharply that they would have something to cry for some day—which did not seem to comfort them much. The Story Girl shed no tears, though the look in her eyes hurt more than weeping.

"After all, perhaps it's for the best," she said drearily. "I've been feeling so badly over having to go away and leave Paddy. No matter how kind you'd all be to him I know he'd miss me terribly. He wasn't like most cats who don't care who comes and goes as long as they get plenty to eat. Paddy wouldn't have been contented without me."

"Oh, no-o-o, oh, no-o-o," wailed Sara Ray lugubriously.

Felix shot a disgusted glance at her.

"I don't see what *you* are making such a fuss about," he said unfeelingly. "He wasn't *your* cat."

"But I l-l-oved him," sobbed Sara, "and I always feel bad when my friends d-do."

"I wish we could believe that cats went to heaven, like people," sighed Cecily. "Do you really think it isn't possible?"

Uncle Blair shook his head.

"I'm afraid not. I'd like to think cats have a chance for heaven, but I can't. There's nothing heavenly about cats, delightful creatures though they are."

"Blair, I'm really surprised to hear the things you say to the children," said Aunt Janet severely.

"Surely you wouldn't prefer me to tell them that cats *do* go to heaven," protested Uncle Blair.

"I think it's wicked to carry on about an animal as those

children do," answered Aunt Janet decidedly, "and you shouldn't encourage them. Here now, children, stop making a fuss. Bury that cat and get off to your apple picking."

We had to go to our work, but Paddy was not to be buried in any such off-hand fashion as that. It was agreed that we should bury him in the orchard at sunset that evening, and Sara Ray, who had to go home, declared she would be back for it, and implored us to wait for her if she didn't come exactly on time.

"I mayn't be able to get away till after milking," she sniffed, "but I don't want to miss it. Even a cat's funeral is better than none at all."

"Horrid thing!" said Felicity, barely waiting until Sara was out of earshot.

We worked with heavy hearts that day; the girls cried bitterly most of the time and we boys whistled defiantly. But as evening drew on we began to feel a sneaking interest in the details of the funeral. As Dan said, the thing should be done properly, since Paddy was no common cat. The Story Girl selected the spot for the grave, in a little corner behind the cherry copse, where early violets enskied the grass in spring, and we boys dug the grave, making it "soft and narrow," as the heroine of the old ballad wanted hers made. Sara Ray, who managed to come in time after all, and Felicity stood and watched us, but Cecily and the Story Girl kept far aloof.

"This time last night you never thought you'd be digging Pat's grave to-night," sighed Felicity.

"We little k-know what a day will bring forth," sobbed Sara. "I've heard the minister say that and it is true."

"Of course it's true. It's in the Bible; but I don't think you should repeat it in connection with a cat," said Felicity dubiously.

When all was in readiness the Story Girl brought her pet through the orchard where he had so often frisked and prowled. No useless coffin enclosed his breast but he reposed in a neat cardboard box.

"I wonder if it would be right to say 'ashes to ashes and dust to dust,'" said Peter.

"No, it wouldn't," averred Felicity. "It would be real wicked."

"I think we ought to sing a hymn, anyway," asseverated Sara Ray.

"Well, we might do that, if it isn't a very religious one," conceded Felicity.

"How would 'Pull for the shore, sailor, pull for the shore,' do?" asked Cecily. "That never seemed to me a very religious hymn."

"But it doesn't seem very appropriate to a funeral occasion either," said Felicity.

"I think 'Lead, kindly light,' would be ever so much more suitable," suggested Sara Ray, "and it is kind of soothing and melancholy too."

"We are not going to sing anything," said the Story Girl coldly. "Do you want to make the affair ridiculous? We will just fill up the grave quietly and put a flat stone over the top."

"It isn't much like my idea of a funeral," muttered Sara Ray discontentedly.

"Never mind, we're going to have a real obituary about him in *Our Magazine,*" whispered Cecily consolingly.

"And Peter is going to cut his name on top of the stone," added Felicity. "Only we mustn't let on to the grown-ups until it is done, because they might say it wasn't right."

We left the orchard, a sober little band, with the wind of the gray twilight blowing round us. Uncle Roger passed us at the gate.

"So the last sad obsequies are over?" he remarked with a grin.

And we hated Uncle Roger. But we loved Uncle Blair because he said quietly,

"And so you've buried your little comrade?"

So much may depend on the way a thing is said. But not even Uncle Blair's sympathy could take the sting out of the fact that there was no Paddy to get the froth that night at milking time. Felicity cried bitterly all the time she was straining the milk. Many human beings have gone to their graves unattended by as much real regret as followed that one gray pussy cat to his.

CHAPTER XXX

Prophecies

"HERE'S a letter for you from father," said Felix, tossing it to me as he came through the orchard gate. We had been picking apples all day, but were taking a mid-afternoon rest around the well, with a cup of its sparkling cold water to refresh us.

I opened the letter rather indifferently, for father, with all his excellent and lovable traits, was but a poor correspondent; his letters were usually very brief and very unimportant.

This letter was brief enough, but it was freighted with a message of weighty import. I sat gazing stupidly at the sheet after I had read it until Felix exclaimed,

"Bev, what's the matter with you? What's in that letter?"

"Father is coming home," I said dazedly. "He is to leave South America in a fortnight and will be here in November to take us back to Toronto."

Everybody gasped. Sara Ray, of course, began to cry, which aggravated me unreasonably.

"Well," said Felix, when he got his second wind, "I'll be awful glad to see father again, but I tell you I don't like the thought of leaving here."

I felt exactly the same but, in view of Sara Ray's tears, admit it I would not; so I sat in grim silence while the other tongues wagged.

"If I were not going away myself I'd feel just terrible," said the Story Girl. "Even as it is I'm real sorry. I'd like to be able to think of you as all here together when I'm gone, having good times and writing me about them."

"It'll be awfully dull when you fellows go," muttered Dan.

"I'm sure I don't know what we're ever going to do here this winter," said Felicity, with the calmness of despair.

"Thank goodness there are no more fathers to come back,"

breathed Cecily with a vicious earnestness that made us all laugh, even in the midst of our dismay.

We worked very half-heartedly the rest of the day, and it was not until we assembled in the orchard in the evening that our spirits recovered something like their wonted level. It was clear and slightly frosty; the sun had declined behind a birch on a distant hill and it seemed a tree with a blazing heart of fire. The great golden willow at the lane gate was laughter-shaken in the wind of evening. Even amid all the changes of our shifting world we could not be hopelessly low-spirited—except Sara Ray, who was often so, and Peter, who was rarely so. But Peter had been sorely vexed in spirit for several days. The time was approaching for the October issue of *Our Magazine* and he had no genuine fiction ready for it. He had taken so much to heart Felicity's taunt that his stories were all true that he had determined to have a really-truly false one in the next number. But the difficulty was to get anyone to write it. He had asked the Story Girl to do it, but she refused; then he appealed to me and I shirked. Finally Peter determined to write a story himself.

"It oughtn't to be any harder than writing a poem and I managed that," he said dolefully.

He worked at it in the evenings in the granary loft, and the rest of us forebore to question him concerning it, because he evidently disliked talking about his literary efforts. But this evening I had to ask him if he would soon have it ready, as I wanted to make up the paper.

"It's done," said Peter, with an air of gloomy triumph. "It don't amount to much, but anyhow I made it all out of my own head. Not one word of it was ever printed or told before, and nobody can say there was."

"Then I guess we have all the stuff in and I'll have *Our Magazine* ready to read by tomorrow night," I said.

"I s'pose it will be the last one we'll have," sighed Cecily. "We can't carry it on after you all go; and it has been such fun."

"Bev will be a real newspaper editor some day," declared the Story Girl, on whom the spirit of prophecy suddenly descended that night.

She was swinging on the bough of an apple tree, with a crimson shawl wrapped about her head, and her eyes were bright with roguish fire.

"How do you know he will?" asked Felicity.

"Oh, I can tell futures," answered the Story Girl mysteriously. "I know what's going to happen to all of you. Shall I tell you?"

"Do, just for the fun of it," I said. "Then some day we'll know just how near you came to guessing right. Go on. What else about me?"

"You'll write books, too, and travel all over the world," continued the Story Girl. "Felix will be fat to the end of his life, and he will be a grandfather before he is fifty, and he will wear a long black beard."

"I won't," cried Felix disgustedly. "I hate whiskers. Maybe I can't help the grandfather part, but I *can* help having a beard."

"You can't. It's written in the stars."

" 'Tain't. The stars can't prevent me from shaving."

"Won't Grandpa Felix sound awful funny?" reflected Felicity.

"Peter will be a minister," went on the Story Girl.

"Well, I might be something worse," remarked Peter, in a not ungratified tone.

"Dan will be a farmer and will marry a girl whose name begins with K and he will have eleven children. And he'll vote Grit."

"I won't," cried scandalized Dan. "You don't know a thing about it. Catch *me* ever voting Grit! As for the rest of it—I don't care. Farming's well enough, though I'd rather be a sailor."

"Don't talk such nonsense," protested Felicity sharply. "What on earth do you want to be a sailor for and be drowned?"

"All sailors aren't drowned," said Dan.

"Most of them are. Look at Uncle Stephen."

"You ain't sure he was drowned."

"Well, he disappeared, and that is worse."

"How do you know? Disappearing might be real easy."

"It's not very easy for your family."

"Hush, let's hear the rest of the predictions," said Cecily.

"Felicity," resumed the Story Girl gravely, "will marry a minister."

Sara Ray giggled and Felicity blushed. Peter tried hard not to look too self-consciously delighted.

"She will be a perfect housekeeper and will teach a Sunday School class and be very happy all her life."

"Will her husband be happy?" queried Dan solemnly.

"I guess he'll be as happy as *your* wife," retorted Felicity reddening.

"He'll be the happiest man in the world," declared Peter warmly.

"What about me?" asked Sara Ray.

The Story Girl looked rather puzzled. It was so hard to imagine Sara Ray as having any kind of future. Yet Sara was plainly anxious to have her fortune told and must be gratified.

"You'll be married," said the Story Girl recklessly, "and you'll live to be nearly a hundred years old, and go to dozens of funerals and have a great many sick spells. You will learn not to cry after you are seventy; but your husband will never go to church."

"I'm glad you warned me," said Sara Ray solemnly, "because now I know I'll make him promise before I marry him that he will go."

"He won't keep the promise," said the Story Girl, shaking her head. "But it is getting cold and Cecily is coughing. Let us go in."

"You haven't told my fortune," protested Cecily disappointedly.

The Story Girl looked very tenderly at Cecily—at the smooth little brown head, at the soft, shining eyes, at the cheeks that were often over-rosy after slight exertion, at the little sunburned hands that were always busy doing faithful work or quiet kindnesses. A very strange look came over the Story Girl's face; her eyes grew sad and far-reaching, as if of a verity they pierced beyond the mists of hidden years.

"I couldn't tell any fortune half good enough for you, dearest," she said, slipping her arm round Cecily. "You deserve everything good and lovely. But you know I've only been in fun—of course I don't know anything about what's going to happen to us."

"Perhaps you know more than you think for," said Sara Ray, who seemed much pleased with her fortune and anxious to believe it, despite the husband who wouldn't go to church.

"But I'd like to be told my fortune, even in fun," persisted Cecily.

"Everybody you meet will love you as long as you live," said the Story Girl. "There that's the very nicest fortune I can tell you, and it will come true whether the others do or not, and now we must go in."

We went, Cecily still a little disappointed. In later years I often wondered why the Story Girl refused to tell her fortune that night. Did some strange gleam of foreknowledge fall for a moment across her mirth-making? Did she realize in a flash of prescience that there was no earthly future for our sweet Cecily? Not for her were to be the lengthening shadows or the fading garland. The end was to come while the rainbow still sparkled on her wine of life, ere a single petal had fallen from her rose of joy. Long life was before all the others who trysted that night in the old homestead orchard; but Cecily's maiden feet were never to leave the golden road.

CHAPTER XXXI

The Last Number of Our Magazine

EDITORIAL

I<small>T</small> is with heartfelt regret that we take up our pen to announce that this will be the last number of *Our Magazine*. We have edited ten numbers of it and it has been successful beyond our expectations. It has to be discontinued by reason of circumstances over which we have no control and not because we have lost interest in it. Everybody has done his or her best for *Our Magazine*. Prince Edward Island expected everyone to do his and her duty and everyone did it.

Mr. Dan King conducted the etiquette department in a way worthy of the *Family Guide* itself. He is especially entitled to commendation because he laboured under the disadvantage of having to furnish most of the questions as well as the answers. Miss Felicity King has edited our helpful household department very ably, and Miss Cecily King's fashion notes were always up to date. The personal column was well looked after by Miss Sara Stanley and the story page has been a marked success under the able management of Mr. Peter Craig, to whose original story in this issue, "The Battle of the Partridge Eggs," we would call especial attention. The Exciting Adventure series has also been very popular.

And now, in closing, we bid farewell to our staff and thank them one and all for their help and co-operation in the past year. We have enjoyed our work and we trust that they have too. We wish them all happiness and success in years to come, and we hope that the recollection of *Our Magazine* will not be held least dear among the memories of their childhood.

(Sobs from the girls): "Indeed it won't!"

OBITUARY

On October eighteenth, Patrick Grayfur departed for that bourne whence no traveller returns. He was only a cat, but he had been our faithful friend for a long time and we aren't ashamed to be sorry for him. There are lots of people who are not as friendly and gentlemanly as Paddy was, and he was a great mouser. We buried all that was mortal of poor Pat in the orchard and we are never going to forget him. We have resolved that whenever the date of his death comes round we'll bow our heads and pronounce his name at the hour of his funeral. If we are anywhere where we can't say the name out loud we'll whisper it.

"Farewell, dearest Paddy, in all the years that are to be
We'll cherish your memory faithfully."[1]

MY MOST EXCITING ADVENTURE

My most exciting adventure was the day I fell off Uncle Roger's loft two years ago. I wasn't excited until it was all over because I hadn't time to be. The Story Girl and I were looking for eggs in the loft. It was filled with wheat straw nearly to the roof and it was an awful distance from us to the floor. And wheat straw is so slippery. I made a little spring and the straw slipped from under my feet and there I was going head first down from the loft. It seemed to me I was an awful long time falling, but the Story Girl says I couldn't have been more than three seconds. But I know that I thought five thoughts and there seemed to be quite a long time between them. The first thing I thought was, what has happened, because I really didn't know at first, it was so sudden. Then after a spell I thought the answer, I am falling off the loft. And then I thought, what will happen to me when I strike the floor, and after another little spell I thought, I'll be killed. And then I thought, well, I don't care. I really wasn't a bit frightened. I just was quite willing to be killed. If there

---

[1] The obituary was written by Mr. Felix King, but the two lines of poetry were composed by Miss Sara Ray.

hadn't been a big pile of chaff on the barn floor these words would never have been written. But there was and I fell on it and wasn't a bit hurt, only my hair and mouth and eyes and ears got all full of chaff. The strange part is that I wasn't a bit frightened when I thought I was going to be killed, but after all the danger was over I was awfully frightened and trembled so the Story Girl had to help me into the house.

FELICITY KING.

THE BATTLE OF THE PARTRIDGE EGGS

Once upon a time there lived about half a mile from a forrest a farmer and his wife and his sons and daughters and a granddaughter. The farmer and his wife loved this little girl very much but she caused them great trouble by running away into the woods and they often spent haf days looking for her. One day she wondered further into the forrest than usual and she begun to be hungry. Then night closed in. She asked a fox where she could get something to eat. The fox told her he knew where there was a partridges nest and a bluejays nest full of eggs. So he led her to the nests and she took five eggs out of each. When the birds came home they missed the eggs and flew into a rage. The bluejay put on his topcoat and was going to the partridge for law when he met the partridge coming to him. They lit up a fire and commenced sining their deeds when they heard a tremendous howl close behind them. They jumped up and put out the fire and were immejutly attacked by five great wolves. The next day the little girl was rambelling through the woods when they saw her and took her prisoner. After she had confessed that she had stole the eggs they told her to raise an army. They would have to fight over the nests of eggs and whoever one would have the eggs. So the partridge raised a great army of all kinds of birds except robins and the little girl got all the robins and foxes and bees and wasps. And best of all the little girl had a gun and plenty of ammunishun. The leader of her army was a wolf. The result of the battle was that all the birds were killed except the partridge and the bluejay and they were taken prisoner and starved to death.

The little girl was then taken prisoner by a witch and cast into a dunjun full of snakes where she died from their bites and people who went through the forrest after that were taken prisoner by her ghost and cast into the same dunjun where they died. About a year after the wood turned into a gold castle and one morning everything had vanished except a piece of a tree.

                                                    PETER CRAIG.

(Dan, with a whistle:—"Well, I guess nobody can say Peter can't write fiction after *that.*"

Sara Ray, wiping away her tears:—"It's a *very* interesting story, but it ends *so* sadly."

Felix:—"What made you call it The Battle of the Partridge Eggs when the bluejay had just as much to do with it?"

Peter, shortly:—"Because it sounded better that way."

Felicity:—"Did she eat the eggs raw?"

Sara Ray:—"Poor little thing, I suppose if you're starving you can't be very particular."

Cecily, sighing:—"I wish you'd let her go home safe, Peter, and not put her to such a cruel death."

Beverley:—"I don't quite understand where the little girl got her gun and ammunition."

Peter, suspecting that he is being made fun of:—"If you could write a better story, why didn't you? I give you the chance."

The Story Girl, with a preternaturally solemn face:—"You shouldn't criticize Peter's story like that. It's a fairy tale, you know, and anything can happen in a fairy tale."

Felicity:—"There isn't a word about fairies in it!"

Cecily:—"Besides, fairy tales always end nicely and this doesn't."

Peter, sulkily:—"I wanted to punish her for running away from home."

Dan:—"Well, I guess you did it all right."

Cecily:—"Oh, well, it was very interesting, and that is all that is really necessary in a story.")

PERSONALS

Mr. Blair Stanley is visiting friends and relatives in Carlisle. He intends returning to Europe shortly. His daughter, Miss Sara, will accompany him.

Mr. Alan King is expected home from South America next month. His sons will return with him to Toronto. Beverley and

Felix have made hosts of friends during their stay in Carlisle and will be much missed in social circles.

The Mission Band of Carlisle Presbyterian Church completed their missionary quilt last week. Miss Cecily King collected the largest sum on her square. Congratulations, Cecily.

Mr. Peter Craig will be residing in Markdale after October and will attend school there this winter. Peter is a good fellow and we all wish him success and prosperity.

Apple picking is almost ended. There was an unusually heavy crop this year. Potatoes, not so good.

HOUSEHOLD DEPARTMENT

Apple pies are the order of the day.

Eggs are a very good price now. Uncle Roger says it isn't fair to have to pay as much for a dozen little eggs as a dozen big ones, but they go just as far.

FELICITY KING.

ETIQUETTE DEPARTMENT

F-l-t-y. Is it considered good form to eat peppermints in church? Ans.; No, not if a witch gives them to you.

No, F-l-x, we would not call Treasure Island or the Pilgrim's Progress dime novels.

Yes, P-t-r, when you call on a young lady and her mother offers you a slice of bread and jam it is quite polite for you to accept it.

DAN KING.

FASHION NOTES

Necklaces of roseberries are very much worn now.

It is considered smart to wear your school hat tilted over your left eye.

Bangs are coming in. Em Frewen has them. She went to Summerside for a visit and came back with them. All the girls in school are going to bang their hair as soon as their mothers will let them. But I do not intend to bang mine.

CECILY KING.

(Sara Ray, despairingly:—"I know ma will never let *me* have bangs.")

FUNNY PARAGRAPHS

D-n. What are details? C-l-y. I am not sure, but I think they are things that are left over.

(Cecily, wonderingly:—"I don't see why that was put among the funny paragraphs. Shouldn't it have gone in the General Information department?")

Old Mr. McIntyre's son on the Markdale Road had been very sick for several years and somebody was sympathizing with him because his son was going to die. "Oh," Mr. McIntyre said, quite easy, "he might as weel be awa'. He's only retarding buzziness."

FELIX KING.

GENERAL INFORMATION BUREAU

P-t-r. What kind of people live in uninhabited places?
Ans.: Cannibals, likely.

FELIX KING.

CHAPTER XXXII

Our Last
Evening
Together

IT was the evening before the day on which the Story Girl and Uncle Blair were to leave us, and we were keeping our last tryst together in the orchard where we had spent so many happy hours. We had made a pilgrimage to all the old haunts—the hill field, the spruce wood, the dairy, Grandfather King's willow, the Pulpit Stone, Pat's grave, and Uncle Stephen's Walk; and now we foregathered in the sere grasses about the old well and feasted on the little jam turnovers Felicity had made that day specially for the occasion.

"I wonder if we'll ever all be together again," sighed Cecily.

"I wonder when I'll get jam turnovers like this again," said the Story Girl, trying to be gay but not making much of a success of it.

"If Paris wasn't so far away I could send you a box of nice things now and then," said Felicity forlornly, "but I suppose there's no use thinking of that. Dear knows what they'll give you to eat over there."

"Oh, the French have the reputation of being the best cooks in the world," rejoined the Story Girl, "but I know they can't beat your jam turnovers and plum puffs, Felicity. Many a time I'll be hankering after them."

"If we ever do meet again you'll be grown up," said Felicity gloomily.

"Well, you won't have stood still yourselves, you know."

"No, but that's just the worst of it. We'll all be different and everything will be changed."

"Just think," said Cecily, "last New Year's Eve we were wondering what would happen this year; and what a lot of things have happened that we never expected. Oh, dear!"

"If things never happened life would be pretty dull," said the Story Girl briskly. "Oh, don't look so dismal, all of you."

"It's hard to be cheerful when everybody's going away," sighed Cecily.

"Well, let's pretend to be, anyway," insisted the Story Girl. "Don't let's think of parting. Let's think instead of how much we've laughed this last year or so. I'm sure I shall never forget this dear old place. We've had so many good times here."

"And some bad times, too," reminded Felix. "Remember when Dan et the bad berries last summer?"

"And the time we were so scared over that bell ringing in the house," grinned Peter.

"And the Judgment Day," added Dan.

"And the time Paddy was bewitched," suggested Sara Ray.

"And when Peter was dying of the measles," said Felicity.

"And the time Jimmy Patterson was lost," said Dan. "Gee-whiz, but that scared me out of a year's growth."

"Do you remember the time we took the magic seed," grinned Peter.

"Weren't we silly?" said Felicity. "I really can never look Billy Robinson in the face when I meet him. I'm always sure he's laughing at me in his sleeve."

"It's Billy Robinson who ought to be ashamed when he meets you or any of us," commented Cecily severely. "I'd rather be cheated than cheat other people."

"Do you mind the time we bought God's picture?" asked Peter.

"I wonder if it's where we buried it yet," speculated Felix.

"I put a stone over it, just as we did over Pat," said Cecily.

"I wish I could forget what God looks like," sighed Sara Ray. "I can't forget it—and I can't forget what the bad place is like either, ever since Peter preached that sermon on it."

"When you get to be a real minister you'll have to preach that sermon over again, Peter," grinned Dan.

"My Aunt Jane used to say that people needed a sermon on that place once in a while," retorted Peter seriously.

"Do you mind the night I et the cucumbers and milk to make me dream?" said Cecily.

And therewith we hunted out our old dream books to read them again, and, forgetful of coming partings, laughed over them till the old orchard echoed to our mirth. When we had finished we stood in a circle around the well and pledged "eternal friendship" in a cup of its unrivalled water.

Then we joined hands and sang "Auld Lang Syne." Sara Ray cried bitterly in lieu of singing.

"Look here," said the Story Girl, as we turned to leave the old orchard, "I want to ask a favour of you all. Don't say good-bye to me tomorrow morning."

"Why not?" demanded Felicity in astonishment.

"Because it's such a hopeless sort of word. Don't let's *say* it at all. Just see me off with a wave of your hands. It won't seem half so bad then. And don't any of you cry if you can help it. I want to remember you all smiling."

We went out of the old orchard where the autumn night wind was beginning to make its weird music in the russet boughs, and shut the little gate behind us. Our revels there were ended.

CHAPTER XXXIII

The
Story Girl
Goes

THE morning dawned, rosy and clear and frosty. Everybody was up early, for the travellers must leave in time to catch the nine o'clock train. The horse was harnessed and Uncle Alec was waiting by the door. Aunt Janet was crying, but everybody else was making a valiant effort not to. The Awkward Man and Mrs. Dale came to see the last of their favourite. Mrs. Dale had brought her a glorious sheaf of chrysanthemums, and the Awkward Man gave her, quite gracefully, another little, old, limp book from his library.

"Read it when you are sad or happy or lonely or discouraged or hopeful," he said gravely.

"He has really improved very much since he got married," whispered Felicity to me.

Sara Stanley wore a smart new travelling suit and a blue felt hat with a white feather. She looked so horribly grown up in it that we felt as if she were lost to us already.

Sara Ray had vowed tearfully the night before that she would be up in the morning to say farewell. But at this juncture Judy Pineau appeared to say that Sara, with her usual luck, had a sore throat, and that her mother consequently would not permit her to come. So Sara had written her parting words in a three-cornered pink note.

"*My own darling friend:*—*Words cannot express* my feelings over not being able to go up this morning to say good-bye to one I so *fondly adore.* When I think that I cannot *see you again* my heart is almost *too full for utterance.* But mother says I cannot and I *must obey.* But I will be present *in spirit.* It just *breaks my heart* that you are going *so far away.* You have always been *so kind* to me and never hurt my feelings *as some do* and I shall miss you *so much.* But I earnestly *hope and pray* that you will be *happy and prosperous* wherever *your lot is cast* and not be seasick on *the great ocean*. I hope you will find time *among your many duties* to write me a letter *once in a while*. I shall *always remember you* and please remember me. I hope we *will meet again* sometime, but if not may we meet in *a far better world* where there are *no sad partings*.

"Your true and loving friend,

"SARA RAY."

"Poor little Sara," said the Story Girl, with a queer catch in her voice, as she slipped the tear-blotted note into her pocket. "She isn't a bad little soul, and I'm sorry I couldn't see her once more, though maybe it's just as well for she'd have to cry and set us all off. I *won't* cry. Felicity, don't you dare. Oh, you dear, darling people, I love you all so much and I'll go on loving you always."

"Mind you write us every week at the very least," said Felicity, winking furiously.

"Blair, Blair, watch over the child well," said Aunt Janet. "Remember, she has no mother."

The Story Girl ran over to the buggy and climbed in. Uncle Blair followed her. Her arms were full of Mrs. Dale's chrysanthemums, held close up to her face, and her beautiful eyes shone softly at us over them. No good-byes were said, as she wished. We all smiled bravely and waved our hands as they drove out of the lane and down the moist red road into the shadows of the fir wood in the valley. But we still stood there, for we knew we should see the Story Girl once more. Beyond the fir wood was an open curve in the road and she had promised to wave a last farewell as they passed around it.

We watched the curve in silence, standing in a sorrowful little group in the sunshine of the autumn morning. The delight of the world had been ours on the golden road. It had enticed us with daisies and rewarded us with roses. Blossom and lyric had waited on our wishes. Thoughts, careless and sweet, had visited us. Laughter had been our comrade and fearless Hope our guide. But now the shadow of change was over it.

"There she is," cried Felicity.

The Story Girl stood up and waved her chrysanthemums at us. We waved wildly back until the buggy had driven around the curve. Then we went slowly and silently back to the house. The Story Girl was gone.

THE END

About the Author

L. M. MONTGOMERY's fascinating accounts of the lives and romances of Anne, Emily, and other well-loved characters have achieved long-lasting popularity the world over. Born in 1874 in Prince Edward Island, Canada, Lucy Maud showed an early flair for storytelling. She soon began to have her writing published in papers and magazines, and when she died in Toronto in 1942 she had written more than twenty novels and a large number of short stories. Most of her books are set in Prince Edward Island, which she loved very much and wrote of most beautifully. *Anne of Green Gables,* her most popular work, has been translated into thirty-six languages, made into a film twice, and has had continuing success as a stage play. Lucy Maud Montgomery's early home in Cavendish, P.E.I., where she is buried, is a much-visited historic site.